The Choice

The First of the Thory's Chronicles

A novel by

DONALD DEISCHER

PAGE PUBLISHING, INC.
New York, NY

First originally published by Page Publishing, Inc. 2016

ISBN 978-1-68289-520-7 (pbk)
ISBN 978-1-68289-522-1 (hbk)
ISBN 978-1-68289-521-4 (digital)

Printed in the United States of America

For Caitlin,
the tiger that inspired this story

Prologue

The mortal world is wide and wonderful. Lisa and Thomas Thory were born into that world. For six years Lisa had a loving mother and father. Three of those she shared with her brother. Their father died on a trip abroad. Soon afterward, in a rage of depression, their mother took her own life.

The brother and sister were brought up and raised by their Aunt Lucile. She loved and took care of them like any Mother would. They led a good and simple life of school and sports, and at home, there were chores and jobs.

Lisa was twenty-two; she had gone through high school with a 4.0 grade average. She had played and captained her high school lacrosse team and won the championship two years in a row. Though she had been accepted into many colleges, she chose to stay close to home. She always remained simple. More than that, she always considered herself rather plain, though to others she had a beauty to her that couldn't be missed. She was five foot seven, athletically built with long light auburn hair. Her eyes were bright blue green. She had a smile that she seemed to share with everyone. But in her spare time she kept to herself and helped her Aunt when she could.

Thomas was taller than Lisa, though he was only nineteen. He too had done well in school and had even managed college courses during summer months. He was the captain of the wrestling team. Thomas was a quiet person, who, despite his good looks, rarely had a girlfriend. His dark brown hair was well groomed and kept short. Looking at him, he wasn't as athletically built as his sister, but he was as strong as an ox. Despite their differences anybody could tell they were siblings.

Perhaps it was from the loss of their parents so early or it may have been from the way their Aunt raised them, but the three of them were very close. It was always family, first and last. The only time her brother had little to do with his sister was mornings before her coffee. Even her Aunt gave her a wide birth till 7:00 when she had finished her coffee and her eyes were open. For the past sixteen years, the Thory's had truly led a simple and happy life. All that was about to change.

The Choice

1

Lisa and Thomas had been running for only a day, though it had seemed longer. Their aunt, only a day before, had died in an accident. They both had survived by some miracle with only a few bruises and cuts, or at least that was what the doctor had said. Lisa had pulled over, tired from running and driving; then as she stared out of the window of her car into the quiet darkness she began thinking and dreaming about how it all started.

Lisa had tried to save her aunt, but she had been too badly cut by a piece of wreckage. Their aunt Lucile had been the only mother they had. Lucile was the only family that she and her brother had ever known. And now she was slipping away, dying, and there was little she could do. But as she lay there, Lucile told her, "You and your brother will have to find your family. Get to them as quick as you can. It won't be safe for you and your brother. Soon others will come for both of you." She took labored breaths and told her, "Lisa, go to Bael. He's the only one who could protect you," as she pointed to the glove box. Inside was a paper with an address and the name Bael, along with a map that Lisa put in her pocket. Her aunt smiled and told them, "I love you so very much, and I wished that I had more time to explain." She gave each of them a hug and kiss, then told them, "Don't stay at the hospital. Once you were looked after, go and find Bael as fast as you can. Trust no one but him, till you reach the family."

"What family?" she asked.

"Bael will explain," she said, and then she passed out. Lisa could hear the siren of the police and the ambulance arriving. As the EMT treated them, Lucile had died.

When they reached the hospital, she and her brother sat together, waiting for the doctor; they were bandaged and x-rayed but seemed fine. A nurse had read their chart and gave them a strange look that Lisa didn't understand. The same nurse went to the desk and nervously dialed the phone. Lisa listened.

"Hello, this is Sarah. Let me speak to mas . . . Doctor Marin. Yes, Doctor. We have a case here that—"

"The name?"

"Tory. T-H-O-R-Y. And Thorn. Yes, sir, Thorn was DOA. The other two have superficial wounds."

" Elisabeth and Thomas Thory?"

"Yes, sir. I will, sir. It will be taken care of, sir." She hung up the phone and quickly went over and said something to the attending doctor, then returned to them.

"How are you feeling?"

"Not too bad," Lisa replied. "All things being considered."

The nurse smiled.

"I have some good news for you. Your x-rays came back clear. Your scans were fine. But there were a few things about your blood tests that the doctor will want to question you about, okay? So just have a seat, and he'll be here to see you soon."

That reminded Lisa to get out as soon as they got checked out. So they nodded to the nurse, but when an ambulance came in, and everyone was busy, they ran for the door. They ran down the street and got on the first bus heading toward home. Hours later Lisa and her brother walked through the front door of their home.

Lisa went to the desk and got out the family's checkbook and the cash that their aunt had put away. Thomas came walking into the room.

"Sis, I know that we're running. I know that we're following what Aunt Lucile said to do. What I don't understand is why?"

Lisa turned to her brother. "Thomas, I'm like you. I don't understand all this, but that nurse was acting funny. No police asked us any questions about the accident. Then we were supposed to wait for a doctor about a blood test. When the doctor that took care of us wasn't even busy. Why couldn't he ask us? After what Aunt Lucy said, it was time to go! Okay? Let's get packed. Just the backpacks I want to get moving. I've got a feeling I just can't shake!"

Minutes later they got into Lisa's car and headed for the address on the paper. Thomas told his sister, "According to the navigator, it's two hundred thirty-six miles out of town. In the middle of nowhere! And who is this Bael guy Aunt Lucile is sending us to?"

"Thomas, I think it's safe to say, I know just as much as you do at this point. So give me a break, huh?" Lisa drove through the night; her brother finally fell asleep. She looked at the clock and thought to herself. Twelve hours, not even twelve hours ago I lost my mother, got my world thrown into a meat grinder. Apparently, someone is after me. For what? I don't know. And now I'm heading off to see someone I never met. To find a family I never knew I had. I feel like I'm cursing myself for saying it, but it can't get much stranger than this I hope.

She was beginning to wear down when she found a place to pull off the road. According to the navigator, they were not far from the address, but she had to rest. She would have too many questions to ask when she got there. She wanted to be awake to ask. So with a few hours till daylight, she pulled over and slept.

It was early that morning when her brother's voice woke her, "Sis! Sis! You've got to wake up and see this!" She shook her head, yawned, and tried to wake up. Thomas jumped into the car.

"What is it, Thomas? And why couldn't it wait till I woke up?"

"Sis, I looked at the navigator and saw how close we were, so I hiked down the road and found the place! You're not gonna believe it!"

"What?"

"The only way I can describe it is a wooden castle. I'm not kidding the place is like a castle."

"Okay, give me a minute, and we can get back on the road, and we'll be there in about ten minutes. Just let me get my eyes open."

"Without your morning coffee. Why don't I just drive?"

"Fine!" Thomas got out of the car; Lisa slid over to the other seat. Thomas got back in and backed out onto the road.

As they drove up the rocky driveway, she saw the house. What a house! There were only three stories, but were so tall it seemed like five. Made like a log cabin. There were figures carved into the wood in front. She could swear that some of the wood was still planted in the ground. There were strange lettering carved on every side of the huge house. And the front doors were at least eleven feet tall. She could see why Thomas said castle. It was beautiful. It was almost surrounded by a broken flower garden. As they stopped and got out of the car, they could hear something from the back of the house. By the sound of it, someone was chopping wood. Lisa told her brother, "Stay with the car. Be ready to leave." As Lisa went around the house, she found a man with a huge ax chopping firewood.

"Excuse me, sir." He swung his ax again into the log.

"Sir!" she said again.

"I hear you. I heard you pulling up. What is it you want?"

"Well . . . sir, my aunt sent us here." He picked up his ax and began to swing again.

"Her name is Lucile Thorn? And I'm looking for someone named Bael." He turned his head and dropped his ax in the log. He smiled. "Then you must be Elisabeth, yes?"

"Yes."

"And your brother is here as well?"

"Yes, back at the car."

"And where is Lucile?"

"There was an accident yesterday, and I'm sorry, but she died."

"It's me that is sorry. Sorry for you and your brother's loss. And if I may, I am Bael. I know why you're here. And I will deliver both of you safe to your house, your family."

"Sir, I hate to say this, but neither I nor my brother has any idea of what family you're talking about. Since the accident, all we've done is follow our aunt's instructions. We were given a card with a name and an address. We were told to get here as fast as we could. We would love it if you could fill us in on what is going on?" Bael looked at her and realized at once she had been told nothing. Bael smiled at her.

"Get your brother and come into the house. I'll try to explain the best that I can."

Bael greeted her brother as if he had known him as a friend his whole life. He led them to the huge front doors and pulled it open as if it had been a screen door. Inside the room, it was amazing. Each floor seemed fifteen feet high. There was a stairwell to the right that you could have brought a grand piano down. It had paintings along the wall to the second floor that wrapped around. From the ceiling of the second floor to the midway of the second floor, a wooden chandelier hung. The room gave the appearance to be almost round, but the corners gave it an octagonal-shape open rooms that led off in three directions. He took their bags and placed them on a table in the center of the room. With all of its size, the whole house was still warm and inviting. They were led to the kitchen where he made them breakfast and coffee. The smell alone made Lisa feel better about the day. Thomas had taken in other things as they came in. A large and heavy sword hung above the door with strange lettering carved boldly beneath it. One of the rooms that led off from the main room was a library with large wooden chairs around the room and another table at its center. Lit from the walls by at first glance were what he thought torches, but had electric lights in the ends. The hallway that led to the kitchen was across from the entrance. Other rooms off from the hallway looked simple and comfortable. Thomas noticed one strange thing: other than the bathroom, there were no doors. The upstairs rooms that you could see were the same. After the meal Thomas asked about the doors. Bael pointed down the hall to the sword above the door.

"Can you read the words below the sword?"

"No, sir." Bael smiled. "Simply put, it says, 'Welcome, friends, and feel safe, enemies shall not enter.'"

"Sir, I understand the welcome but not the doors." Again, he smiled. "'You do not shut your friends out, friends respect privacy and do not need doors. Here there are no secrets. If you want to know, simply ask.'" Both Thomas and Lisa had never heard anything put so well. Every entranceway seemed to make them feel closer after that. They walked from the kitchen down to the library where they all sat and relaxed.

Now, his eyes went over his guests. "Where to start? First. If you can, I need you to keep an open mind. Very open. Your family is very different from most. There is strength in you and your family that others don't have. It is truly in your blood. How can I say this? Well . . . this will sound crazy, but you come from a line of *vampires*. And before you give me the looks, I'm not talking about monsters or glittery Adonis's. No. What I am saying is true *vampires*. But you are not vampires. In your blood, there is something special. It lets you heal faster, move quicker, see, and hear farther."

Lisa and her brother were trying to be polite. "Sir, I don't want to be rude, but are you serious or are you trying to make a joke?" Bael nodded his head, understanding how crazy it sounded.

"You were in an accident yesterday one that fatally wounded your aunt? What injuries did you and your brother receive?"

"We had some cuts and bruises. We were lucky?"

"What was the worst cut you received?"

"My leg had a gash in it. Why?"

"Take the bandage off. I'm sure by now it's only a scar. And for the record, I see no bruises anywhere on either of you. In high school, were you athletic?"

"Yes."

"And how easy was it for you?"

"We both played sports, and we're team captains. So what? As for us healing, we have a good metabolism, that's all!"

"I understand your doubt, but if you would allow me to finish?"

"Fine."

"Many vampire families have a human bloodline as well. Ones that have had human children that were born before they became vampires. Those children grew up, had children, and on the line went. When they reach a certain age, they are given a choice. Right now there are two families that are trying to take that choice from you."

"Why?"

"To increase the strength of their house. They will feed off you and become stronger. Up until now you have been carefully watched and taken care of. Hidden from the families. Even your own. You should be told. Your aunt was not your aunt by blood.

"She was a blackthorn. They watch over the human bloodlines. Which brings me to some good news. She isn't actually dead by your way of thinking, merely gone dormant to heal. It may take several years, but she will be back to see you. The blackthorns aren't vampires either, just caretakers. Now, I will be looking after you. At least till we reach your family." Lisa sat in silence trying to take in what she was being told. Thomas had questions to ask. "Okay first, who are you? Or should I say what are you?"

"I am Bael. Think of me as a sheriff or marshal for all the non-human races. I make sure everyone keeps to the code of conduct—which are laws, rules, and guidelines to which we live. Most would be too much for the police to deal with."

"Okay but who are *you*?"

"I am Bael, son of Beowulf and grandson of one of the first gods, Bael. I have lived for thousands of years and my father, much longer. We have been putting down those you would call evil for all of that time. Protecting those who need it, and your friend."

"You say that as if you know us?"

"I do. I have known you and your mother before that and her father and mother before that. I would have thought Lucile had at least mentioned me?"

Thomas shook his head. "Not that I can recall. Sorry?"

Bael waved at the two of them. "It's fine. You're here now, and safe."

"Thank you. What choice is it we have to make?" Thomas asked.

"You still have time. Your sister not so much. First, you must decide whether or not to remain human. Then you must choose a family. You have until your twenty-third year."

"What if I choose to remain human?" Thomas replied.

"You will be taken somewhere until it can be made safe for you."

"You said all nonhuman races. How many races are there?" the boy continued to ask.

"Oh . . . many. The *vampires*, the *werepeople*, the *farae*, the *sub-farae*, the *watchers*. And a few others that keep to themselves."

"How many of them do you call friend?"

"Those who keep to the code or keep the peace."

"How many enemies do you have?"

Bael paused. "This I do not know. Enemies do not always make themselves known, do they?"

Lisa finally had enough. "Thomas, you're asking questions like you believe this! Don't tell me you're buying into this?"

"Hold on, sis. I'm not saying I believe it or not, but he started by asking us to keep an open mind. So I think he knew it would sound outrageous. Which makes me think there might be more to this. There is one other thing to think about."

"What?" his sister asked.

"You." He pointed to his sister. "You have had a running record of knowing things. And don't try selling me on that guessing thing. I know better. So let me ask this! Putting the story aside, how do you feel about him?"

She looked at her brother angrily. "Thomas?"

"Elisabeth, please?" Lisa went silent and looked over Bael almost through him. She got a look on her face, just before. "*Shit!* All I get from him is a feeling of trust. It just doesn't make sense."

Thomas shook his head. "Over the last twenty-four hours can you name one thing that has?"

Lisa thought for a moment. Yes, she had. Only what Bael said about the doors. "*Shit!*"

Her brother tried to comfort her. "It'll be all right, sis. We just need to stick together. Sir, the one thing Lisa needs right now is sleep. She's on overload, and only slept a few hours this morning."

Bael smiled. "A very good idea." He led them upstairs to the guest rooms. Lisa was asleep before her head hit the pillow.

"So, Thomas, what if I may ask, do you believe?"

"I believe in my sister. She thought someone was after us. She believed our aunt enough to come here. And she and I get a sense of trust from you. But the story is way too farfetched to suit me." Bael nodded. "Fair enough for now. Do you want to get some sleep as well?"

Thomas waved it off. "No, I think a little fresh air at this point might be better."

"Good. You can help with the firewood."

"Gee, thanks," Thomas replied.

The two went out to the back of the house. Thomas looked at the huge ax. "You don't want me to swing that thing, do yah?"

"If you knew how much power or strength you truly had, I would say yes. For now, take the wood to the backdoor and pile it with the rest."

Thomas watched as this man who didn't look like Conan, all big and muscular lift this ax from hell and with one swing powered his way through the tree lying on a pair of logging horses. "I'll say this, as far as you being the grandson of a god, you got my vote." A raven came down from the trees a few minutes later and sat on the log. It bowed its head and began to squawk at Bael. And Bael listened. As if he understood what it was cawing about. He turned to Thomas. "It seems we may have some company later tonight. Start taking the wood in the house and stack it by the hearth you'll see where. I want to get a message to someone. Pile it up to the red mark on the wall. When I return, I'll fix us a big dinner, okay?"

With that he jumped high into the trees. Grabbing one, then pushing off. Seconds later, he was gone. Thomas stood, looking at the trees. "Definitely more to the story," he said to himself. Then he started collecting the wood.

Within an hour, he had finished. Thomas went in the house and cleaned up. He changed his clothes. He even found an old washer to wash his clothes in. Afterward, he went into the library again. So many beautiful books. Then he found books on some of the races Bael had mentioned. When he finished the book, he looked at the clock. It had been three hours since Bael had left. It was 1:15 p.m. He read another book to pass the time and get some perspective on what he was told. At 2:20 p.m. the door at the back of the house opened and shut. Thomas was relieved to find Bael in the kitchen cooking.

"Is turkey all right with you and your sister?"

"Great!" the boy replied.

"Good I have one prepared. I just need to warm it up." He made some diced vegetables rice and dressing. It smelled wonderful. By 4:00 p.m., the dinner was ready. Lisa had slept for six hours. Though she could use another eight, her brother wanted her to get something to eat in case there was trouble with whatever guest would arrive. Thomas shook his sister lightly till she opened her eyes. When she realized where she was, she said, "Shit . . . I was hoping it was a bad dream."

"No, but wake up. Dinner is ready."

The smell hit her nose. "Turkey?"

"Yeah, and it looks delicious."

She was scratching her head. "How long was I out?" She yawned.

"All day, sis. I got a lot of things to tell ya, and you're not gonna like it."

"What?"

"Well . . . as far as Bael being the grandson of a god? Give him the benefit of the doubt. And as for the rest, I hate to say it, but I think I believe him."

His sister looked frustrated. "What? Why?"

"Sorry, but I think you will to."

They sat in the kitchen and enjoyed the meal. Then Lisa figured it was time for her to ask some questions. "Bael, Thomas says that while I was asleep, a lot of things must have happened?"

"Oh, I suppose they have," Bael replied.

"Yes, my brother seems to have been won over to your story. Or at least some of it. So you're the grandson of a god? What else happened?"

Bael pushed his chair back. "I had some information brought to me by a friend. They are coming to see you tonight. The families that I told you about."

"Coming here?" she asked.

"Well, one is."

Lisa got excited. "Are you going to take care of this guy?"

"No," Bael said. I will take care of you and your brother."

Her frustration was breaking. "But I thought?"

"Don't worry, *Master Maris* has a flare for theatrics, so he wants to make a gesture of power to save face. When he arrives, do not show any fear. But also do not for any reason step from this house. He will try to goad you, or intimidate you. But hear in these walls, you must remain calm and sure. Outthink him."

Lisa looked at Bael. "What about you? Why don't you just stake the guy?"

Bael shook his head. "The rules, laws, and even traditions. Besides, whatever he's thinking, the other family is as well."

Thomas smiled. "I get it. See what he says, and maybe, he'll give us his plans."

"Well done, Thomas." With that, Bael took a chair out to the front porch and set out a small table with a glass of water on it facing inside. "He may get a surprise himself tonight? One never knows?"

The sun was still shining. When Bael came from upstairs with a book in his arms, Lisa asked, "What is that?"

"This is our law book. I sometimes need to refresh the memories of certain individuals. He should be here soon."

"But it's still daylight?" Lisa looked confused.

"Lisa, this isn't the movies. Vampires don't sleep in coffins. And a stake through the heart doesn't kill one either. For now just sit and relax."

Minutes later they heard in the distance a crow cawing. "He's here, guys. Remember what I told you."

"And what could that have been?" said a voice on the porch. Out of the shadow, he stood, a tall lean man. He had dark gray eyes and dressed in a blue suit.

"My dearest Bael, how good to see you. And these of course are the Thorys. I've been looking forward to meeting you both for quite some time."

Bael smiled at the man. "If it isn't good old Maris! Come in, won't you?"

Maris rolled his eyes to the top of the door to see the sword. "I . . . ah . . . think not."

"Than by all means have a seat." He bowed and sat down. "Do you really think that I would cross that sword of your fathers? *Please* give me credit for being smarter than that." Maris smiled deeply.

"Now to the business at hand. Miss Thory, if I may, please understand that I need you, and your brother, of course. You see, I'm trying to look out for my people. *You* could help make them strong. Your family is already very powerful whereas mine. Well . . . other than myself, we are. How shall I say this?"

"Thieves! And apparently, you are weak ones at that," Thomas said angrily.

"Thieves? We are no thieves, I assure you," he said, putting his hand to his chest. "That is why I have come to offer you an opportunity."

"And this opportunity, how would it leave us?" Lisa started in.

Maris's smile was sickening. "Weakened of course, but once concluded, I am sure your strength would return," Thomas cleared his throat.

"Actually, no. you see, I read up on what it takes to do what you've asked and found that not only would it kill us, but you know very well that it would. As that is how you became, what was it? Oh yes, master of your house."

Maris stood up. "Be careful, boy, Bael is powerful, but he can't be everywhere at once. Can you? It is very far to your . . ." Maris stopped and looked questioningly at Lisa. "Miss Thory, would you do something for me *please*?"

"What now?"

"Simply raise your hand towards me so that I may see your palm." Lisa looked at Bael. He nodded. She raised her hand, spreading her fingers. Maris's face began to twist angrily at Bael. "DID YOU KNOW?"

"Not until after I met them," Bael replied. Maris shook his head and paced at the front doors. "It's not possible!"

"Oh yes, Miss Thory, you are indeed special."

"You *will* be busy, won't you, Bael? And the boy is he as well?" Bael nodded.

Lisa turned and looked at Bael questioningly. Maris watched. "This can't be. You, children, don't know! This is priceless!" He laughed.

"My dear Miss Thory, I am sorry. I don't mean any offense to you or your brother. Bael, tell them I speak the truth. PLEASE."

Bael nodded again. With that he crossed the threshold into the house. He took Lisa by the hand and gently kissed her hand. Which she quickly pulled back.

"Miss Thory, I wish you well on your trip. But understand this: soon you both will be sought by *every* vampire, till you reach the father of your house. Myself included. I am sorry." He walked to Bael and whispered to him, "My friend, you cannot protect them alone. Without you having to . . . There are so few you can trust with a treasure this size." He turned to leave. Standing in the doorway stood another man. He had long black-and-white hair and bright blue eyes. He's an older gentleman, but *he* looked bigger and in better shape than Conan. He's dressed for the woods. But well dressed. Maris looked back over his shoulder at Bael." Well played, but unnecessary." As he walked past the man, he nodded his head. "Nick, how's the latest litter?"

"Just fine, Maris."

"Good night to all." And Maris was gone. Bael laughed. "Nicola, I see you got my message. Great timing. Lisa, Thomas, I would like to introduce you to one of my best friends and family, Nicola Lazar."

"Nice to meet you, sir." They shook his hand. He took them by the shoulders for a bear hug.

"Ha-ha. I am happy to meet you as well. So why have you called me to your house? Usually you come to me."

"I have a problem." Bael said as he looked at his guests. "Nicola, these are the last of the Tepes, Basarab line." Nicola shrugged his shoulders.

"You should handle easy enough?"

Bael slightly shook his head. "They're marked, Nicola."

"That's not possible. Is it?"

"Look who you're asking."

Nicola nodded his head. "I will call the family, of course, but you know we can't go back to Russia?"

Bael began to pace. "Yes, but I will have to take the long route to keep them safe. The royals are the only vampires I can trust."

Nicola stopped Bael. "There are others, you know? They too are family. They must. Maliki isn't too far. And I would suggest Remi. They should be enough to get to Alec. I will call Sasha and Katja."

Bael looked up from the floor. "Not Katja, I—"

Nicola cut him off, "Bael it has been long enough, my friend. Too long. And now I ask, is there anyone who would fight by your side harder? Even my Sasha cares more for you, I think, than for her father. You know this, yes? Your problem, *you* must overcome."

Bael nodded. "You're right. Call them."

Nicola went into an office on the other side of the house. Lisa and Thomas stared at Bael, waiting for an explanation.

"Bael, are you going to tell me what the deal is with my hand or what?"

"I'm sorry. In our world, whenever two different families or races have children, the most dominant survives, the other does not. Your blood line is intact. And yet you are marked by your father." Bael took her hand. "You see, these lines in your hand?"

"Yes."

"In most human hands, they are broken. Life lines, love lines, and others all broken on human hands. Yours are connected and make a pattern called a mark."

Lisa looked at her hand. "So what mark is it? What family this time?"

"It is not a curse mark as in our world. It is a sorcerer's mark. A magic mark. This doesn't usually happen. There hasn't been an occurrence in over a thousand years. It is something worth breaking the laws for. It means many vampires will be tempted to come for you two."

"Who is our father?" Thomas asked.

"I'm not sure."

"But you have an idea, don't you?"

"Years ago there was an accident. A sorcerer, a *natural sorcerer*, went to stop an eruption thought to be a natural event. It wasn't. It was caused by a curse by an island witch, or sorcerer. In the end, they both died. If I'm correct, he was your father, Thomas Oaken."

"What's the difference between a natural sorcerer and some other kind?"

"Some sorcerers are born to magic, knowing the art from birth. Others study for years. Then there are *naturals*. They have a magic within them. They need nothing, yet if they study, their spells, curses, and all that, they become very powerful. That is a part of your bloodline as well. But it shouldn't be."

Thomas looked at his hand the pattern connected. Bael closed the doors. The sun was down. The winter evening brought a chill, so more wood was thrown into the hearth, till all were warm again.

Nicola returned to the room. "They will all be here tomorrow. Not till late, but all are on their way." Nicola grabbed up Lisa and Thomas again. "It has been a big night for you. Tomorrow there will be much to do. You should try to sleep now. Yes?"

There was something about Nicola. Lisa hugged him hard and then Bael. Thomas said goodnight. Up the stairs, they went. Bael and Nicola sat by the hearth, staring at the flames. Nicola leaned forward. "I said nothing in front of children, but there is another who could help in all this."

Bael looked at him. "No. He would be a help, but after all this time, I just wouldn't feel right."

"Bael, he is family, your son. End this stupidity. Call. He will come."

"Are you sure?"

"Of course I am."

"How can you be?"

"If your father called, you would go to him."

"I don't even know where he is. I've heard nothing since that message at his grandson's birth." Nicola smiled and began to softly laugh. "You would still go, yes?"

"Yes, I would go."

"Come, my friend, you too must sleep." They climbed the stairs and went to their rooms. Minutes later the house was filled with the sound of Nicola's snoring. Lisa and Thomas stared at the ceiling and silently started laughing. They laughed for a while till they were back asleep.

2

In the morning, the events of the evening seemed almost forgotten. Lisa slept in. Thomas was reading in the library, and Bael was putting posts around the house like a fence, but with nothing between them. Then he went to his cellar and returned with a jar, spreading a black powder between the posts. He then placed his hands together as if in prayer then spread them wide; when he brought them together again, there was a flash and some smoke. This startled Thomas from reading, who quickly got to his feet and went to the front doors to see what was happening. Bael saw Thomas and said, "Sorry, Thomas, but you can come out now, at least to the posts."

"Okay? Yes, thanks. I'll tell Lisa if she ever wakes up."

Bael scratched his head. "Why don't you make some coffee? I'll be in soon to make us breakfast."

"Deal," Thomas replied. "Oh, where's Nicola?"

"In the woods, hunting his breakfast."

Later the coffee was brewed. Breakfast was cooking in the pan. Yawning, Lisa came slowly down the stairs. At the bottom of the stairs, she stopped and looked down the hallway to the kitchen. She shook her head. The house and events seemed crazy, yet she felt as if she were home, as if this was how it was supposed to be. She walked into the kitchen and was handed her coffee. "Where's Nicola?"

"Out, but he should be back soon."

"So what's on the agenda for today?"

Bael put down his toast. "Well . . . let's see. We need to pack and get you two some new clothes for the trip. Something a little more durable. I'm thinking some jeans and warm shirts a good coat or jacket. Oh, and a great pair of boots."

"What, are we going on a trip or safari?"

"A little of both, I'm afraid."

"Okay great," she replied.

Thomas looked at his sister. "Sis, you're okay with that?"

She put her hands up in the air. "Sure, I think I'm starting to get used to these little surprises. I'll go get showered and dressed, and we can get going." She got up from the table and started for the stairs. When the front door opened, a huge tiger walked in. "Huh?" She walked up to the tiger and gave it a hug around the neck.

"Morning, Nicola!" she said and went up the stairs. Bael who had been watching the whole time just shook his head. Thomas who was standing behind him said, "Is that really Nicola?"

"Yes, but I don't know how she knew." The tiger followed her up the stairs. She went to the bathroom, and the tiger to one of the bedrooms. Bael looked at Thomas. "Should I be worried about this, or happy?"

"I really don't know. I was going to ask you." They both went into the library. Thomas picked up a book. "Bael, I've been reading up on what you've said over the past two days. As best I can make out, we're in a lot of trouble, aren't we?"

"Actually it depends on who is on our side. It's going to be a long journey. Come on over to the maps here, and I'll give you an idea of the route I have in mind." Bael rolled out a map from a barrel next to his desk on the table in the center of the room.

"We are about here. On the border of California and Oregon, we leave by foot over the mountains to Nevada. We'll get transportation at the bottom to Utah. Then again, we take the mountains on foot. On the other side, I'll find transportation again and take that to St. Louis. At St. Louis, other transportation will be waiting. We pick up the last member of our team there and head north to Canada."

"Why take the mountains by foot?"

"Because it will be easier to lose any who would track us," Nicola said as he entered the room. "Also, vampires hate snow and ice."

Thomas nodded.

"So . . . North it is, huh?"

Bael smiled. "Yes, Nicola, what time should they arrive?"

"The girls, around one. The boys, three."

"Then we'll leave in the morning after breakfast." Lisa, arriving late to the party, asked, "What are we doing after breakfast?"

"Leaving tomorrow morning," Thomas replied.

"Now, if you're ready," Bael says, "we'll go do some shopping."

Bael looked at her car. "I think my truck may be a better fit."

"What truck?"

"It's behind the barn." They all walked down to the barn. As beautiful as the house and barn were, she expected to see a beautiful black truck shiny and glistening with chrome. What she saw was a ten-year-old dodge truck. It was a burgundy quad cab in great shape but a little disappointing to what she built up.

"Guys, you get up front with me. Nicola, the backseat is yours to give you some room." When everyone was seated, off they went. Lisa looked up at Bael. "How long will it take to reach our family?"

"Well . . . you see, it's going to take a while. We can't take an airplane do to the airports. And the longer we stay off the roads, the better. To be safe it's best to walk as much as possible. That way they won't know which way we left or which way to look."

"What's wrong with airports?"

"A couple of things. One, we can't bring the equipment we'll need. Two, with the crowds, it would be far too easy to lose one of you. And third, you just don't want to see an air-sick tiger." Lisa and Thomas held back the laugh the best they could.

"Who, or maybe, what are we waiting for?"

"Nicola's daughters and two friends of ours."

"And what are your friends?"

"Were people that I trust to get us there."

"Wolf or tiger?"

"Maliki and Remi are bears."

"No wolves? Damn!"

Bael looked at Lisa and Thomas. "We need to keep the team kind of small. Wolves usually travel in a pack. As it is nine won't be very invisible."

"Nine?"

"Yeah. On the way we're picking up my son."

"Oh! And what is he like?"

"Ask his grandfather."

"His grandfather?"

Nicola put his arms together. "Yes, grandfather. And I'm very proud of him. He is brave and strong. Very smart and handsome like his mother. Oh, and his father. It has been too long since I have seen him."

"How long?" asked Thomas. "Almost ten years."

"What about you Bael?" Lisa asked. "When was the last time—"

Nicola cut her off. "Nyet . . . this is something better left alone, little one."

"It's okay, Nicola," Bael said. "It's been two hundred years."

"Wow!" Lisa yelled. "And now you're going to see him because of us?" Lisa smiled a big grin and then gave a nod. "Good!" The rest of the trip to the store was quiet.

The store was a nice country store just off a side road. It was larger than most general stores, but nowhere near the size of a city mart. Lisa walked in and started to look around. When Bael put a hand on her shoulder. "Lisa, Thomas, I know the store may seem safe, but from now on, you two stay close. All right?" he asked.

"Sure," they said and both nodded. An old woman with glasses came walking up to them with a smile. "Oh, Bael, I didn't hear you come in. Who are all your guests you've brought to see me?"

Bael smiled back. "Annie, I'd like you to meet Thomas and Lisa Thory, my family from California. The tall gentleman is Nicola. I think I've mentioned him to you before."

The woman blushed slightly. "Of course you have. He's the father-in-law, right?"

"Yes."

"Well, I'm glad to meet you all. I was beginning to think he made up having a family. Hell, I only know a few friends that he has around here. So what can I get for you all today?"

"Well, Ann, we need four pairs of jeans, four thermal shirts. Some socks and a great pair of boots for both."

Annie looked them over. "I got what you need, but I've got some flannel shirts that the kids would like better. Their just as warm and look good on girls with the colors I got."

"Fine, but at least two thermals." Anne left to collect the clothes. Lisa looked in the jewelry case at the front counter. Thomas and Bael were looking at belts when Nicola came up behind Lisa. She saw his reflection in the glass and smiled.

"What do you see?" Nicola asked.

"Oh nothing, just looking." Anne came back with a basketful of clothes and set two boxes on the counter. "Now," she said, "I got a man's boot in size 11 and a woman's size 7 1/2. As for the clothes, I never get 'em wrong, do I, Bael?"

"No, and we'll take these belts too."

She presses buttons on her register. "That comes to $602.47."

Bael took out his wallet and paid her.

Lisa whispered to Bael, "How did she know our sizes?"

"She's been sizing people up for years."

They walk for the door and turn to say good-bye and thanks to Annie. As they're walking to the car, Nicola stopped. "Oh . . . I'm sorry I forgot. I too may need socks. Go ahead I'll be right back."

Nicola went back in and, minutes later, came running out with his socks. He got in the backseat.

"Bael, you will hold for me in your bag?"

"Sure." On their way back to the cabin, Lisa fell asleep, looking out the window. She awoke to her brother, saying, "Come on, sis, wake up. We need to get out!"

She opened the door and got out. She started for the house when she noticed that around her neck was a necklace of turquoise and white gold. She turned to the others. With a big smile, she ran up to Nicola and gave him a big hug and kiss.

"Thank you, Nicola. How did you know which one I was looking at? "It was the most beautiful."

"Ah, but next to you . . . You make it even more so." Bael gave him a wink, and as Bael passes him, said, "Nice job." Nicola laughs as they enters the house.

All were busy in the house. Lisa and Bael were working on a huge meal of venison with vegetable dressing. A duck or two from the smokehouse in the barn and a big berry and apple pie for dessert. Nicola was down in the cellar working on something, and

Thomas was reading again till he fell asleep in the big chair. A little after twelve, they heard a vehicle drive up. Out of the van came two women and a man. Nicola grabbed up the girls with his usual zest, kissing them both. Then went up to the man. Lisa thought Nicola was big. But this man was even taller. Nicola turned and introduced them to his daughters Katja and Sasha. They looked almost exactly alike. Except for their hair and eyes. Sasha had light brown hair and eyes. Katja had black-and-white hair and blue eyes like her father. Then he introduced them to Maliki, a huge man with white hair and black eyes. He had a soft smile and kind face. He took her hand so gently, bent down, and kissed it.

Lisa blushed and said how nice it was to meet them all. The girls greeted Thomas and Lisa, but went over to Bael and each gave him a hug and kiss. Though Katja's seemed to last a little longer. She slid off him till her feet were both planted again. Bael looked a little sad yet happy. "It's nice to see you two again. I've missed you. Come on inside. I hope you're all hungry. We made dinner."

Lisa didn't know what was wrong, but Bael seemed off somehow. She whispered to Bael, "Are you okay?"

"I'm fine, Lisa, really."

"You don't look real fine. You look like you just got ran over."

"It's okay, Lisa. I promise to explain later."

"Okay, sure. I just worry, that's all." Bael gave her an easy smile. "Come on, let's go in and get to know each other better. Okay?"

"Oh . . . kay," Lisa replies. And they all go into the house.

The ladies walked in and went to work, setting the table and bringing in the food from the kitchen. Maliki and Nicola went into the library. Bael and Thomas started to follow, but Bael went to the kitchen to help with dinner. Lisa had made the meal with Bael, so she went into the kitchen as well. Sasha made her feel welcome by calling her over to help with the venison getting it to the table. Katja grabbed some flour and a bowl and started mixing. Buy the time the ducks had finished cooking, the dough had risen and into the oven went the bread. The rice went out. The whole kitchen was a machine.

In the library, Thomas was explaining the route on the map to Maliki and Nicola. Maliki suggested going through Canada and

Alaska over the ice and taking a boat to Russia. Nicola reminded him of the problems in Russian territory for him and his daughters. To which Maliki apologized. He looked at the map again. "Are you going to see Alec and that hard-headed brother of his?"

"It will be safe shelter for the children." Thomas didn't like being called child all the time. Then he considered the age of everyone else in the room. *Yeah, I guess child does kind of fit?* Bael came into the library to tell them that dinner was almost ready. When they all heard an engine, and someone yelling out in front of the house, Maliki looked at Nicola with a frustrated look. "Remi? Is *that* coming with us?" Nicola shook his head at Maliki. "My friend you are too hard on Remi. He is sometimes getting carried away. But what would he do if someone insulted one of your girls?"

"True. And he is family?" Nicola laughs. "Now go and welcome him in." Before he could get to the door, it pulled open. "Hello, mon'ame." In came Remi like a wind. Another tall man with a beard. He had brown hair and eyes. He had an attitude that shined through the room. "Where are my kittens? He sees Maliki. Ah and how are you? You old bear? I have missed you as well."

Katja and Sasha ran from the kitchen. "Cousin Remi!" they shouted and jumped to his arms.

"Ah . . . look at you as beautiful as ever. And Bael, where is he? Have you caught him yet, mon' cher's?" With that Katja let go and slid down.

"I am sorry, little one, if I spoke out of turn. He still struggles with his heart? Come let us lighten the mood. Now where are these troublesome two, huh?" Thomas and Lisa stood together and walk toward him. Lisa looks up high into his eyes. "It's nice to meet you. I am Lisa and this is my brother, Thomas."

Thomas put his hand out. Remi shook his hand. He took Lisa by hand and kissed it as Maliki had. Again, she blushes. Bael stood at the back of the room with his hands on his hips.

"What? No greeting for me, you big shaggy bear?"

Still holding Sasha in his arm, he walks over and grabs his head and kisses his cheeks. "It is so good to see you, my friend. I have news for you."

"Can it wait till after dinner?"

He looks at the table and spots Katja's bread. "Aye . . . it can wait. There is nothing to do anyway."

They take their seats. And all hold hands around the table. "We thank the earth for all its bounty, and the gods who provided it." Then everyone takes a different dish and the meat gets carved. Plates are made for Lisa and Thomas who were beginning to wonder if there would be enough for everyone. Katja's bread was gone before anyone knew what happened. Remi poured honey over it, and it just seemed to disappear. As for the venison, Nicola and his girls were enjoying it. Thomas and Maliki had the ducks down to the wishbone. Bael and Lisa had their plates, and that was all. Neither seemed too hungry despite the great food.

After the meal, Thomas and Remi, along with Nicola, cleaned up the table and the dishes. Everything was put away. Bael went to the cellar and came back with a large backpack. He then went around the house getting it ready. Clothes and some things from the bathroom, some utensils for cooking were all placed in the bag. He sent the girls out to the barn, and they came back with rope and equipment. Items were put in the bag for hours. Lisa began to realize how long this trip might take. When Bael had finished, Remi took him by the arm and led him to the office. "My friend, I still have news for you." Bael sat down with Remi. "What news?"

"The word has gotten out about the children. Montgomery is saying that due to them being marked that there is no choice to make for them. Their family's father wanted to speak for them, but Montgomery says that marks have no voice. He is pushing for their confinement."

Bael looks puzzled. "They can't be put in confinement without going before the royals?"

"Montgomery is saying that marks are not and cannot be set before the houses."

"When will the royals meet?"

"Monty is pushing so . . . soon, I would think."

"That was what he meant."

"Who?"

"Maris! He and his house were my original concern," he said. "I couldn't be in two places at once." I can't go before the royals and watch over them."

"With this many after them, even our group couldn't fight and look after them!"

"What about your son? They wouldn't be so bold as to oppose you both? Or either of you, would they?" Bael sits back in the chair.

"What bothers me is who is backing Montgomery? He wouldn't make moves like this without someone backing him? Someone he seems to fear more than me." Remi put his hand on the arm of the chair.

"In our world, *you* keep the peace. You have the power it takes to enforce the rules. And yet you do not interfere with the families or the races. I don't know who it could be." They came out of the office, and Bael shouted to them all, "Ladies and gentlemen, it's time for us all to get some sleep. I want to leave out of here by four thirty in the morning, so . . . everyone to bed."

Slowly they all got up and went up to their rooms. Bael stayed downstairs and checked the posts outside. He walked back in and saw the sword above the door. "Oh . . . Father, how I miss you. Especially now, two lives are at stake." He turns out the lights and stokes up the fire. Then he goes to his room to sleep.

3

The next morning, hours before daylight, everyone started to rise. All except one: Lisa was still fast asleep. The coffee brewing didn't even wake her up. Bael went to Nicola. "I think you should go and wake her this morning. She had a long day, and I think she's more comfortable around you."

"Of course I will wake her, but what makes you think so?"

"When she first saw your change? It's the way she knew it was you." Nicola nodded his head and went upstairs. He knocked on the outside of her doorway.

"Elisavetta? he called quietly into her room. Elisavetta?" he called again. He went into her bedroom. She was still deep in sleep. He gently began to shake her. "Come, little one. It's almost time to leave." She slowly opened her eyes to see Nicola. She yawned and stretched. "Good morning," she finally said. "I'm sorry, Nicola. I'm just not a morning person." She smiled. "I'll shower and be right down. Okay?"

She got up on the bed and gave him a kiss on the cheek, then jumped down and ran for the shower. "You must hurry, Elisavetta. Bael is rushing to leave!"

"Okay, I'll be fast." Nicola went back downstairs. He looked at Bael. "She is showering and will join us soon." Thomas looked out the window, at the darkness. "You woke her?"

"Yes." Thomas walked up to Bael and whispered, "He got her up this early? He's the god performing miracles. I've seen her glance, sour milk, waking up at six for school. It's not even four? I'll wait in the library till she's had her coffee."

Bael laughs. "Okay we'll call you in when she's ready."

A few minutes later, Lisa came down the staircase. Hopping on one leg, trying to get her boots on. "I'm sorry you had to wait." Bael had a hot cup of coffee waiting on the table in the middle of the room. "Thank you! I need this!" She drank it as fast as she dared and put on her backpack. Thomas came in and did the same. Bael looks at them sternly. "Now this is a long journey, so if you're having trouble, shout out and we'll stop or help."

"Okay," they agreed, and they all set off.

Thomas, Lisa, and Bael carries the gear. Bael sends Remi and Sasha ahead to make sure the way was clear. Katja moved behind them, watching and listening. Nicola said that there was nothing that could sneak up on her for miles. Bael agreed. Lisa kept noticing that Bael, every once in a while, looked sick again. Lisa started to walk with Bael. "Are you going to explain why you keep getting run over? Or keep me guessing?"

Bael looked at Lisa. "I'm sorry. I did promise an explanation, didn't I? Lisa . . . , you see how Katja and Sasha look alike?"

"Yes."

"Well . . . their sister Tara looked exactly the same as Katja."

"Their triplets, I get it."

"Yes, but Tara was my wife."

"Oh . . . so she reminds you of her, huh?"

"Yes, but there's more to it."

Nicola interrupted, "You see, little one, all of my daughters love Bael. But two had his affections. Till he chose and married my Tara. There was problem at the birth of my grandson. And my Tara died years later due to that problem. Bael mourned his wife. But he has denied himself to love again."

"Nicola!" Bael shouted. But Nicola continued, "You see, he still loves Tara and her sister Katja. Tara herself told both of them to be happy?"

"*FATHER, THAT'S ENOUGH!*" Katja came from behind. "Right now we have enough to deal with. Lisa, this all happened long ago. *Please* drop the subject."

Hours went by. Walking seemed better than talking, even on the eggshells, everyone seemed to be on. Till finally, Thomas could take the quiet no more. "It's bad enough to have to climb all day without all this silence. Bael, if you don't mind, I still have some questions?"

"Go ahead, Thomas."

"Who is this Alec we're going to see?"

"A good friend and a sorcerer. He's not used to guests, but his home is as safe as mine."

"What's his stake in all this?"

"None really."

"You know I looked through that law book of yours till I fell asleep."

"Yes, I've noticed you spend a lot of time reading up on the way we do things?"

"My sister deals with surprises as they happen. I'm more apt for being prepared."

"My brother the Boy Scout," Lisa added. Thomas gave her a grim look. "Saying all we have to do is ask is great. But if we don't know what to ask, we still won't know anything. For instance, why are we so valuable, worth breaking the laws? And if this mark isn't supposed to happen, what are they planning to do with us? And how come a guy who wouldn't come in under that sword one minute walks in without a care the next? Not to mention—"

Bael stopped him by holding up his hand. "I get your point. Guys, let's take a little break, huh?" Bael took a deep breath. "First . . . about Maris. When he got to the house as you know, his plans would have killed you. That made him an enemy. Crossing that sword would have cost him his head and life. When he saw that mark, you were more than just a power boost to his house. You were something he could use. He was no longer a threat to your life. The sword would let him enter."

"The sword would let him?"

"Yes. If you could be bound, you could be used. 'Quite the treasure' as he put it. As for what the royals are going to do, I'm not sure, but I will have a say in the end. That I promise."

Sasha and Remi came back to the group. "They're out there, keeping their distance but there. If you want to stop for lunch now would be as good time as any?" Remi suggests. Sasha smiles at Thomas. "How are you keeping up?"

"Fine, thanks."

Bael reached in his bag and pulled out sandwiches; Nicola shakes his head. "I will find something later tonight." After eating they continued up the mountainside. The conversations went from schools to family and family to jobs. Lisa found out that Nicola was a doctor and a great one from what Bael had said. Katja was a photographer for many magazines, and a newspaper, working all around the world. Sasha had been in the navy as a pilot. Remi worked for the government as a ranger, but he had been in the US navy as well. He had been living in Louisiana and moved to Canada after he got out of the navy.

Lisa turned to Bael. "Do you have a job?"

The others laughed. As did Bael.

"Sorry, Lisa, it's just that my job keeps me very busy."

"How do you pay for things?" Nicola looks at Lisa. "I thought you knew Bael is a prince. He no longer claims the crown or title. He like his father, he battled from place to place for thousands of years. Countries and nations have paid him to solve their problems. He is quite well-off as far as money is concerned." Lisa sat there, a little stunned. "So . . . the grandson of a god, a prince, a kind of a marshal, or sheriff? Anything else?"

"Well yes . . . actually, your legal guardian."

"You're joking?"

"No. Your mother put me in charge of you when she chose. Lucile was your watcher. She reported to me everything you've done over the years. She didn't work for a job. How do you think she paid the bills?"

"Mom's estate? I thought."

"Dear, your mother isn't dead. Well . . . , technically, she's undead. But still alive. But she couldn't stay with you. The families would have known. You understand, don't you?"

"No. That is, I didn't. We had always assumed she was dead. When you said family, I thought . . . I . . . I . . . I just thought." She looked at her brother who had lost all the expression on his face.

Sasha who was trying to be serious looked at Bael. "I think you broke 'em this time."

Everyone stopped. Nicola asked for some water for them though vodka would be better. Bael sat Lisa down and then Thomas. "No. He doesn't take surprises well, does he?" Sasha asked. Bael got a fire started. Katja went out and brought back some dinner. Camp was up. Thomas and Lisa weren't.

Lisa woke to the smell of coffee and what was left of dinner. It was night. The light from fire was warm and inviting. She sat up and shook her head.

"How are you feeling?" Bael asks.

"Better, I hope."

"Yeah. I just . . . I . . . oh, I don't know anymore!" Lisa looked around. "Where is everyone?"

Bael sighed. "Well . . . , your brother is sleeping on the other side of the fire. He went out about the same time you left us. Nicola and the girls are watching the perimeter. Remi is up the mountain, keeping watch, and Maliki is sleeping till three o'clock. I am here with you. Welcome back, Alice, the hatter's been waiting."

"Very funny, Bael. How long was I out?"

"About seven hours and some change."

"I'm sorry. I didn't . . . "

"Lisa, your brother is still out. You have nothing to be sorry about. Myself on the other hand. I am sorry. I thought you understood more than you and your brother had."

She put her hands to her face. "I really thought I was getting used to this. I did, you know. So do I call you Uncle Bael or what?"

"Just Bael."

"Well . . . Bael, I don't know what else you got planned, but can I have some coffee before we start?"

"Sure."

"How about some aspirin?"

"Got you covered." And he threw her a bottle. Lisa took the pills and drank her coffee. After a while she felt more herself again. "She's alive? I can't believe it." She watched the fire and started to cry.

Katja came into the camp.

"Bael, why don't you go for a walk?" He nodded his head and left. Katja sat next to Lisa. She put her arm around her shoulders.

"I've known Bael a very long time. No matter how bad things seem. I know he is always there for . . . us. He looks after an entire world, but never forgets his family. And that's you. And that's your brother. So everything will work out. You've known my father for a few days now? He wouldn't have it any other way."

Lisa turns and hugs Katja, still crying. In a muffled voice, she hears Lisa, "You know, I've only known your father a little while, but I can't help it. I love him and your family so much."

"Well . . . Lisa, we're right here." Katja patted her back.

"I know. I just don't want to lose any of you." Katja laughs. "Little one, calm yourself. Tomorrow will come, and we will still be here. Okay?" But no answer came. She had fallen asleep again. Katja laid her back down, covered her up, and rubbed her shoulder. "We are becoming very fond of you too, little one. Very fond."

"Your father wouldn't want to admit it. But I think it was love at first sight. They took to each other so fast." Bael walked out of the shadows. "Sorry, but I had to stay close." Katja looked up. "Yes, I know. Bael, you keep forgetting they are still human, very human."

"Yeah, I don't have the whole subtle thing down yet, do I?"

"Bael, you are strong, powerful, and a genius in a fight. But when it comes to dealing with emotions and loved ones."

"That sword is rusty, huh?" Bael sighed. Katja got up, and walked over to him.

"Bael, it's not just these kids. You've been avoiding me for so long. I understand. I do. I loved her too. That's not going to change. But I love you too, and that's not going to change either. Is it? Think of all the problems. I know you love me. So did my sister. The day you were married, I was so happy for you and Tara. She didn't betray me to marry you. I wanted you both happy. And you were. Well . . . you might be happy again. You used to be in touch with your emotions. You loved your wife and son. You were family. My father's family as well. You saw us all the time. Then you shut yourself off, and as a result, what happened? We don't see you hardly ever. Your son hasn't seen you in two hundred years. Do you remember what you said to me? Time heals. Love never dies. Yet look at us. It struggles to live at all. You're killing it, and fear is growing in its place. Fear of losing what's gone. What would your mother say?"

Bael looked at Katja. "I just can't let go."

"Bael?" Lisa called. "I never forgot my mother. Yet you know Lucile was my mother. I felt that loss too. Your wife is you. There is nothing to hold on to. It's just there." Bael shook his head. "Both of them are coming back to you."

"But I didn't know that." Bael looked at the girl on the ground as she fell back to sleep. Bael held Katja and kissed her. "I do still love you. I haven't forgotten. Though my heart hasn't healed, perhaps *we* can heal it? If you don't mind working on a tough project, do you?" Katja kissed him. "I only work with the best." She started to kiss him again. But her head popped up. Her nose caught a scent. *Damn! I need to get back out there.* She kisses him. "Don't forget I've signed on."

"I won't." Katja leaped into the air and came down on a paw. She ran off into the dark woods. Bael started to lie back down. He paused. "What do you know it's beating again?" He lies back and fell asleep, smiling.

The morning came with a drop of rain hitting Thomas on the nose. "Huh? What the . . . uh . . . man, it figures."

"Good morning, sunshine." Lisa had been up for an hour. She got the coffee on. The camp packed up and was determined to have a good day. Bael walked into camp from the perimeter. "Well, Miss Thory, you seem better than the last we spoke."

"I am and thanks."

"I think this. Thanks is on me."

"What do you mean?"

"Do you remember waking up and giving me advice?"

"Oh god, that happened. I thought I was dreaming. Hey wait, that means you . . . "

"Lisa, why don't you give everyone a chance to wake up?" Bael gave her a wink.

"Fine, I'll shut up." Thomas shook his head. "Did I hear right? My sister is shutting up? What did I miss?"

Lisa shook a big stick at Thomas. "Tom, it's only a little after five. Don't push it."

"Got it!" Thomas responds. Maliki was out cold as was Sasha and Katja. Nicola and Remi were still out. Lisa stopped drinking long enough to notice. "Does Remi ever sleep? He never came in last night." Nicola came strolling in. "There's my tiger!" Lisa ran up and gave the tiger a bear hug. Nicola purred, yawned, and lay down with a thump! Bael turned to Lisa. "Okay. I got good news and bad news. Which do you want first?" Lisa circles a wave in. "Shoot me the bad first."

"We've got fifty-six miles to walk today."

"What's the good news quick?"

"Only two are uphill. And it's getting colder. This light rain will probably turn to snow within the hour."

"Great, just great," Thomas grumbled. Lisa decided to stay positive. "Sounds fine. But let's give everyone a little more sack time. They earned it."

Everyone began to wake up at around seven. Lisa had more coffee ready for everybody. Bael had the backpack ready, except for what they were sleeping on. Remi came walking into camp. "Bonjour, my friends!"

"How are you so cheerful without sleep?" Lisa asks.

"Me? I slept fine. I found a place up there on the cliffs to watch over the camp for miles. My ears and nose work when my eyes must close. A trick I learned centuries ago." The rain had gotten colder. Snow was on its way. Bael went to Nicola and whispered in his ear. Then Bael did the same to Maliki.

"Okay, guys, it's two miles to the top then. I have an idea for getting down the other side. As for the two miles, I think we could cover the ground faster if you two ride."

"Ride what?" Nicola and Maliki changed forms before them.

"Well . . . there are no horses, but then horses couldn't move as well across this ground." The snow began to come down in large flakes. Lisa and Thomas smiled.

"Are you sure about this?" Nicola rubbed his nose against her hand. Bael laughed. "Go ahead. Climb on. And hold on tight." They climbed up. Lisa put her right hand around his neck, and the other behind his front leg to keep steady. Whereas Thomas, he rode like a jockey. Lisa looked at Bael. "What about you?"

Thomas laughs. "I think he'll be able to keep up!"

Bael picked up the big backpack and leaped to a branch high in the trees. The polar bear let out a roar heard for miles. Then he took off at a run; Thomas straining to hold on. Lisa hugs her big white tiger. "Don't forget I'm here, Nicola." And the large tiger leaps into a run. Remi bowed to the girls. "Shall we dance, Mon'chers?" They changed to their animal forms and chased after the others. Bael watched from above, keeping an eye out for the vampires who were following them, and keeping their distance.

They reached the top within an hour. Bael was waiting for them. He had knocked down a tree and split it with his knife and hand. When they arrived, he was finishing, rounding off the front to make a makeshift sled. It was long and hard, but fast down the steep side of the mountain. The snow was getting deeper as they raced down the hillsides. The cold taking its effect on the kids. Thomas turned his head, and Bael noticed how red and cold they were getting. He brought the sled to a stop, and he dug into the backpack, until out came his hand with folded fur hats. He grabbed one of their shirts and said to use it as a scarf. When they seemed warm enough, he started down again. He had obviously been this way before. Two hours or more later, they reached the lower part of the mountain. The snow had thinned, but they were still going at a good clip of speed. From time to time, Lisa would catch sight of something running off in the distance. It wasn't part of their group. By noon they were coming to the bottom. They could see a small town a couple of miles away.

It was two thirty by the time they got to a restaurant in town. Lisa and Thomas's feet were killing them. The waitress came over and asked, "What would you all like today?"

"Eight coffees?" Bael asked.

Thomas corrected him, "Seven and a coke, please?"

"Sure thing, sweetie." She left and returned with the drinks.

Bael asked the waitress, "Is there a place in town to rent a vehicle?"

"Sure is. The phone book is over there. Help yourself." Bael found the rentals easy enough. He called and asked for a large van. They had none. The man on the phone had a suggestion of the dealership on the corner. It had a window bus on the lot and might be able to get it for a reasonable price this time of year. The man didn't know the number but told him the name. After they warmed up and had something to eat, they walked down to the dealership. Bael felt they were being watched, but it wasn't a vampire. It felt different. Bael pulled at Sasha and whispered in her ear. Sasha stopped. "Guys I forgot my bag at the diner! I'll hurry back and get it and catch up." Sasha left running, and the others walked on. Lisa saw the bus down the street. She brought Bael's attention to it. Seconds later they heard a kind of small roar behind them. They walked to a backstreet where Sasha had grabbed a man by the throat. "I got him. You were right. He was watching us as we went down the street." The man disappeared from her hand and reappeared in front of Bael. He bowed and began to explain, "I am sorry, but I chose this town due to its remoteness. Then after twenty years, I felt the presence of magic. I was merely curious. Then I saw you, Your Highness, and I got worried."

Bael looked at the man. "I thought I knew everyone in this reagent. Who are you?"

"My apologies." He bowed again. "I go by the name Goume, sir. I am a puck. I live here now. If I may? I have a shop here selling antiques to humans."

"Why so remote?"

"I like the quiet, sir."

"Well, enjoy your quiet. We're just passing through picking up a vehicle and leaving."

"Buying a car, sir?"

"Yes."

"At the dealer, on the corner, sir?"

"Yes."

"I may be able to help you there, sir? You see, I am friends with the salesman there."

Bael laughs. "A puck friends with a used car salesman."

"Sir?"

"I'm sorry, Goume. Truly, but pucks and salesmen are both notorious tricksters."

"Sir, I am a puck. Not *the* puck. Generations of pucks have done far more with our power than play jokes."

"I know that, Goume, and I am sorry. I meant no offense."

"That, sir, is one of the reasons I came here. The old clichés are forgotten here. Some of the humans here even know what I am. And don't care." Bael bowed his head. "Sir, I do apologize again. It's been a troubling few days. I seem to find amusement where there is none far more often lately."

Goume bowed back. "I hope that I may ease your problems, sir. Let's see if I can perhaps get you a good bargain with my friend, shall we?"

They went to the dealership, and Goume talked to his friend. Goume and his friend came out of the office. "Sir, my friend here is Mr. Parks, and he would be willing to lower the price for you two thousand off the sticker." Bael looked over and saw a bank. "I can get you cash?"

Mr. Parks looked over the group. "Well . . . we'll say three then and call it a deal. I'll have the paperwork done by the time you get back." Bael shook his hand. "Thank you, sir. And, Goume, thank you as well."

"Not at all, sir." Bael shook his hand, and leaned in. "You may call me Bael, if you wish."

"Thank you, yes. I would."

Bael and Lisa went to the bank and cashed a check and made a call on their phone. When they returned, Bael signed some papers and handed the money over. The bus was warmed up, and they got on board. There was room for all and then some. Goume came to say good-bye.

"Bael, it has been a pleasure meeting you."

Bael bowed his head. "And you, Goume, have been the most Noble farae I have met in years."

Goume smiled, and a tear rolled down his cheek. "Thank you. Sir, if I may." He made a sign in the air, then pointed his finger, and the bus gave a small shake. "It will get you where you need to go much easier now."

"Thank you again, Goume."

"Not at all, sir, and to you and yours, good journeys."

"Good-bye!" they said. And they all waved.

4

On the road they rested the cold evening air, and the warm bus put most to sleep. Remi and Bael sat up at the front of the bus, driving and talking. "Have you been thinking about who might be behind Montgomery?" Remi asked.

"Yes, but I can't come up with anyone with that much power."

Remi shook his head. "*The old ones—(The fare folk, or Farae)*— have too much respect for you. What about the *Eblis [dark Jinn]*? They have the power." Bael nodded. "True, but they deal with themselves through the *Jinn (genies, or poss. fallen angels)*. I can't see either getting too involved. Besides first and foremost is the question. Who deals with the *vampires?*"

Remi turned to Bael. "I've got a thought that worries me." Bael listened. "What is it?"

"What if it's not just about the children? What if it's deeper? Could someone be setting you up? Trying to push you?"

"Possible, but again, who?"

"What about Sorrow? Perhaps he could find out something?"

"Pull over and I'll see." Remi slowly pulled to the side of the road. Bael got off the bus and put his arm out and whistled. From high above the bus, a large raven came down to rest on his arm. Bael spoke to the bird and then it took flight. Bael got back on board. And Remi started off again. "He'll see what he can find out. I think our best chance will be *Alec.*"

After a few hours, Bael was driving. Remi went back to get some sleep. Thomas and Lisa had woken up since their little nap the other day, which gave them some energy. They went up front to talk with Bael.

"How's the bus doing?" Lisa asked.

"Just great."

Thomas asked if he could take over for a while.

"Actually that would be great." Bael set the cruise and got up holding on to the wheel. Thomas took the seat and wheel. "Just stay on this road!" Thomas nodded. Bael sat next to Lisa. "How are you doing?"

"Fine I guess."

"That man in town?"

"He said he was a *puck?*"

"Yes."

"Would you care to elaborate some?"

"Sure. The puck are farae or fairies, and there are many different kinds of fairies. They are also called the old ones as they were here before humans. They lived with them for many years. Their king, Prince Oberon, took most back to live on a separate plane on an island called Avalon, the green island of apples, a type of paradise. Many pleaded to stay here. Humans usually don't see or notice them. The human mind will tend to block out what it can't perceive as real. Over the centuries some of the subfarae have developed the same way of dealing with humans. They simply don't see each other."

"Why did he start crying?" Bael dropped his head. "You see, the old ones struggle with most human words. One however transcends all boundaries. The word *noble*. It is an old word. It means so much to us. You know this word don't you?"

"Yes, but we don't use it much. We have honor that gets used well especially with our military."

"This too is an old word and a good one. In the human world, *nobility* has been twisted. That is one of the reasons most of us have left our nations and countries. You fight a war with honor. Nobility is how all should be dealt with after. Humans have twisted every word and meaning throughout their history—countries, politics, families, and religion. Any story ever written will be rewritten till it is socially acceptable for that time, place, or people. Take my name Bael. My grandfather's name, yet it was originally Bel, then changed to Baal, then to Bael. Other religions came along and took the same god and changed his name to Asmodai and Samael. Later, other religions add that there is only one god that is good. Therefore, the others must be evil. Even the word *evil* has been changed from its origins. The original gods were a triad. Now brought to two. At other times, the Greeks had a triad—Zeus, Hades, and Poseidon. And the Norse had Odin, frigia, and so many others. My grandfather was known as the god of wisdom and fertility. His brother *An* the god of creation and light. Their sister *Ea* the goddess of water and life. These names are forgotten by man as was their messages. Time and again given. Time and again twisted." Lisa listened to Bael. Through everything he said, he was never angry but disappointed. Lisa looked up at Bael. "It seems like . . . well, do you like humans at all?"

Bael put his arm around her. "I love them all. You see, they also have the honor and nobility. They show it at the strangest of times. A soldier gets a medal, but believes it should go to others. That is nobility. Those that would talk out a problem without anger and find the quick resolution so others stay safe. That is noble. And showing manners in the face of an insult and not retaliate whether the insult was meant or not. That is noble."

"Humans have greatness in them, a hope. And that is what I love about them. And you." He hugs her harder and kisses her head.

Lisa thought over what Bael told her. Her mother Lucile was the embodiment of nobility. Maybe that was why they loved her so much. And why it hurt to find out their maternal mother was alive. Lisa couldn't even ask any questions about her. She wasn't sure she wanted to know.

As they drove through the night, Thomas enjoyed driving. Before the sun came up, he saw lights ahead. It was a city. *Salt Lake City most likely,* he thought. He looked at the gauges. They could use some fuel and a soda would be nice. He thought of far too many reasons to stop. As he drove into the city, he looked for a gas station. He pulled in next to the pump, got out, and started filling the tank.

"How are you this evening, Thomas?" Before he turned his head. He knew the voice. The boy was pulled away and into the air. Finally, coming to rest on a rooftop across the street, Thomas looked up. Master Maris stood there, smiling a most sickening smile.

"So . . . Master Thomas, where I wonder would you and your companions be heading?" Thomas said nothing. "Do you think you've come a long way? Well . . . you haven't. No. you have very far to go. Oh, I know very well where you are heading. By now you must be wondering why I don't just take you now and be done with it? As I told you, I need you and your sister.

"However, that's not going to happen if you continue to make foolish mistakes. I need you to learn and learn quickly without your friends down there. How long do you last?

"Thomas, listen to me. Stay closer to them. And if you reach the robed wonder, ask for *affirmation*. Do not tell the others of this conversation. When we return, get your soda. And take your balling out from Bael. If you tell them about me before you're affirmed, you won't make it. I promise you." With that he pulled Thomas back into the air and returned him beside the bus and vanished. He finished refueling and got his sodas and a coffee for his sister, then shut the bus door. He took a deep breath and settled his nerves. As he pulled away and left the lot, a bump woke Bael and the others. \

"Sorry didn't mean to wake you. I just had to get some fuel!" Bael was furious. "Are you out of your mind? Leaving the bus alone, do you have any idea what could have happened to you?"

"SORRY! I just stopped for a minute. I'm fine! Sis, I got you a coffee." Lisa took the cup and shook her head. "What were you thinking?" Remi took over the driver's seat, and Thomas went back to a seat in the rear. Bael went to Thomas. "Thomas, you have no idea how fast a vampire can move. You could have been taken in the blink of an eye. That's why we stay together."

"I understand! Believe me, it won't happen again."

"Good." Bael nodded. Thomas drank his sodas and thought about what had happened. He started looking out the window for answers.

Thousands of miles away, night was coming to a small town. A private tavern within the town stood as it had for hundreds of years in the Romanian hillsides. Inside the tavern, a man waited in the shadows of light at the back of the room. Walking quickly down the pathway was a man dressed in a gray suit and high polished shoes, he had the appearance of a banker. With narrow features, and a dark thin mustache at the end of his narrow nose. As he reached the door of the tavern, he looked around nervously before he slipped inside. The room was empty except for a bartender and a gentleman at the back table.

"Ah . . . Montgomery, I trust things are going well?" Montgomery walked to the corner table. "Uh . . . well, yes, sir, but there were a few complications. As you expected, the queen has given her support to the children. However, their family father, Lord Basarab, is not backing down, nor has the Magyar." The man in the shadows tapped his ring on the table.

"I thought you were the voice of the Magyar?"

"I am, sir, but one of three. However, the rest of the families have agreed." The shadowed man took his glass in his hand. "Who are the other families that are holding their ground?"

"The Bathorys and the Ravennas, but their families are voicing a different opinion, sir. Sir, if I may? Perhaps we should wait for a more opportune time to challenge Bael."

"You let me worry about Bael. I have waited for this game for a very long time. Not all the pieces are on the board yet, so . . .Do as you're told and work on the families."

"Yes, mea lord."

"Oh . . . and, Montgomery, as much as I like your work, if you question me again . . ." Montgomery saw the smile on his face in the shadows, and fear cut through him. "Do we understand each other?"

"Yes, sir. Of course, sir."

"Where are they now?"

"*They*, sir?"

"Bael and his friends."

"They should be nearing the Rockies I would think, sir. As you ordered, all are keeping their distance."

"Prepare the thralls you have. I want them and as many underlings as you can spare. Put up a fight for them to get in to see the sorcerer. Once in, I'll send some subfarae to keep them there."

"But, sir . . . I . . . yes, sir." The man in the shadows waved to the bartender. "Two more, George, my friend, Here needs something for his nerves."

"Of course, sir," the bartender replied and soon brought the glasses to the table. Montgomery took the drink. "What about the *Royals*, sir?"

"Do what you can, but I have a surprise for them as well. Now, finish your scotch and go back to work."

"Very well, sir." Montgomery finished and left. The man got up from the table and threw a gold coin to bartender. "Good evening, George!"

"Have a good evening, sir." He walked into the night air. "Yes . . . just a few more pieces, Bael. A few more pieces." And the man vanished in a shimmer.

Remi called out to Bael, "The town is up ahead, Mon'ami." Bael went to the others. "Soon we'll get to the mountains again. It's going to be much harder this time than last."

Lisa sighs. "Bael, I know this is supposed to make things harder for those following us but Thomas and I aren't exactly used to this kind of thing."

Bael smiles sympathetically. "I know, but the cold throws them off some, and we can track them easier." Thomas thought to himself, *I'm not so sure about that.*

Bael continued, "Once we get on the other side, we'll be driving the rest of the way."

They started packing up their things as they drove through the town. Without any warning, Remi came to a stop. He put on the break and stood up. "Ladies and gentleman, there will be a slight change in plans."

Nicola yelled out, "Have you lost your senses, Remi. You could have killed them."

"My apologies, little ones. Bael, look here." And Remi pointed out the window. Standing on the corner outside a café was a young man in his thirties—tall, muscular, with long light hair and bright blue eyes. Bael could hardly believe his eyes. Nicola smiled as Lisa had never seen.

"Who is that?" she asked. Nicola put his hand on her shoulder. "That, my dear, is my grandson, Beowulf."

"Oh . . ." Lisa tried to fix her hair, but it was no use. They all got off the bus. Before Bael could say a word, Sasha ran across the street and picked up Beowulf in her arms. "So . . . how is my nephew these days? Eh . . . give your aunt Sasha a hug and kiss! Oh. How I've missed you."

Bael and the others walked over. "Sasha put him down."

"Hello, Father." Bael looked at him, hesitating for a moment, then gave him a hug, nearly smothering him. Finally, giving him a kiss. "I've missed you, son. More than I have the words for. Can you forgive me? I'm so sorry for closing you off after your mother passed away. I can't explain why it happened. Except to say I was a fool."

"Father." Beowulf put his hand on his father's shoulder. "I knew what you were going through. I was going through it as well. But I had the family to help me through. I'm just glad you're here now."

Bael smiled at his son. Then Bael looked confused. "How did you know to meet us here?"

"Well . . . first, I got told the situation with the Thorys. Then I was told you were on your way to me. Since I figured you'd try losing your problems in the mountains. I came here because you used to take me up the mountain from here."

"How long have you been here?"

"Not long."

"Who told you we were coming."

"The first message came from Alec through his owl Sebastian. Then grandfather sent me a message to pack up and get started to meet you through old gray his hawk. And last, was Sorrow on his way to Salem to get information for you. He was the one who told me where I might find you."

Bael looked cold and away from his son. "You've heard from your grandfather?"

"Sure!" Bael turned. "I wasn't even sure he was alive."

"Yeah. Well . . . he didn't want to fight. And you know what happens when you're together?" Nicola interrupts. "Bael I know this is shock for you. But I haven't hugged my grandson yet, and we have far to go to get reacquainted yes?"

"Yes. Bael replied. Let's get on the bus and I'll make introductions on the way."

After everyone was back in their seats, Bael called up front to Remi, "Well, Remi, I guess take a left turn and head to Alec's!"

"Where to now?" asked Lisa. "To Canada, to meet an old friend. Bael replied. "He's perhaps the best sorcerer I've met." Nicola laughs. "Yes, the great robed wonder, haw . . . haw . . . Him and his brother Jason the ever resolute." Bael clears his throat. "If you don't mind Nicola I would like to introduce our friends. Lisa, Thomas I would like you to met my son Beowulf." Beowulf walks to the children and kisses Lisa's hand, and bows to Thomas before shaking his hand. "It is wonderful to meet you both." Bael lightly interrupts. "Beowulf, this is Elisavetta and Thomas Thory, your godsister and -brother."

"Please call me Lisa." Lisa asks.

"Of course, if you wish. You may call me Beowulf. Unless my grandfather is around, then I would prefer BW. But little wulf is how I am usually called."

Thomas smiles. "It could be worse. We are referred to as children. But given the age of most in the room, it's understandable."

"Thank you for disburdening my nickname."

"How is your namesake?" Bael asks. "Grandfather's fine. He misses you though."

"Where is he nowadays?"

"Right now, I'm not sure."

"What have you been up too?"

"Father, I have been busy. For many years, I traveled, learning about different people and cultures. Then I went and spent fifteen years with Grandfather on and off. Came back to the United States for the First World War. Met some of the *werepeople* in the army. After that, I did research and found out more about our history. It was then I got a visit from Great-grandfather! What a surprise that was!"

"You met Bael? The . . . original Bael."

"Oh . . . He'd like that, 'the original.' Yeah, but he didn't let me know who he was for over a week. You might be surprised, but you met him too once upon a time. As a matter of fact, several times. He keeps an eye on all of us in different forms. But he can't get too involved in our lives."

For the first time, Bael was the one in a state of shock. "Really?"

"Yeah, Grandfather knew too. But he never mentioned it."

"Yes, that sounds like my father."

"Father, Please don't start on Grandpa."

"GRANDPA!" Bael shouted.

"That was just a slip. He prefers grandfather. Grandpa Nicola is the only grandpa." Lisa turns to Katja. "Did I look like that when I got my surprise news?" Lisa pointed at Bael.

"No, dear, you went into shock that put you out for a few hours."

"Oh yeah . . . right. I forgot." Bael put his hand on his head. "I knew Dad was alive, but I didn't know you were keeping in touch. And then my grandfather who I've apparently met but never introduced himself. How do you know the one calling himself Bael is the true Bael?"

"Grandfather confirmed it was him."

"Oh . . . I guess I've missed a lot keeping everyone at arm's length. Well . . . that's going to stop—from now on son. What have you been up to lately?"

"The last two years I've been taking it easy, catching up on my studies."

Thomas's head popped up. "What studies?"

"Magic and history, but Dad's the expert. How much has he taught you two so far?"

"Wulf, nyet." Nicola said to his grandson.

"Sorry didn't mean to start anything," Beowulf apologized.

"It's fine, son. I'm not planning on teaching them until we get all this trouble settled."

Lisa looked questioningly at Bael. "Are you a sorcerer too?"

Bael sighed. "Yes, but that's not what I am."

"Father!" Beowulf tried to interrupt but was stopped by his father. "Beowulf, my place is keeping order and protecting those that need it. I do the job now. You know that, right?"

Lisa went up to Katja. "This would be a bad time to ask him what's going on, huh?"

"Elisavetta, you're getting much better on your timing."

"May I ask you a question privately?"

"Not here and now, when we stop tonight."

"Where are we stopping tonight?"

Remi yelled out, "Butte Montana Cher. Tonight you will have a roof over your head. And body in a bed."

Sasha leaned over to Lisa and whispered, "And a bath."

Bael looked around and smiled. "Guys, get your sleep now. Tonight, we're on guard, while the ladies sleep."

Remi called back, "In that case, Sasha, Katja, one of you take over the wheel, my dears."

Sasha went and relieved him. As Remi came to the back, Lisa spoke up, "You know, Remi, I can drive this bus as well as my brother."

"It's true, Cher, you could. But I know my kittens well. And your brother got in trouble, no?"

Lisa said no more.

5

Later that night, at the lodge outside Butte, Bael and everyone found their cabins. It's a nice cabin, with all the amenities. The girls got one cabin, Thomas and Maliki the other. The girls weren't the only ones who wanted a bath. Thomas filled the huge tub with hot water and turned on the jets. Katja made Bael put a kind of spell on their cabin so she and Lisa could talk privately. After driving the bus, Sasha was the first in their tub. Nicola and Remi watched over the girls' cabin. Bael and Beowulf watched the boys. Lisa, finally having her privacy, asks Katja. "What was going on today?"

"What was going on was Bael took over the job of keeping order from his father, Beowulf. Because of a disagreement. But Bael didn't want his son doing the job with him."

"Why?"

"No one knows. However, Bael trained him in magic and history and to defend himself. Then he taught him about their powers and abilities as *gods* or *demigods*. Beowulf had no idea his father possessed so much strength and power.

"You see, Lisa, it's hard to control something without practice. But using that much power can be even more dangerous when it's practiced. His *demigod abilities* are compounded with *magic* that he got from his mother. His father rarely ever had used his power. Which was even stronger. He had other abilities that got the job done without using his powers. But Bael didn't think his father's way was right.

"Bael's father was drawn to darkness. He would take from that darkness and feed his own power, then destroy it. After many centuries, the body count was so high. Bael asked why some couldn't be imprisoned.

"Beowulf simply stated his sentence was equal to all.

"Every time they're together, the fight would start all over again. Finally, Bael got his way. Beowulf retired and left Bael to do as he felt right."

Lisa looked at Katja. "So when are you going to let the cat out of the bag?"

The bathroom door opened. Sasha came out. "What cat out of a bag?" Katja gave Lisa a look of panic. Lisa shrugged her shoulders, put her hands up to show she was sorry.

"Well . . . is someone going to fill me in or just leave me in the dark?" Sasha asked.

Lisa looked at Katja questioningly. Katja reluctantly nodded her head. Lisa turned to Sasha. "Katja's trying to keep it a secret, but I don't know why. So don't let the whole world know yet. Okay?" Sasha nodded.

"Sure, what's up?"

"The other night," Lisa started. "Bael and Katja were talking, and he finally broke down and admitted he still loved her."

"That's not a secret," Sasha replied.

Lisa smiled. "No, but them being a couple is."

Sasha looked at her sister with shock and surprise. "Really? Did he kiss you? What happened? And where was I? How does Lisa know what happened when your sister doesn't?"

Katja finally cut her off, "The other night, after Lisa and Thomas had their little freak out, Bael tried to give Lisa some comfort. But it didn't come out very well, as you can imagine. So . . . I went in to help. She got settled down, and Bael came back. He felt bad that he couldn't deal with Lisa or anyone when it came to the emotional side. The way he used to. Lisa woke up, and it was she who put things into perspective for him. Then he asked me if I would join him to heal his heart; together. I agreed, we kissed, and then I had to get back on patrol because I caught a scent. But he kissed me again before I left."

Sasha turns to Lisa. "So what *did* you say to him?"

Lisa shrugged her shoulder. "I honestly . . . I'm not sure what I said."

Katja smiles. "It's okay. You were a little out of it."

Sasha got up and walked over to the mirror. "I take it that Dad doesn't know yet?"

"No, and you best not tell him!"

Sasha smiles at the mirror and winked. "Sasha, I want more time, *please?*"

"Sis, I wouldn't do that to you or Bael. I know the way Dad is. He'll have the wedding before the date. Lisa, as for you"—Sasha put her hands on her hips—"know more slips."

Sasha looked to Katja. "There is one thing I am going to bring up. What is little wulf going to think?"

Katja hadn't thought about her nephew. She loved him so much, and she didn't want to hurt him. Honestly the thought of a wedding hit her hard, the reality of it. Now what might happen to her relationship with her nephew? Lisa saw the look on Katja's face.

"Katja, BW is how old?" Sasha responded.

"He's a little over fifteen hundred."

"Sasha said it wasn't much of a secret, right?"

"Yes?

"Well, I would think, after this much time, he would feel relieved."

"You might be right, but it's still my nephew. Sasha, what do you think?" asked Katja.

Sasha thought a minute. "I have to say I'm with Lisa. "He's a grown man. Let him deal with it."

The ladies laugh for a while, then took their baths and got to sleep.

In the other cabin, sleep did not come so easily. Maliki was snoring while Thomas thought more and more about what Maris had said. And the events that led up to the crash that started the trouble.

The week began well enough. School was great. Lisa had finished her second year of college and was home. He had been waiting to hear from some of the colleges he had applied to. Wednesday things changed. Aunt Lucile said she had gotten some news in the mail and left us overnight but wouldn't say where she was going. On

Thursday, she came in, in a panic. Lisa had gone to the store. So she missed the excitement, but he filled her in later. Lucile put a roll of cash in a jar on a desk. Made sure everything was easy to get to on the desk. Got on the phone, making long distance calls to places he didn't know. When he asked her about them, she shushed him out of the room. Lisa came home to find Lucile in tears. Lisa asked what was wrong. But got no real answers from Lucile. Friday morning, Lucile got up, made them breakfast, and told them that they were going on a trip to see a friend of the family. A Miss Murray. That they would leave as soon as she called back. As if the past day's events never happened. They left the house about an hour later. When Lucile got off the phone, she seemed worried. She said something about the damn drive messed up everything. Then they were off. Lisa in the front seat with Lucile him in the back with his books. The road was wet from a sprinkle of rain that morning and into the afternoon. By the time it was six, we were getting tired. He had just closed his eyes when he heard the bang of a tire blowing and saw the truck plow into them. Knocked off the road, they flipped down the hill, coming to stop at the bottom. Lucile was hurt but told us what to do. What was the worry Lucile had about the hospital, and us getting out of it? Who was Miss Murray that they never got to? What drive messed it all up to begin with? Then he thought about Maris. Affirmation? To what? And who's side was he on? Well, that one was easy . . . *his*. But why say nothing till they got to where they're going? Thomas always loved a mystery, but real life kept getting in the way of him thinking. His sleep was restless nightmares of Maris, Lucile, Lisa, and the others all swirling in his dream, falling from nowhere into a pool of blood from the wreck, then being ripped from everyone. Back and forth, he rolled and fought his way clear of the car, the nurse, Maris. Then he felt a pressure on him, holding him, calming him. He woke in a sweat. Maliki had been woken and tried to settle his tossing. He held Thomas. "Your dreams are getting the better of you perhaps."

Thomas wiped the sweat off his head. "Dreams, no. Nightmares, yes. I've just got too many questions."

DONALD DEISCHER

Maliki looked down at him. "The answers will come, most likely when you don't ask them. Some you already have, but your mind won't let you have them."

"So . . . I get nightmares."

"Calm yourself and the answers will come." Maliki tucked him in, which made him feel more like a kid than ever, but it felt good to know he was there.

"Maliki?"

"Yes."

"Thanks, thanks a lot."

"Sleep well, Thomas. Tomorrow will be better."

In the morning, the sun came in through the window blinds. Little by little, everyone started waking up. Thomas found Beowulf sleeping in the other bed and Remi asleep on the floor. He got up and tiptoed around them to the bathroom, showered, shaved, and dressed. He looked out the window and saw Bael. He walked outside. "I'm glad to see you looking before you came out!" Bael said loudly.

Thomas shook his head. "Quiet. Do you want to wake everyone? Look before the others wake up? Why don't we get the girls and get some breakfast?"

Maliki came around the corner of the hotel. "Breakfast does sound good, Bael. "And I smell fish from the diner."

Bael threw his hands up. "Fine. Are the girls awake?"

Maliki put his ear to the air. "Lisa and Katja are, but Sasha is still sleeping well."

Bael knocked on the door lightly. Bael turned to Maliki. "How did you hear them. I had a spell over their cabin for privacy?"

"And a good one it was too," Maliki replied. "But it faded in the rising of the sun."

"Oh yeah. When we changed shifts, I wanted to hear whether or not they needed help."

Lisa heard what Bael had said. "Well, it was nice of you to inform us of it." Lisa had gotten up early, which shocked Thomas.

Katja came out of the room, stretching and yawning.

58

"Good morning, ladies!" Thomas and Bael said at the same time.

Thomas smiles and asks, "Would you, ladies, care to go to the diner for coffee and breakfast?"

Lisa put her hands on her hips. "Are you serious? Of course, I want coffee."

They got the group together and went into the diner.

The door opened with a bell. And they went in. The sign said to "seat yourself," so they found a table.

Bael noticed something was wrong first, then Lisa, and finally the others. There were people in the diner, but no one moved or spoke. Then Bael saw two men sitting in a corner booth. One of the men looked at Bael and started laughing. The laughing man got up and was followed by the other. Bael gestured to tip a hat that he wasn't wearing.

"Good morning, Peter and David. Always a pleasure."

"Ah, Bael I rushed as fast as I could when I heard the news. Are these the Thorys? I must admit I see what all the fuss is about. She will make a beautiful vampire. The light auburn hair, the green eyes—oh my, yes."

Bael looked around the room. Everyone's motionless. "Your work I take it?"

"Of course, I couldn't do business in front of everyone, could I? Don't worry, I'll put them back later."

Bael stood up. "Thomas, Lisa Thory, meet Peter and David Ravenna. Two friends of your family up till now."

"Bael, now that's not fair. I'm here to fill you in. By now you've heard about Montgomery? But someone is pulling his strings. I don't know who, but I will. I just had to see for myself. An amped-up vamp. Two yet. And, ah yes, he smells the air. They do smell intoxicating."

Lisa stood. "So you're here for us too?

"Well, I've just about had it with all this chasing I'm tired of. Of. Of. So back off."

"Oh, I like her brother. She has more fire than Valerie, and she's still human," David said as he came around Peter. David bowed his head. "My dear, while it's true you would be welcomed into our family, I'm afraid you don't have all the facts. The other families either want you for your power or your life. Right now, most just want you dead."

"Why not you?"

"Because, for one reason. We owe Bael far too much to go against him. For another, our family has been friends of your house for hundreds of years. It would not be right. And last, of course, is we are not fools or puppets. *No one* pulls our strings. Like that cur Montgomery."

Peter turned to Bael. "From what I understand, they will put up a fight before you are allowed to enter Alec's. But there will be a force there to keep you there once inside."

"How do you know so much?"

"After Montgomery's unofficial meeting of the royals, he seemed upset because there were families voting against him. So he was unofficially followed when he left the city. He met with someone at the old tavern in Romania and given orders. By whom? I don't know, but he knows your limitations."

"Why, what were the orders?"

"Look around you."

"Their using thralls."

Peter nodded. "They will not know what they are doing, but you may only stop them. Not harm them."

"What about once we're in?"

"Sum of the subfarae, thralls, and what else, I can only guess."

Lisa looked at Peter. "Why are you helping though?"

"My dear Miss Thory, there is nothing more fun than sticking it to someone who has it coming to him. Montgomery will be furious when he finds out we told Bael his plans."

"Who's going to tell him?" Lisa asked.

The brothers look at each other questioningly and then back at Lisa. "Why, we will of course. Bael, there is one thing. He won't get anywhere till he convinces Lilith, and I have to think whoever is pulling his strings has thought of that. So who could turn the queen? When you have that answer, you'll have the next move."

Bael tried to think. Thomas finally asked Bael, "Who does she listen to?"

"That's just it, no one!"

Peter gave a smirk at Bael. "She listens to you, to Lord Basarab, Prince Oberon, from time to time. She always heeded your father's words."

Bael chimed in, "That was fear."

Thomas, listening, said under his breath, "Wow, it's good to be the king."

Bael stopped and paused. "You may have something, Thomas." He turned to Peter and David. "How fast could you get a message to the queen?" David spoke with a smile, "She would have it by morning if need be."

"No, it can be later than that, and I need it delivered in secrecy. You can't know of its contents either. I will have a different letter for you, but don't read it till the official gathering of the royals. If I'm right, you'll know what to say when the time comes."

Katja came from behind the counter with two envelopes and paper. Bael wrote quickly. On the back of an envelope he wrote along the seal Lilith. He licked his ring and pressed it to the envelope. "Give this to her when we leave Alec's. That should be several days yet, so take your time." Bael handed Peter the letters.

Peter bowed his head. "You have the word of the Ravenna house."

Bael smiled at the brothers. "Will you be joining us for breakfast?"

Peter looked around the diner. "Alas, *no*. Our dietary needs at the moment are strained. We shall make other arrangements. Goodbye, my friends, and may I say again, my dear, you will make a beautiful vampire. As for you, sir"—he looked at Thomas—"you would make a father proud. Farewell, my friends." And they walked out the door. As the door closed, everyone in the diner began their routine movements. All was back to normal. As for their group, everyone was waiting to be filled in by Bael.

Lisa asked, "Do you want tell us what's going on?"

Bael looked at Lisa. "Not just yet. I'm not even sure myself yet, but things are making more sense."

"Oh, then definitely leave me out of it," Lisa said. "I hate it when things make sense." She paused. "Are you really keeping it to yourself?"

Maliki put his hand on her shoulder. "Your mind and mine can be read by some vampires. For now it is best we not know."

"Well, why didn't he say that?"

After the meal, Lisa bought a few items for the road and walked to the bus with a big paper bag. She set it in the back, and they all went back to the cabins.

By 10:00 a.m., the bus was getting loaded up. Remi was still half asleep. Nicola was yawning loud enough it should have woken the rest of the cabins. Thomas got behind the wheel again. While the rest got comfortable in back, Maliki had gotten a few books and was reading; Lisa was sitting with Nicola. Remi was huddled next to the luggage, still trying to wake up. Katja sat next to Bael. The doors closed, and Thomas yelled out, "Which way now?"

Bael shouted back, "Right out of lot, and when you reach the highway, north." Bael sat back and pulled Katja close, his arm around her. He hadn't meant to, but he gave his little secret away when he looked at Katja. Nicola eyed them for a while, waiting. Finally, he smiled and closed his eyes.

Thomas looked in the mirror and saw his sister sleeping, resting on Nicola. He was happy to see her so at ease. Thomas felt at times like a fifth wheel around his sister. Although she acted tough, it was Thomas that usually fought for her. He just made sure she didn't find out. Bael was right about that. By the age of twelve, Thomas had a punch that could knock out most, and he did. Only recently had she done her own fighting. She had broken up with her college boyfriend, good' ole Mike. Till he got dumped, then he hit her. Then his sister, the lacrosse girl, turned around and knocked him on his ass. Then she gave him a kick that would have Thomas singing her praises for years. Mike would be singing too at a much higher pitch. He had always been proud of his sister. Trusted her decisions, she usually made the right choice; it was uncanny. That more than any other reason was why all of this made sense to him. Not the whole vamp thing. But *magic*, yeah, that made sense. She always knew things before they'd happen. The day of the accident, she had made sure we were all buckled in. She didn't know what was going to happen, but she knew something was. Before this *magic* was a guy pulling a rabbit from a hat, or something on a movie. Now it put the puzzle together. *Sister Sorcerer*, he thought and smiled. *I dare anyone to call her a witch.*

Town after town went by. Thomas saw another coming and decided to ask Bael for a break. Bael! Thomas called back, "This should be the last town before the border could we stop and stretch our legs a little." Bael knew the town well. "Sure, there's a truck stop on the outside of town. Pull in there." Everyone had been resting throughout the trip and woke up feeling much better. Remi came walking to the front. "When we start up again, I will take over for a while, Mon'ami."

"Thanks, Remi. I was getting a little stiff. How much longer would you say we have?"

"Fear not, my friend. We will be there tonight." Thomas stopped the bus at the pumps. He waited for the others and got off the bus. Every step was a stretch in the right direction. Lisa bought some fresh baked bread for Remi and a bag of fresh caught fish from the local rivers and streams, or so it read. It was burgers and fries for the rest. Lisa liked it when they stopped. They stayed together; it gave her a sense of family. Bael was showing more and more the truth about himself and Katja. So much so that Sasha made the joke. "We are watching the kids still, right?" she said to Bael. Katja blushed. Lisa gave Sasha a nudge.

"Okay, no jokes."

Everyone used the facilities and got some refreshments. They all took a short walk and got back on the bus. Remi had taken the wheel again. Thomas sat with Maliki and talked about the mystery that they were all wrapped up in. As they pulled out of the station, Thomas saw a sign for the first-aid station. "THAT'S IT!" Thomas shouted.

"I know what started this mess." Lisa and Bael turned.

"What started all this?" Lisa asked.

"Aunt Lucile was complaining about the damn drive. I thought she was talking about the running around she was doing. That wasn't it. It was the blood drive they had at our schools. The nurse at the hospital said there was a test they had to run. The blood drive must have tested one of our samples and got our names. There was a Miss Murray that we were going to when the accident happened. I don't know what part she played."

Bael cut Thomas off, "I think I can shed some light on Miss Murray. She is an assistant of Alec's and has a safe house in California."

Thomas started up again, "My guess is Lucile didn't want you involved yet, but when the accident happened, she knew the hospital would have our faces. So she said to run to you, Bael!"

Maliki nodded at the boy. "I told you, it would come. As for the rest of the mystery, I'll just have to wait and see."

Within the hour, they were across the border into Canada. Bael noticed a bird flying outside the bus. It was his raven or crow, Sorrow. Bael told Remi to stop if he saw a place to get off the road. After some time, he found a truck park and pulled in. Bael told everyone to stay on the bus. He got off, and the bird flew to his side. The bird began to caw and crack at Bael.

Lisa went to Nicola. "Can you understand what its saying?"

Nicola laughed. "No, little one. I do not understand birds or their language. Only the godly or those few sorcerers can speak with them."

All of a sudden, something moved very quickly. Like a shadow, it moved, and then another. Finally, there were many moving around the bus. You could see no figures, only the outline or a blur. The bus began to shake. Nikola placed a hand on Lisa's shoulder. "Don't worry, little one, they are just trying to . . ." He looked at his daughter for the word. Katja held on to piece of metal. "Get a rise out of us. Draw us away from the bus. The vampires got angry when they saw that their plan wasn't working." One got bold and boarded the bus as fast as he could and tried to grab the kids. Sasha put out a hand in transition to paw and caught him by the arm and throat. She crushed it in her hand, and the figure went limp. She threw him out of the bus. He started to heal as he lay on the ground. Bael put his foot on his back and pushed the vampire into the ground. He moved his foot and placed his hand over the figure's body and began to make a fist. As the fist got tighter, the bones of the vampire began to crack his body contorted as he writhed in pain. Bael put out his other hand, and with a gesture, the others fell to the ground.

"This is my first and last warning. Trouble me again and your family will need new members! Do you understand me?"

They moaned a yes. He turned his hand, and it was as if a wind was scooping them up. He opened his hand wide and released them. Lisa and Thomas were stunned. Lisa looked to Nicola. Was that magic, or god powers?" Nicola pulled her to him. This is not magic Elisavetta. Bael looked down at the bold vampire, still being crushed by his hand. Bael pulled him off the ground without laying a hand on him. He looked him in the face racked with pain. His fist grew tighter. You could hear his muscles as they pulled and bones crushed. Bael did not seem himself. He was angry.

"I don't know you. What house are you? You're not neo. You're Magyar?"

"No, Vampyr," he answered.

"Oh. Why have the Vampyrs decided to insult and attack me? Your loyalty has never been in question before. Why now would you risk so much?"

"MMMMY LLLORD, PLEASE!"

His fist tightened again. "You're lord? You would call me lord after this?" He raised his fist and the vamp with it. "I will be in the court soon, and your father will have much to answer for."

"HHHE DDOEESSS NOT KKNOW!" Higher and higher he rose. Now he could see Bael's eyes. The white of his eyes seemed to glow while his pupils went black.

"So you attack your lord, disrespect your father, and endanger your families' name. *Why?*"

A whisper of a voice came from the blood-soaked face. "We were told to by Montgomery." Blood fell from his face. "My lord, others are coming."

Bael leaned forward. "I know," he whispered. Nicola stepped off the bus. "Bael, it is enough!"

Bael threw him to the ground and turned to the bus. "He'll live." Bael got back on the bus.

"Is everyone all right?"

Katja put her hand on his. "We're fine. Are you okay?"

His head hung low as he passed. "I'm fine. Remi, let's get back on the road." Bael walked to the back of the bus and fell asleep. Katja went and held him.

Lisa went to Nicola. "Is he all right?"

"Yes, little one. He will be fine. He just needs to rest. Bael has not been emotional for a very long time. Now all that he cares about is here. He is a protector. A great protector. But all his emotions are strained. So they all came out at once as rage."

Lisa looked back at Bael. "I'm so sorry for him."

"No, little one. This is good."

"Why?"

"His heart has returned."

Beowulf looked at his father and Aunt Katja. After a few minutes, he smiled. As he lay down over a few seats, he softly said to himself, *Well . . . I'll be damned.*

6

Lisa spent hours thinking about what she saw. Bael had shown a power or magic. She wasn't convinced which, and yet, as she looked at her palm, she wondered what could, or would she be able to do. If what Bael said was true, she had the possibility of being a *sorceress*. What did that mean? She looked at Bael asleep with Katja. She so wanted to ask him. *No,* she thought. He said he would teach them when the time was right. As she passed over the people in the bus, she realized, these were the people she trusted. Truly trusted. In a matter of a week, she had come to trust and love them as much as her brother and aunt. Around Nicola she felt like a kid again. She almost laughed. *My tiger,* she thought. Remi, she worried about him getting enough sleep. She cared for him the way she had Thomas for years. Knowing full well he could take care of himself but worried anyway. Sasha and Katja, she wasn't sure how she felt about them. Not like sisters, but more than friends. Then there was Maliki. He seemed closer to Thomas. She thought, *I should spend more time with him, but I think that will come in time.* As for Bael, well . . . it seemed like he was a little of everything already. Putting a label on him might be pulling that rubber band to tight.

Walking down a great stone hallway, three figures moved in haste. One trailing just behind the others. The others were wishing to leave him far behind. Montgomery was trying to get their attention.

"Gentlemen, please, if I may speak to you a moment. This unpleasant situation with illegal marks and trying to bring them here before the royal houses, it's undignified."

"Perhaps," the men replied. "But the queen has spoken. The house mother has put her voice with the queens. Bael is bringing them here, and they will be heard. The mother spoke for the house. Now, if you will. Excuse us, we must go."

"I was merely suggesting that someone put a word in milady's ear." The older looking of the two gentlemen turned. "Yes, I think *you* should." And the men disappeared into a running dash.

The bus came to a stop at the top of a hill they had gone off the road for a while, but this was as far as it could go. The northern forest stood in front of them. A light snow was on the ground. Remi called back to Bael, "Bael, come you must see this." The light of the sun was fading. In the ground, in front of them, he saw them, footprints. Lots of prints in the snow. "Thralls, Vampiric thralls. Can you tell how many?"

Remi studied the prints. "At least a hundred, but over there, they seem to have come from nowhere."

Bael shook his head. "A portal? Where are they getting magical help from?"

Lisa broke in, "Are you sure this Alec is on our side?"

"Yes!" Sasha stepped outside and put her nose to the air. "Katja, come here. Something doesn't smell right. I just can't place it."

Katja joined her sister. "I smell it, musty, or moldy?" Remi followed with Thomas behind him.

"Mon' due, I know that smell. It's the bayou, back-swamp Mississippi, or Louisiana? I don't know why, but that's the smell all right."

Bael looked at the portal. "The only thing I can think of is they found a local talent to open one here, and wait." Remi thought and tapped his chin. "There's been a lot of voodoo back o' them swamps, but magic like that. I just don't recall any."

Bael put his hand on Remi's shoulder. "When were you there last?"

"Oh, about sixty, seventy years ago, give or take."

"Well . . . someone's gotten better." Beowulf stepped off the bus.

"I can feel something else out there. It's dark but human. It's fast. I feel them moving. I just can't . . ." Beowulf lost his focus. "Father, their mixed in with the thralls."

Bael walked to his son. "What do you mean you feel them?"

"Can't you feel them?"

"No."

"Grandfather taught me, so I would know."

"Know what?"

"Who were the right ones to kill."

"You haven't been killing, have you?"

"Only with Grandfather."

Bael shook his head.

"Father, I was out in the world. If Grandfather hadn't taught me, I wouldn't know who to trust or where my enemies were to avoid. Like now, I know where they are. I can help hold them off while the Thorys get to the door. You don't know the difference between thralls and whatever these things I'm syncing are. Hold them all back, and I'll take care of the others."

Bael was about to object when Nicola stopped him. He put his hand on Bael's arm. "Bael, he's right. You cannot tell the difference."

Bael gave a nod and closed his eyes and again put his arms out, hands open. A finger on each hand folded into his palm. He reached out, and the trees seemed to move slightly to form a path. There was a ripple in the air as if heat were moving through the cold air from his hands. His eyes opened. Like before white with light yet black in the center. The blue of his eyes had disappeared. Beowulf began running, and he jumped into the woods. As Katja had done days earlier, as he landed, he had changed to tiger, but on two legs. Off he ran and disappeared.

"Go!" yelled Bael. Nicola grabbed Lisa and flung her on his back as he changed to his tiger form. Maliki did the same to Thomas, and down the path, they raced. Katja and Sasha had changed yet were running on two legs. They had grabbed the backpacks, Lisa's and Bael's. Lisa looked back at Bael as they ran. She could see the power emanating from him. Remi had run astride of Nicola till a wall of stones could be seen. The stones made an archway with a huge wooden door in it. Remi ran ahead; Lisa could hear his breath as he ran. When he reached the wall of stones, he jumped over it. A moment later, the door opened, and Remi was holding it open. In the forest around them, Lisa and Thomas heard wailing and scream-ing. Thomas had shut his eyes. Lisa looked back for Bael, now com-pletely out of sight. As they came flying through the door, the ground changed beneath their feet to a stone floor and a carpet on it. As the ladies came through, Remi shut the door. Lisa called out, "What about Bael and Beowulf?" Laughter came from the dark hallway in front of them. "My dear Miss Thory, they will be along shortly. Have no fear of that."

From the dark hallway, Lisa heard the shuffling of footsteps. First, she saw an outline of a man about six foot high, perhaps a little taller. Then she made out his robe. And last, as he stepped into the light, his face, it was a kind face, with salt and pepper hair. His dark mustache faded to a gray beard surrounding his smile; in his left hand, he held a long curved pipe. His right, he extended to shake hands with everyone.

"Ah. Good to see you all. Now, Miss Thory," he said as he turned to meet her, "let me see what all the fuss is about. Come to the light, my dear, and you, sir, don't hide yourself. I don't bite."

"No" came a voice from above and behind them. "That would be me that *bites*." Another man was standing on a staircase; his hair was more gray than dark and was thinning on top.

Just then Lisa saw a shimmer or wave in the air and then there was Bael, and then a second, Beowulf appeared.

"Ahh . . . at last, the false prince arrives. Be a good lad. And be so kind as to put the cats out."

"Jason, that will be enough of that." Alec raised his hand as a warning. "Our friends are our guests."

The man came down the steps. "Very well, I suggest we split up the group and give them the tour." Alec nodded a small bow.

"Thomas, you, the bears, and Beowulf, come with me."

Bael looked to Alec. "Alec, for right now, I would just like to rest a bit. I'm feeling a little weak."

Alec nodded. "Well, you go into the parlor and rest then. You know the way."

Katja took his arm. "I'll give him a hand."

"Well then," Alec said. "Jason, you take Miss Thory and Sasha, and the rest, follow me."

Thomas and the others followed Alec down the hallway. Alec made a gesture with his hand, and the hall lit up with torches. Bael and Katja moved off to a room left of the entrance. When all had gone, Sasha went up to Jason and rubbed the top of his head. "That had better be the last of the cat jokes, you big fibber."

"Now, Sasha, you know very well."

"What, that you, you're actually a big softy? Yeah, I know."

"Sasha, you know I don't like company." They started walking up the stairs. Lisa followed, a little puzzled. Sasha kissed his cheek. "Want us to go?"

She looked back at Lisa and gave her a wink. He stomped quickly to the top of the stairs and turned.

"If I acted like I wanted them here, they might show up all the time. I'd prefer to be feared and disliked!" Sasha kept walking up with Lisa behind her. They came to a large room filled with herbs in boxes and all kinds of things in jars. There were books from one side of the room to the other. It was at least three stories tall. It had a large table or desk in the corner of the room with an oval mirror in the top. Glass cases and wooden chests.

"Well, at any rate, welcome back to . . ." As he turned around with his hands in the air, he saw Lisa. "Oh."

He dropped his hands. "Miss Thory, I had forgotten you were with us. My apologies."

Lisa smiled.

He raised his hand, and the lights got brighter. "Allow me to introduce myself. *I am Jason Ashmoore*, sorcerer and your host. Welcome to our home."

Lisa smiled and gave a small curtsy. As Ashmoore bowed back, he straightened his tie and cleared his throat. "Miss Thory, I hope you will be so kind as to keep my secret?"

"Secret? What secret would that be?"

Sasha gave her another wink. Ashmoore nodded. "Thank you. As you can see, this is my private library and study, though you are most welcome. May I offer a refreshment?" A tray with drinks and sandwiches floated to his hand. They took one of the drinks and thanked him.

"So how have you been?" Sasha asks Jason.

"I haven't been chased by every vampire in the area, so not too bad."

"Why didn't you help us out there?"

"You know full well I'm forbidden to help Bael."

"Not him. Help us?"

"Hmm . . . I don't know if there's a loophole there or not. I'll ask Alec later."

"You're giving us shelter now!"

"Hmm . . . good point. Perhaps we should have."

Sasha laughs. "I'm just messin' with you. We were fine."

He walks over to Lisa. "So you're what all the troubles about. Yes, I can see why they're fighting over you."

Lisa blushes. "You're very beautiful, dear, and when you change. I dare say you'll be more radiant than the queen herself. Don't you think, Sasha?"

Her head nodded, but Jason could see something was wrong. Jason took a paper out of the desk. "Now here, Miss Thory, is a map of the entire house."

She looked at the map and the many halls and rooms, stairs, and balconies.

Balconies, oh no, she thought. And the look on her face made Jason laugh.

"My dear, don't worry about anyone getting in the house. It isn't there."

"What do you mean it isn't there? I'm here. It must be there."

"You're thinking mortal, dear. It's a bad habit to get into. You see, if you look outside." Jason led Lisa to the window. Everything out the window was a brilliant blue or black outline. "You see, this isn't you're earth. This is another plane altogether."

"It's so beautiful." Lisa sighed.

Jason smiles and nods. "All of this we'll explain to you both this week. For now, know that you are safe."

"I hope you like our home, Master Thomas. It's a bit drafty from time to time, but it is off-the-beaten path."

Thomas cleared his throat. "Sir, if I may, I know your name is Alec, but all the same, who are you?"

"I am sorry, where are my manners? I am Alexander Chartwell and my brother, the other man you saw was Jason, Jason Ashmoore. We are sorcerers of the first house and not affiliated with the order."

Thomas nodded his head. "I see. Well, not really. What is the first house, and what is the order?"

Alec turned to Thomas. "Ah yes, well. The first house is just as it sounds. We were the first sorcerers. Before the others that came so much later. It was they who formed the order, or whatever their calling themselves these days. You see, they have a set of rules to adhere to we . . . well, not so much."

"Okay," said Thomas. "I understand a little better. But why do you and your brother have different last names?"

"I must say you ask good questions for one so young. You see, my brother and I are very old. So old in fact, that when we were born, people didn't have last names. They were called by what they did and their name. Like, say, Thomas the 'Ship Builder,' or Thomas, 'the Baker.' Later, when last names were added, at first it was only the leaders that had them then a few others. We had lived through all that. And while we were separated for a while exploring, we had chosen our names. I chose mine due to how I would help others find their way to places and people, Chartwell. My brother has never told me how he chose his last name. So I don't know, to tell you. Over the years, we all get known by other names anyway. It helps our anonymity."

They passed through many rooms for almost an hour. Alec was showing off his home to its best advantage. Finally, they came to what Thomas would call a living room. Alec called it the parlor. There asleep on a kind of old sofa was Bael. Sitting by his side was Katja, almost asleep herself. Little by little they all began to show up and find a place to sit around a large fireplace in the center of the room. As Nicola passed Katja, he bent down and kissed her forehead.

"I'm very happy," he said so very quietly. And he sat in large wooden chair next to her.

Alec looked to his brother, who, in turn, gave a single nod. Alec addressed the room in kind voice, "I'm glad you are all here and safe. I wish I had more news to give you. I have no idea who is behind all the new troubles. We are being blocked from seeing so much. Right now, even parts of your journey we could not break through to see. Whoever it is is very powerful. I have put forth a request to the prince of the farae to see if he may know how we are being blocked. But have heard nothing. Our only fear, my brother and I have is that whoever it is knows Bael's powers and perhaps weaknesses. As for the royals, the gathering has been scheduled by order of the queen for the end of the month. That will give us three weeks to train you. So that you will be ready no matter what they decide."

Lisa stood. "I still don't understand what it is their deciding."

Thomas took his sisters hand. "They're going to decide what we are, and the possibility of what we could be. They decide whether or not we are a danger to the way of things by their standards."

"Very well stated, Master Thomas," Alec replied.

Thomas turned to Alec and his brother. "What if we had affirmation before we arrived at the royals' meeting?"

"That would be impossible, wouldn't it, Jason?"

Jason smiled at Thomas. "Who told you about affirmation, boy?"

"It was just mentioned once I think," Jason began, laughing.

"It's possible, dangerous, but possible." Alec got a puzzled look on his face.

"Oh, my dear brother," Jason said, laughing, "you don't understand. The boy means '*the stone, the Paragon stone.*" Alec's face went pale. At the mention of it, Bael woke from his sleep. "What are you talking about?" he asked.

Jason stood and walked over to Bael. "The boy has found a way out of their problems."

"I'm afraid you won't be able to help them though. We take them to Anun, and they go before the Paragon stone. If they survive, no one, not the royals, not the gods themselves, would say a word against them."

Jason continued to laugh. The others were not so pleased. Nicola went to Bael. "He's right, but to take them to that place, to the stone."

Lisa was confused and scared from the others reactions. "What is this place and stone that has everyone upset?"

Jason stopped his laughter and took her hand. "I'm sorry, Elisabeth, my dear, it's not funny, of course, and you don't understand. Anun is a kind of city or town that once was a paradise on earth. The stone was whole then. Those that went before it were looking for wisdom, power, and truth. The stone is alive. It holds such a force yet gave of itself to all. Humans were made by god or gods. As were the angels and demons. The farae, the old ones, were made of magic, a power of the stone. Over time it was found that the farae could in some cases mate with humans as did angels and demons. Everything went well for many years. But the human nature began to fight and war as it does now. The angelic nefilem were the mating of man and angel, very powerful but were destroyed by archangels. The farae took their half children and went to another plain. Some however asked to stay and were allowed, providing that their interaction with humans be limited. The humans continued to war outside the city. A woman had made her way through the battles to the city. The paradise she found gave her shelter and hope. There were those at the city who wanted knowledge and to learn. To stay in the city, she was brought before the stone. The truth was shown to her that her husband was looking for her and, finding the house empty, listened to rumors from others. He was in a rage and, when found, would kill her. She was with child and wanted it saved. The stone pulled the child from the mother and, through the stone itself, as the children's feet found the floor, they stood. For the woman carried twins. The children were given from the stone some of all that it was. Two human children born of magic. They could speak, walk, think as an adult, but the wisdom they were given had shown them the ways of man and to leave them to their wars till they learned a better way. The mother of the children gave them all the love she could for three months and then left to return to her husband, where she died by his hands. In time the warring humans found the city themselves. Blood was spilled by men. Buildings destroyed. At last the stone used its power to shift the city to another plain. The humans were dissolved. All, but the children. They were brought to Avalon home of the farae and raised there for many years. When they were young adults, they were taken to the world of men and wondered amongst them. They saw men's wars. How they lived. The humans had begun to use magic as well in their wars. Fearing that the humans might find the stone. It separated itself. That which held its power formed a crystal and found its home with the farae. The stone of knowledge hid itself between two plains so it could not be found. The Paragon stone remained in the city. Over the years, few have gone to it. Affirmation has come at a terrible price for some. They again dissolved into nothing."

Jason stopped his story. "We can take you there, but it's the cost I fear. So few have gone and returned, the city is a myth even to the farae these days."

Lisa sat and thought over the story. She had heard. She looked at Alec and Jason. "You were the twins? Weren't you? And you saw the others dissolve? All they could do was lower their heads. How do you know, or do you know what would happen to me or my brother?"

Jason looked up to see Lisa's eyes, tearing up. "We don't, my dear, and that's why we are all so worried now. It does solve our current problems, but we don't want to lose either of you in the process."

Lisa turned to her brother. "Thomas, I want you to tell me the whole truth. Where did you learn about this affirmation from?"

Thomas looked over the group. Maliki came to him. "Is there a reason you hesitate telling us?"

Thomas looked up to the face of his friend. "Yes, I would tell you if I could. When we return, I'll tell you I swear."

Maliki smiled. "If Thomas said there's a reason, then there is. Have patience. He will tell us when he can."

Alec stood. "Before we do anything, may I suggest that we wait till the morning? You have all had a long trip, and there is far too much to do tomorrow as it is. For now, let's get some sleep so that we will be fresh for tomorrow."

Bael and the others all nodded. "Good, follow me, and I'll show you to your rooms."

Alec led them to a hallway again. He raised his hand, and the light in the hallway brightened. Lisa looked throughout the hallway. There were no lights—not at all. Just an illumination to the hall. She tried looking for her shadow to get a sense of where the light was coming from, but there was no shadow. Each door in the hall was arched with a beautifully carved door. Alec stopped in the middle of the hall. "I hope these rooms will be comfortable. There are two beds to a room, but if you prefer, you may sleep alone of course. There are plenty of rooms here."

Thomas opened one the bedrooms. The room had two huge beds and a dresser with a large mirror each had a bedside table with a lamp. At the end of each bed was a large wooden box filled with blankets and linen. "There are clothes in the dresser for you in the morning. I'm afraid it's one bathroom for two rooms, through the door between them. If you get hungry, the kitchen is to the right through the living room and look to the light. It's on all night."

The group began to split up and pair up. Thomas and Maliki, Remi and Nicola, Sasha and Lisa, the others decided to have their own rooms. Bael, Beowulf, and Katja took the room next to Lisa and Sasha, though by now, everyone knew where she would have preferred sleep. Lisa raced to the bathroom and was relieved when she found it had an enormous bathtub. She started filling it. Then she went to Katja's room next door. She knocked and heard Katja say "come in." She opened the door. "Hey, Katja, if you don't mind, I'm gonna take a bath before bed. If you need the bathroom for anything first."

"Thanks, but I'm fine. You go take your bath and relax."

"How are you doing? with Bael, I mean."

"We're fine, as matter of fact, we're getting close again."

"I'm glad you look good together." Lisa looked back at her tub. "Well . . . I'll get back to my bath. Good night, Katja. Sleep tight. I love you." And she closed the door. Katja smiled at the door. "I love you too, little one." Lisa hadn't realized it till later in the tub. She had said good night to Katja as she had to her aunt and brother. She lay back in the tub. More and more she felt closer to the group, not just safe, but family. Nicola was like her dad, and felt better knowing he was close. Katja and Sasha felt like sisters, or her aunt. Bael was her uncle or second father. Remi and Maliki were cousins, or uncles. She felt warm, not because of the water; Bael was taking her to her family. She felt as though she had arrived. She had giggled at the thought of it.

Sasha had left the room and gone after Jason in the living room. "Jason, I'm glad you're still here. You weren't serious before, were you? You wouldn't take them to the stone?"

Jason turned grimus to her. "I hate to say this, but it would help if they were affirmed before they went to the royals. It should prove their case."

"And what if they don't come back?"

"Sasha," Jason sighed. "I can see you've gotten attached to them, but I don't think there's a better solution." Sasha began to cry. "Jason, I can't lose them. We can't lose them. Bael would go back to stone. My father has lost so much, though I'm not supposed to know. Katja loves Lisa so much. Not to mention Maliki who looks after Thomas as a cub. You know Remi may act carefree, but it would crush him too."

Jason took her hand. "And you . . ." Sasha stops her panic, and tears. "What about you? Why can't you lose them? Even if they make it back from the stone, you're taking them to their family. Vampires and the werepeople don't socialize as they used to. You will lose them eventually. I just want you to be practical."

Sasha took his hand. "But they will be alive! Oh, Jason, please!" She began to cry again. Jason held her face and then pulled her close as she cried. "Oh my, sweet kitten. I will do whatever I can to keep them safe, but the stone decides who comes back from the city. Still, I will try." She cried in his arms for a while, and then he wiped her face with a cloth from his pocket.

"Now you go back to your room and get some sleep. We'll see what can be done tomorrow." She nodded and gave him a hug and returned to her room. Jason walked slowly to his study, muttering to himself. "There must be something else. But what?"

Remi and Nicola take turns pacing in their room. Remi was near rage and having problems keeping his rants from Nicola. "I can't believe them talking about that damned city, taking the children there to the stone. I have been to the city. It still smells of blood and war. I held my tongue in front of the little ones, but the brothers they know, they know the horror that place has become."

"Of course they know." Nicola jumped in. And I would think they would put down such a foolish plan. What I don't understand is where Thomas found out about the stone or being affirmed."

"Affirmed?" Remi looked at Nicola; he saw him knawing on something. Nicola repeating, affirmed time and time again. Remi finally asked, "What is it, my friend? What are you thinking?"

Nicola looked at Remi. "How many books at Bael's house talk of the Paragon stone? And then I ask this, how many would refer to affirmation?"

Remi sat and thought. "I'm sure Bael has a few in his library. Perhaps three or even four in passing that mention it."

Nicola put his hand on Remi's shoulder. "To mention affirmation by name?"

"None?"

"So where did he hear that term? No one in our group has even thought of it."

Remi started pacing again. "When has he met anyone outside our group in the last week?"

Nicola made a fist and clutched it with the other. "Only one manipulating son of a . . ." He began to curse in Russian.

"Who?" Nicola turned to Remi. "Maris, only he would suggest going to that pit."

Remi stared at the floor. "Why though, if they are affirmed? Wouldn't that be better for us? And if they don't come back, he would lose his chance to use them as well, right?" Nicola shook his head. Maris had much to gain in helping us if the timing was right. If we knew nothing of him now, and the children were destroyed, he did the one behind this a favor. If they got affirmed, he did the children and their house a favor. He's playing both sides, either way he gains.

Remi nodded. "When could he have told him though?" Remi paused.

When Thomas stopped and got gas at that station, he was very quiet after that. "But why would he have not just taken the boy?" Nicola smiled. "Where would he have taken him to? He isn't old enough yet to turn, or the royals would have his head. Montgomery wants the boy dead as do some of the others. Bael would be hunting him as well, and then there is something else. I think he actually likes the children. Elisavetta especially it was in his manners at the house when he met them."

Remi looks in shock. "Maris, are you joking Mon'ami that snake going against orders because he likes them? Mon'due, now I have heard it all." Nicola nodded his head.

"I hate to say it, but it makes sense." They heard the chime of the clock in the room. Nicola looked at the clock. "It's getting late. Tomorrow there is much to do. Let us sleep tonight, and in the morning, tell Bael about our idea." They turned off the light and got into bed. Later as they calmed and slept, they reverted to their animal forms.

In another castle far, from Canada in the European mountains near Finland and Sweden, word has reached the ears of *King Draugur*, the Father of the *Magyars*, a family of vampires—very old and powerful. The father sat on his throne and was being told of the attack on Bael and the others and, more importantly, who gave his people those orders. His page was shaking as he informed his majesty. The father scowled down at his page. "Bring me Lord Montgomery at once. I would have a conversation with him. Send Seidrich and two guards to bring him here. Now! Then ask my wife to attend me as soon as she can. Then inform the Magyars responsible for the attack to return to the castle."

The page bowed. "Yes, Your Majesty at once," and quickly left the chamber.

A short time later, a tall beautiful woman and attendants came into the chamber. As she saw her husband, she stopped and sent her attendants away. The father sat as a statue with a scowl on his face. He bore no crown, but there was no mistaking he was king. The queen took the seat next to him and took his hand. "What is it, dear? What has you so angry?"

He tried to calm himself as he took her hand. "Our subjects and the Vampyrs have attacked Lord Bael and his charges. They have done so at the behest of Montgomery. It is my understanding that they used thralls and even windigoes to the attack. Actually, there were two separate attacks. I have sent for those responsible and for Montgomery as well. My love, if we do not make this right by Lord Bael, after this problem with the *marks* is over, so may we be."

"My king and husband, be calm. Bael has long been an honored friend of this house. He must know we would not back that fool Montgomery! As for the others, I fear we have been slack in our obligations to our people. We must bring our house in order. Those that would take orders from Montgomery, or anyone, without the consent of the thrones, must be dealt with, regardless of Lord Bael."

"What about Lord Montgomery? What will you do about his insolence?"

The king clutched his throne as he stood. "Worthless as that sniveling cur is, he is a father of his house . . ." He turned his head around to the queen. "I hope he will not be too missed."

Across the Adriatic and Mediterranean seas, thousands of miles from the castle of the Magyars across the sands of Egypt was the home of the queen of all the vampires *Lilith.* She waited to hear of some word. Of how Bael and the others were after the attack. Her maid came to attend her with news of an arrival of guests.

"My queen, two emissaries from the house of Ravenna are here to see you, ma'am, masters Peter and David."

Lilith looked at the men at the entrance to her chamber. "Come in, gentlemen. There is no need for ceremony." She gave her maid a nod, and she exited the room. Peter Ravenna, followed by his brother, bows to the queen.

"Your Majesty," he began in his usual tone, but as he and his brother approached, his voice lowered to a whisper. This was given to us by Lord Bael to give to you."

They placed an envelope in her hand. "He requests that it not be opened until after he and the others are on their way from the house of the brothers. Upon his arrival in the Royal Court, he has entrusted us with a letter as well. I believe I know the reason for us to wait to open the letters, You're Highness. Even now there are those that would try to know your thoughts."

She tilted her head and gave them a slight bow of acknowledgment. "It will be a long month for all of us. She said as she walked through the room. Lord Bael, I hope will have everything in hand when he arrives." As she sat on her throne, her skin was pale as the stone of her chamber. The age of a vampire is seen in the color of their skin. Over time it became white even translucent and seems to have a glow. None of the vampires truly know how powerful she is. And the Question, while often thought; is never asked. David steps forward. "Your highness we have met the children. Marks or not they seem very . . . impressive. The girl has a spirit not unlike Lord Basarab, and the boy has a mind for knowledge. The girl's beauty she is unaware of; and when she takes the change she will be magnificent." The queen smiled softly. "You seem to be quite taken with them."

"Milady when you meet them you will understand. Yes, we both like them very much. As I believe you will as well. My queen what are you going to do about Lord Montgomery? His actions against Lord Bael are intolerable."

"As queen of all my hands are tied. I must remain neutral till they stand before the royals. I have no say in the politics of the Magyars, and he stood as one of the three fathers of that tribe. He went after the *Marks*, until they stand before the court, they are technically illegal to exist. Therefore legal to hunt." There were fast footsteps coming down the hall and into the chamber. The queen's page bowed to the queen. "They are all safely inside the sorcerer's castle, You're Majesty."

"Good, thank you. You may go." He bows and leaves.

Peter also bows to the queen. "Milady, we must return home."

"Of course, gentlemen, thank you for your service." They bow and exit.

The morning came slowly to the home of Alec and his brother. All of its borders had a restless sleep for most of the night. It was nine o'clock by the time Lisa and her brother had awoken and dressed. They met in the hall and went to the kitchen looking for her coffee. Alec sat at the table in the corner reading a paper and drinking tea. Lisa knocked on the entranceway. "Good morning, Alec, where is everyone?"

"Oh. The werepeople went out to get some air. They're not used to being inside so much and needed to hunt up some food for themselves. Bael is in the library looking for an alternative way for you two to be affirmed. I and Jason have already thought about it, but could think of nothing." Lisa looked back at Thomas, then to Alec. "Is there any coffee?"

"No, I'm afraid not. My brother and I drink tea, but you're welcome to have some if you like."

"Ah . . . no, thank you. Where is the large backpack of Bael's?"

"I believe it's still in the main chamber entrance." Lisa smiled and left. A few minutes later, she returned with coffee and pot. She filled it with water from the pump in the kitchen, added the coffee, and placed it on the hot stove. As the aroma filled the room she began to relax. Thomas saw Alec watching his sister as she moved around the room. "You'll have to forgive my sister. Until she's had her first cup in the morning, she isn't very social. What are you doing?"

"Trying to get some information on how the vampires are dealing with yesterday's events. It seems that you two have caused quite a stir amongst the families. As Marks, many are asking for your lives, and yet others who still have a human bloodline are more supportive of imprisonment. That aside, the attack on you by the vampires yesterday has caused the head of the Magyar family to call the fathers and mothers of the individual families for a meeting of their own. An attack on Lord Bael has been met with charges. However, the attackers are saying that the attack was meant for you, and your sister, though I doubt that will help their case." Bael entered the kitchen looking worried, but smiling. "I smelt the coffee and knew you were awake."

Lisa poured two cups and handed one to Bael. "Well, did you find anything this morning?"

"No, but there must be some other way. The thought of you going to Anun is not my first choice. Thomas however you found out about affirmation. I wish they had given you a suggestion on how?" Thomas sat, staring at the table, wondering what he should do. Alec, seeing the boy stressing over what Bael had said, got up from his seat and pat his back. "Don't worry about it, Bael. It's done. At least now we have a plan. As for you, I think it's time you embrace your abilities as the grandson of a god. Someone is behind all of this. Whoever it is knows your abilities and weaknesses. It's time you learn what you are capable of. It may be their best chance to survive what's coming. For now, let Jason work with the children. He knows how their powers work, and you come and work with me. There isn't much time, and there is much to learn for you and them."

Bael looked questioningly at Alec, but followed him out of the room and out of the castle. They walked for miles till they reached foot of a mountain.

"First things first."

Lisa and Thomas were joined by Jason in the large living room. They were given small chairs that made them feel as though they were sitting on the floor. Jason sat next to the fireplace in the center of the room. "Now, tell me what you know about your powers?" Lisa looked at her brother who shrugged his shoulders. Lisa then shrugged herself. "Not that much. I know our father was a natural sorcerer, but I'm not even sure what that means."

"I've been told that Thomas gets a better understanding from books. So I will start with you, Lisa. Face the fireplace. She turned her chair. Now watch the fire itself, the flame within the fire. I want you to try and feel that flame, but not by its heat. By its presence, it's force. Think of it as a friend you've just met. And you're feeling them out."

Lisa leaned forward and looked deep within the flame and saw a small flame at its core. Before she could think about it, she realized she could feel it, as a living being. She got a strange look on her face, and Jason smiled.

"You feel it don't you?"

She nodded.

"Now, call it out. Call it to you."

She leaned in farther and called it with her finger. "Come here, come on. It's okay."

Slowly, a small flame broke from the fire and moved toward her. She talked to it as you would a child or a pet coaxing it to her. The flame left the fireplace and seemed to almost walk to her.

"Now, put out your hand on the floor. Let it come to you."

She did as she's told, and soon, the small flame was in her hand. It seemed to dance along her fingers and kissed her palm. She moved her hand toward her face and looked deeper into it.

"You're so beautiful." Jason nodded with approval.

"Okay, let it feel you. Let it feed from your strength and power."

Slowly the flame grew; when it was about a foot tall, Jason smiled. Thomas all the while watched with his mouth open.

"That's good. Now gently place it back in the hearth."

She reached forward till her hand was inside the flame and lowered it to a log. "There you are," she said. "Safe and sound." She pulled her hand from the fire. Jason sat back in his chair.

"Very good, Lisa. I'm impressed. It came very natural to you." He looked to Thomas. "Would you care to try now, Thomas?"

He nodded quickly and faced the fire. He looked deeper and deeper into the fire. He tried to get a sense of it, but had a problem focusing on the flame. In his frustration, all of a sudden, there was a flash from the fire. It shocked him back in his seat. "Oh, why can't I do this?"

Jason got up from the fireplace. "Because, Thomas, you are more like me. You need time to understand certain concepts in magic. What's in front of you is more than what you see. You have to learn to feel your way. Don't worry, I was born through magic, and it took me years to realize what I was doing wrong. You'll get it and, in the end, probably be very good at it. Remember, you have a lot on your mind right now as well."

Thomas gave a half smile. "Thanks, I hope you're right."

"Here, I have something that will help." He handed Thomas two large books. "These are what made me understand. Read and enjoy. As for you, Miss Thory, let us try a few other things while you're brother reads."

Bael looked around and took in the area. "Alec, why did you bring me all the way out here?"

"Because this is where you need to be for *these* lessons. First, we start with something." Alec took Bael by the shoulder and faced him toward the mountain face. "Let's start with this." And he pointed to the mountainside. "You want me to climb to the top?"

"No, I want you to pick it up. Carefully. Then I want you to place it back again carefully." Bael looks to the top of the rock face. He knew that the mountain was much higher than the first ridge. "Alec . . . while I know I'm stronger than I look, I can't move mountains."

"Oh no, just the one." Alec waved his hand at the mountain face.

"Oh . . . just the one?"

"Yes, put your hands under it. Feel the mountain, push your fingers through as though they were as long. Well . . . enough to reach the other side. And lift."

Seriously, Alec, I can't move a mountain!" There was a shimmer in the air, and a man walked from thin air.

"Have you ever tried? You can. But you must use your gifts, and not you're magic." The man turned his attention to Alec. "He's always been so stubborn when it comes to using his abilities." He turned back to Bael. "I know your father started to teach you about your abilities, but you fought him at every turn. Well . . . that will have to stop if you're to save your charges."

Bael, looking rather puzzled at the man, said, "Who are you? I don't believe we've met."

"Oh . . . we've met several times, but it has been awhile. Perhaps an introduction is in order?"

Alec gave the gentleman a small bow and turned to Bael. "Lord Bael, it is my pleasure to introduce to you, your grandfather, *Lord Baal*, god of wisdom and fertility."

Bael stood still for a moment, then dropped his head and bowed. The man before him was his *grandfather*, but he no more looked like a god than he did, yet he did seem to radiate a sense of power. He was a tall man of six foot three or so; he wore a suit nicely cut in blue. He had a strong build, blue eyes, average nose, mustache, and well-trimmed beard. But what stood out to Bael the most was the soft, warm smile that he gave to his grandson. Baal bowed with a nod to Alec. "Thank you, my friend, but the grandstanding isn't quiet my style. Nevertheless, I am your grandfather, and I'm very glad to see you. He walked to Bael and put out his arms. "I don't suppose you'd consider giving the old god a hug. Or would you?"

Bael stepped forward to give a hug but stopped. "Grandfather? I suppose you are, since Alec says so, but why have you waited till now to come and see me? My son has seen you more than I have. And now you expect affection."

Baal lowered his arms as Bael spoke. "You're right. I should have revealed myself to you long ago. But in fairness, I have been watching and waiting. I have been in your life since you were born. Our laws say that I must keep my distance, but I had to see you over the years. I've taken the form of people in your life, like certain generals, or other troops you worked with in your youth. The cat that came to your cabin has been me. From time to time, I take the place of your friend Annie. The simple fact is you haven't wanted to see the family that much over the years, so you didn't. I however did want to see you. Now that you're starting to train yourself, I thought I could help."

Bael stared at the ground, thinking. In truth, he knew his grandfather was right, and he had trouble looking him in the eye. He felt a hand on his shoulder and saw his grandfather's shoes. "Bael, always know, I love and care for family even when I must be away from them." Bael looked up and gave his grandfather a hug as tight as he could.

"Gentlemen, as touching as this is, we have far too much training to do and too little time to waste." Alec spoke sternly, but with a smile. They broke their embrace and turned to Alec.

"Right . . . now, Bael, go ahead and lift the mountain for Alec."
Bael stared at his hands a moment. "Are you sure I can do something
like this?"

"Well, it doesn't come up too often, but yes, you have the ability. Think of what you told Thomas about the ax at the cabin." Bael
thought back.

"If you knew how much power and strength you had" was what
he told Thomas. "I guess it is my turn, huh?" Bael bent down and
pushed his hands into the solid rock face of the mountain. He tried
to lift as he was told, but only a large piece of the face came off and
was lifted.

"No!" Alec shouted. "Not a peace the whole thing."

"Look, I can't help that the rock breaks, can I?"

Alec turned to Baal. "He doesn't understand. I don't know why
he doesn't, but he doesn't."

Baal waved off and nodded to Alec. "You said you could teach
him. Well . . . make him understand."

Alec lowered his head, frustrated. "I need to put this in human
terms so you can get the concept." He paused and thought. "Ah, I
have it. In a fight, when you plant your feet and someone large came
at you, you aren't actually heavier, are you? No, you simply center
yourself and focus yourself to one location. As a result, you are harder
to move. What I want you to do is think of the mountain as a whole.
Yet not as planted so you can move it as a whole. Get under it, plant
your feet. Feel not just what's in your hands but the whole mountain.
Do you understand?"

Bael walked back over to the rock face. He planted his feet
firmly; he grabbed at the base of the mountain. He strained this time
to raise himself. Soon he felt a shift in the rock all the while straining.
He felt the foot of the mountain break free and reached beneath to
raise himself up. He felt the hard stone against his cheek and began
to stand. As he got to his feet, he realized he didn't know how much
of the rock he'd lifted.

Bael called to Alec, "Well . . . how much did I get up?" He was
still holding the stone in his hands. Alec called back to him, "Now
remember, gently place the stone back." Bael rolled his eyes and

slowly began to place it back. Just before it's down, it loosened from his fingers. As it hit the ground, there was a huge bang and grumble. The ground shook a moment and dust rose through the air. Bael looked around to Alec and his grandfather, who were brushing the dirt off themselves, smiling. "I did not lift that entire mountain? I couldn't, could I? No . . . how much did I pick up?"

Inside the castle, the others were shocked at the house shaking and the loud boom could be heard throughout the castle.

"What the hell was that?" Lisa shouted! Jason looked out the window and saw a cloud of dust. "That, Miss Thory, is a success. So come and get on with your lesson."

"I don't understand what you want me to do." Jason shook his head. "Just as you had done with the flame. I want you to feel the water in the bowl, not the water itself, but as a friend."

"But it's not the same. I tried, but it doesn't work the same."

"What's so different?"

"I don't know. I can't put my finger on it." Thomas cleared his throat.

"Sir, I think I know what the problem is."

"By all means, Master Thomas, what is it?"

"She can't see the heart of the water, as she did with the flame."

"You may be right, Master Thomas. Lisa, is that it?"

"Maybe. I just don't know where to look in the bowl."

"I see . . . let's try this. Though you can't see its heart, it floats through it. Therefore, all of it is its heart, and none of it is. It just is." Lisa looks again inside the bowl. Jason dips his hand in, and took it out letting the water fall in drops from his hand. "Follow the drops to the water watch as they ripple. Find its heart. Feel the drops as they hit the rest of the water." She did feel something or had a sense of something. It felt like fun she thought. As the drops hit the water it felt like laughter. The ripples were like a tickle. She began to feel the water. "I can, I can feel it. It's still different but I feel something."

"Good, now shape it. Let the water feel you. Let it know what shape you want it to take." Lisa continued to try, but struggled. Jason and Thomas watched the bowl of water as drop after drop fell from Jason's hand. Thomas was the first to notice that the drops were fall-

ing slower until one droplet fell to the water but didn't become part
of it. It sat on top of the water. The other drops had stopped. Slowly
Lisa talked to it and began to call it to her. The droplet began to
move across the water, till it reached the side of the bowl. "Oh, come
on," Lisa said to it. "You can do it." She placed her hand just outside
the bowl. The droplet began to get larger from the water in the bowl.
Slowly it seemed to climb out onto Lisa's hand. "That's it. Oh . . .
it worked." The droplet slid to the palm of her hand, then began to
shape itself till soon it took the form of a swan. Jason looked at the
water. "Is that the shape you wanted?"

"It's what I was thinking of when I thought about the water."

"Yes, but is it the shape you wanted?"

"No."

Jason shook his head. "I thought not. We'll have to work on it,
but well done for a starting attempt." Thomas sat back and marveled
at his sister, then went back to reading. "That was great, sis. I hope I
get the hang of it soon."

Jason clasped his hands. "You do quite well with the elements.
Shall we try something a little more difficult? The air around you
isn't just air, nor is the ground just ground. In all things, even the elements there is more to them. Inside every atom everywhere is *magic*.
It's not a trick or illusion. It exists. Everywhere all at once. Now once
you understand that, truly understand, then like the water in your
hand and the flame before, it will respond to you."

Lisa released the water from her hand, and it poured back into
the bowl. She moved her hand through the air, still wet from the
water. Jason again watched as Lisa tried to understand the lesson.
"I do wish you children didn't think so . . . human. It's very hard to
change your way of thinking to our way of understanding. How do
I help you understand about magic? Understanding magic . . ." he
repeated again and again. "Perhaps it is time for a break till I can
think of how to translate the information."

Lisa smiled. "That would be great. I haven't seen the others for
hours." Thomas continued to read while Lisa found her way out to
the grounds. This plane that they were on was nothing like the world
they knew. At night the ground seemed to almost glow with a blue

light. Now . . . during the day, the ground was yellow, the leaves in the trees were bright red and orange as an Indian summer or fall, yet she knew it was winter. "It's like another world here," she said to herself. She heard a rustling, and as she turned around out from the high bushes came a huge bear.

"Good morning, Remi. How are you this morning?" The big bear shook his head. Very quickly he reverted to his human form. "It's like an inner light consumes you and someone else comes out the other side, all in a blink of an eye." Remi grabbed his clothes and put them on. "It's just how it's done, Cher. I really don't think about it anymore." Lisa gave him a hug. "You would not believe the morning I've had. I've been practicing magic with Thomas and Jason. It was great!" Remi rubbed his head. "I'm glad you had fun, but there's still a lot for you to learn."

"I know. Remi, how many werepeople are there? I mean, different kinds?"

Remi scratched his head. "Well, let me see." He started, trying to count. "Lisa, I can't be sure, but over fifty or more. Why?"

"I had been wondering for a while. Do werepeople and vampires ever . . . hang out? You know, be friends?"

"Of course, at one time. They counted on each other, at times they still do."

"Good, I was worried a little."

"What, about losing your friends? Don't be. Your families' father has known Nicola since he was a cub. I'm sure you can visit with him any time you want."

"Do you think our father would mind if he stayed with us once in a while?"

"Lisa, I thought you knew? Nicola cannot go into Russian territory anymore. He's been in exile for years."

Lisa shook her head puzzled. "What do you mean exile? How?"

"Lisa, you have enough to worry about now before you start worrying about Nicola's exile. He's fine for now and has been for some time."

"Fine, don't tell me. I'm sure Sasha will tell me." Remi looked at Lisa, cocking his head and closing one eye trying to size her up. "You just don't let go of something, do you, cheri?" He sighed. "Okay, Nicola was king of his territory for thousands of years. Every mating season, other males challenge for his crown. A hundred or so years ago, he lost the challenge. The one who took the crown banished him from the territory. His daughters left with him, and his wives were forfeit."

"Can't he challenge and win it back?"

"He could if he was allowed back to the territory, but that most likely will not happen."

"I don't get this why didn't he just go back with the other males instead of exile?"

Remi took her hand. "Because the new king was his eldest brother Alexi. When a family member took the throne from another, it can cause civil war. If there are those who think the other was a better leader. Everyone takes a side and divides the pride, or Ambush, and weakens it. Sometimes the new king will kill the loser. It was Nicola's wife that pleaded for exile."

"So is Alexi a good king?"

"Actually, yes, and loves his brother. He and Nicola still see each other from time to time. Nicola is very proud of his brother, but there are others that think Nicola should have the throne. Nicola will not divide the Ambush."

Lisa nodded her head "At least I get it now. Can he ever go back?" Remi gave her hand a pat. "I don't know. Perhaps one day."

Just then they felt a tremor under their feet shaking everything around them. "What was that?"

"If I were to guess, I would say Bael is trying to understand his power better. Alec took him out to practice this morning. As for practice, shouldn't you return to your studies?"

"I suppose so." Lisa went back into the castle reluctantly and was greeted by a woman at the door, leading her to the kitchen. "Well, you must be Lisa Thory. Correct? Or am I mistaken?"

"No, you're not mistaken, but I'm afraid I don't know who you are?"

"Oh, I'm sorry, dear. I'm Miss Murray, Harriet Murray. But around here, they call me Harry. I look after the brothers and the castle, sort of keep them in line as it were. I was hoping your aunt would be here. Till I was told what happened. Little wolf filled me in and brought me up-to-date. I'm so happy to finally have met you. Your aunt has been telling me about you for years. Come in and have a seat. I'll see if I can't fill in any gaps you might still have. I know you were thrown into the deep end. I'm glad to see you still afloat." Lisa smiled at the lady and went inside. As Lisa sat at the kitchen table, the woman poured some tea. "Well, Elisabeth, where would you like me to start."

"As far back as you can, if you don't mind?"

"Well then, you're mother and father fell in love before they knew what each other was in fact your mother knew less than you do now. She was twenty years old when she married your father. She didn't know about her family line or about any part of our world. Your father was a great sorcerer and a good man he told your mother about the magic and his abilities, which she took in stride. You were born nine months after the honeymoon. She loved you so much. Now came the tricky part. Your mother hadn't been told anything because she went missing when she'd found out about your dad. She kept him a secret from her blackthorn your aunt Lucile. She even managed to keep you a secret for two years, but then Lucile told her about her family and the line and about the choice she had to make. That was when your mother told Lucile she was married and about you, and lastly, that she was pregnant with your brother. Lucile sat down with your mom and dad to figure out what to do. They knew that there would be a problem when you both had the marks on your hands and later you both were found to have the royal bloodline. You were both tested in secret. Your mother put off making the choice, and your father was kept secret. Bael had known your family for years, but Lucile told her what he actually was. Of course he was already your godfather. After your brother was born, she was told she had two years to make her choice. It was at that time your father was called away to take care of problem in the Pacific. An eruption on an island causing damage all over, and he went to help, and it cost him his life. Your mother went into a depression. Lucile took care of you kids more and more. Finally, she made her choice, and Lucile stepped in for your mother."

"Why didn't Bael know about our marks?"

"Because he was never told who your father was. Though I expect he figured it out when he saw the marks."

"Yes, but Bael could have prepared if he'd had known."

"Elisabeth. you two were already a sought-after commodity had it been known that you had marks. I shudder to think what might have happened to you. So only Lucile and myself knew the truth."

"What if someone had read your thoughts?"

"Dear, no one has any effect on me. I'm a negative or nel. Magic has no effect, nor do I have any reaction from vampire or the were-people. In fact, even Bael's power rarely has any effect. Of course, as a human, Bael's power is limited to me anyway."

"Bael said something about that when we were attacked. That they were using human thralls against him. I don't understand even at the diner. Bael didn't break the vampires control over the people around us."

"Elisabeth, everyone has rules to adhere to even the gods. Admittedly, they wrote the rules, but they follow them just the same. Gods and demigods alike have limited power with people. They must have permission to deal with them by those that they affect. That is why people pray. It gave god's permission to help those that they can. Vampires on the other hand can impose their will on humans and control them. You see, for the gods, it is most important that the people have a freedom of choice so that they may know in which plain their spirit resides after their life has ended, or whether it should end at all."

Lisa has a puzzled look on her face. "I know it seems confusing, but don't worry as a mark and part of the bloodline, you should live a very long time to figure it all out." The calm and kind way she spoke put Lisa at ease.

"You mentioned that we were commodities and Maris has shown an interest in us, and Bael said others wanted us, but I understand we wouldn't like what they had planned. Now everyone has different plans for us. Some want us dead, others want us under some

THE CHOICE, THE FIRST OF THE THORY'S CHRONICLES

kind of control, and that doesn't sound pleasant either. Quite frankly it sounds like no matter who wins we lose."

Harriet smiles and gave her a hug. "I promise, dear, if you make it to the royals court, you will be fine. You and your brother both will be just fine."

Jason came in and scowled at Lisa. "Miss Thory, are you going to return to your practice or retire for the day? I don't waste my time nor do let others waste it for me."

Harriet turned with a scowl of her own. "Oh, is that right? Now you listen to me, you old windbag, I've been waiting a long time to see this girl and will not be interrupted by anyone in this house while I am. Is that perfectly clear?"

Harriet grabbed him by the ear and turned him to the door. "I said am I clear?"

"Yes."

"Yes what?"

"Yes, Harry, you're clear." Jason left the room, and Harriet went back to Lisa.

"Dear, in a few minutes, you should return to your practice. I'll be in later to help as well. Lisa looked at Harriet questioningly.

"Oh yes, dear, I'm a sorceress as well." She smiled again and finished her tea. Lisa did her best to hold in a small giggle, thinking to herself, "She does keep them in line."

Meanwhile, Bael had begun another lesson. His grandfather's frustration was beginning to show. Bael had made several tries, but produced no results. So they began again. "Now, Bael, I know this seems impossible for you, but believe me, you are capable of creating. Just concentrate and realize your ability. Close your fist and visualize a seed in your mind. See? It's beginning, let it take shape."

Bael closed his eyes and listened to his grandfather; his concentration making his voice seem farther and farther away, but still he heard his voice strong in his mind.

"Then feel it there. In your mind. Use your will to move it from your mind to your hand. Then feel it take shape again. This time in your hand. Will the energy from the air. Bring it in and through you to form the seed." Soon Bael did feel something. He felt the energy through him. The hair on his arm rose in a wave. Bael opened his eyes and his fist. In his palm, there was a wave of energy and a swirl of the air as they merged it formed an object. Bael and his grandfather watched as from nothing it formed a seed, a real seed. Bael continued to concentrate while his grandfather was now silently watching with pride. The seed now solid opened. It continued to grow, feeding from Bael's energy. Bael for the first time looked up at his grandfather and Alec—both smiling with pride at him. Bael watched as a small stalk began to rise from the seed. Alec reached down and moved away some of the soil to make a small hole.

"Bael, place the seed here," said Alec. Bael placed it in the ground and covered the base. His grandfather patting him on the back. "So what will it be, my boy?" Bael looked questioningly at his grandfather.

"I . . . I don't know. I just thought of a seed not what it would be."

"Ah . . . well, it must become something. What would you most like to see a flower, a plant, or perhaps a tree?"

Bael looked down at his creation, then looked around at the forest next to the mountain.

"Yes. A tree would be nice. An oak, a tall oak tree with beautiful green leaves."

His grandfather looked at the forest as well, with its red, orange, and yellow colors. "Bael, there are no oak trees on this plain. It would stand alone here. Are you sure that would be wise?"

"But after a while it may join with the others and become something else. Something new. Maybe better?"

"Perhaps, but what if it destroys the harmony of what's already here?" Bael thought about what his grandfather had said for a moment. Then he thought of the children. He couldn't stop the thought in his head.

"Grandfather, I have to believe that something new can be something good, maybe something special, but things around it may in the end have to adapt, or maybe the new tree will adapt to them." His grandfather looked down at the seedling as it still rushed to grow from Bael's energy.

"Then I suppose an oak it will be." Bael looked at his grandfather and Alec when he began to feel tired and weak. Alec took hold of him. Baal put his hand on Bael's shoulder, and soon, Bael began to feel better and got back to his feet. Baal pointed to the castle. "Take him back in and let him rest. He's drained for now. After all, he is doing things new to him. It will come easier later."

Alec and Bael started for the castle when Bael stopped and looked around for his grandfather, but he was gone. Bael turned back to the path, mumbling under his breath, "He could have said goodbye." To this, Alec just laughed "Why are you so sure he's gone? There is an old saying that translates to all religions you should remember 'God is in the breeze' even when he's not here, he's here."

Bael and Alec returned to the castle where Katja put him to bed.

Lisa and Thomas continued their lessons throughout the day. Thomas had begun to understand after reading Jason's books how the magic worked. By the evening Thomas had gained and passed his sister's abilities. Jason, Alec, and Harry were impressed by how fast they seemed to come to the magic within them. By three o'clock, Jason left them to work on their lessons by themselves. Alec nodded to his brother and Harry. They left the room to the children and went to the kitchen. Jason was shaking his head as they entered.

"I don't understand how, but they seem to have their father's gift for magic." Harry nodded as she started making a pot of tea. "Oh, I'm impressed, but not all together shocked. Their family line has been one of the strongest as well, you know." Alec turned in his seat.

"Yes, the Basarab's line, strong though it may be, has little to do with magic. Accept for that great grandson that dealt with those gypsies and their unique magic, but that cost him dearly." Harry poured her tea and sat at the table. "That is not the line I'm speaking of." Jason and Alec gave Harry their complete attention. "The Oaken family line is strong as well. The line goes back to Albert Wick, 'the Woodland Sorcerer' and son of Albrecht. Albert was Albrecht's secret human son."

Jason's head popped up. "Albrecht had no human sons. He was a dwarf."

"Ah, but Albrecht met Eleanor Wick and fell in love her. And that was that."

"But Albert had no sons or daughters when he died? He was a good friend. He would have mentioned any children?"

"Elisa Oaken, the black hills witch or enchantress, had one son. Albert Wick was the father though he never knew."

"And just how do you know all this?"

"When Lucile found out about the marriage and the children, she had me look into Thomas Oaken's family. I ran into a wall in the blackhills forest, so I went to the watchers. They got me over the wall." Alec and Jason sat, stunned. Then Alec had a thought that made him jump to his feet. "I know why the children can have both bloodlines. The blood from Albrecht, it was a catalyst. It let the bloodlines flow together instead of one being dominant and the other fade out. They truly have the ability to be both. Jason and Alec think." Alec stopped and looked at the living room, then at his brother. "We'll leave in the morning."

"Where?"

There was an emptiness in Alec's voice.

"Anun."

7

It was one thirty in the morning at the home of Lord Basarab, father of his house, the Vampyrs. He walks the corridors, waiting for news. Those that passed him gave him a bow or a low nod. His anger and frustration over not being able to step in on those that had attacked his human bloodline was reaching its limits. Suddenly, he heard a ring and stopped. His servant answered the phone. After a few minutes of "yes sirs" and "no sirs," he heard the servant, "His highness will be relieved to hear it, sir. I will relay the message as fast as I can, sir. Thank you."

The servant walked down the hall to his lordship. "Sir, the king of the Magyars has called for all involved with the attack back to their palace, and Lord Montgomery is being escorted back to king by his guards for punishment. It's understood that the children are fine, sir."

"Well, that's something. Bascom, I'm going out to the tomb to check on their mother. I'm worried she will find out what's happening. If someone should call, come for me, but say nothing."

"Yes, Father, I'll come as soon as I know something, sir."

He walked out the door to the gardens, down the walkway to a domed building. He opened the large metal door. Inside were stone pedestals around the room. He walked to a stairwell and followed it down till he reached the bottom. There in the dark room he sat as he had many times over the years. It was the crypt of Elisa Thory Oaken. Fifteen years ago, she entered and went into what the vampires called a shadowing. A shadowing is a deep sleep beneath the earth, often called a sleep of stone. A tomb will be filled with earth after a vampire begins its long rest. This usually lasts up to a year, while they sleep their body, and their mind changes. Their skin grows paler, stronger. Their senses sharpen, yet they cannot move and are taken as dead by the human world. Elisa had been in this state for fifteen years. Lord Basarab came and spoke to her, often changing the earth to make her comfortable. He cared for her as he did all his children, but she worried him to be under so long.

"My lovely Elisa, I know why you have taken this measure. I have always known how hard you took the loss of your family when you chose your fate, but the children are coming of age. You should be there for them. I will as always do my best to keep them safe, but please wake for them."

Lord Basarab waited and listened for some sound that she'd heard him. But as every time he had tried, nothing came from the tomb. He rose and returned to the house. In the study, he looked at the pictures on the wall. Queen Lilith had taken a shadowing once long ago. She had slept much longer than Elisa. It was rumored that she had been in shadow for over a hundred years, but no one survived her awakening to say whether it was true or not. He himself had gone into shadow for five years and awakened to find himself drained from hunger, but his strength had increased tenfold. As he walked the wall of portraits, he wondered what he could do about his human line. His fist came down on the oak desk leaving a deeply lasting imprint on it.

"Montgomery, be glad you face your king's wraith and not mine. You damned fool. Though I expect his leniency will not be much more than mine."

The castle of the Magyar king was busy below the royal chambers. Lord Draugur's anger had not decreased. His queen waited patiently for the right time to put an end to the storm that her husband had unleashed in the castle's personal chambers. Finally, he called for wine, and she brought in the tray herself. "Good evening, dear, I'm so glad to see you're in a better humor." He turned, clearing his throat, "Yes. Well . . . why are you bringing my wine? Where are the servants?"

She placed the tray on the table. "I will not have the servants bullied by your foul mood. Nor will I have them see you like this." She was waving her hand to the room. "Now make yourself presentable and I'll have the staff clean this room."

He took her hand and kissed her. "Mara, my love, what would I ever do without you?"

"You'll never have to. Now, change your clothes, and I'll find out what's keeping Seidrich and Montgomery." The queen rang for her maid, and moments later, she arrived. "Ahh . . . Rina, tell William to bring me the phone and then prepare the room."

"Yes, Mother, right away." And she scurried from the room. William returned with the phone. He placed it on the desk and plugged it in. "Thank you, William. Please ring up Seidrich, and that should be all, William." He dialed the phone and handed it to the queen then left. "Seidrich, is everything in hand?"

"No, ma'am. I have informed our people to report to the palace, and they have already left by plane. They should arrive soon. As for Lord Montgomery, his whereabouts are unknown, but I have trackers working on the problem."

"Thank you, Seidrich, if you can *bring him back*."

"Of course, ma'am. While I'm here, would you care for me to relate a message to Lord Bael?" She thought for a moment. "Yes, give him our apologies for the incident and inform him of your mission. Let him understand Lord Montgomery's actions will not be tolerated."

"I understand, Mother. Good-bye."

"Good-bye, Seidrich. Be careful in dealing with him." She hung up and informed her husband. "Very well. First, I will deal with our subjects, then when Montgomery is found, I will deal with him. As for Lord Bael, I'm certain Seidrich can explain easily enough." The king's temper had cooled due to his wife's counsel.

As the sun came up at the castle of Alec Chartwell, all was quiet; the fire in the hearth crackled. Thomas had fallen asleep on the sofa, reading. Maliki was sleeping in the corner of the room, still watching over him even in this safe haven. All of the guests were still sleeping soundly. By seven o'clock Sasha, Katja, and Bael were up, and in the kitchen, Bael made coffee and started on breakfast. Alec and Jason had been up for hours. Harry came into the kitchen watching as everyone buzzed about. Katja had begun making her bread, for she hoped everyone. Alec looked so solemn and worried that caught

Bael's attention. "What's got you so quiet this morning?" Alec looked at Jason, and then Jason looked up at Bael. "You and the children are coming with us this morning."

"Where are you taking us?" He was looking serious himself now. "We leave for Anun once the children awaken. You are coming because you must face the stone as well. It's time you face your own truth, Bael. Who and what you are."

Bael said nothing and walked from the room. He thought about his long life and his family. The recent events of the last week. His son that was back in his life. That was the thought that made his mind up. If he couldn't face what he was, what about his son?

The smell of coffee was in the air. He smiled, Lisa would soon be up. He looked down at Thomas sleeping with a book in his hands. He had known them for years. But now he had grown close to them. He was so proud of them, and now worried if they were ready. What would the stone do with them? With all these thoughts, he didn't notice Lisa had gotten up and walked in. Her voice startled him. "Morning, Bael. What's on your mind this morning? You look a little out of it?" He gave her a faded smile.

"I'm fine, dear, just thinking. Go get yourself some coffee. We're getting an early start today."

"Okay. Is everyone up yet?"

"No, Nicola and Remi are still in bed, and you can see Maliki and Thomas are not yet with us. So go in and get started while I wake Nicola. I'll be back in a few minutes."

Bael returned from waking the others and informing Nicola of the morning's activities. By the time he returned, it was apparent the news had been broken. Thomas and Lisa had gone to get dressed. Katja was doing her best keeping her emotions in check. Alec and Jason began preparations to open a path to the city. Two large circles were drawn on a blank wall with a chalky stone. Than both brothers began to write words or a spell between the inner and outer circles. Finally, Alec came to Lisa and Thomas. "Before I open the way to the city, remember to stay with Jason and myself. Don't leave the group because you see something. Do you understand?"

They nodded and stood back as Alec placed his hand in the center and whispered something that Thomas didn't understand. The inner circle dissolved like sand, falling to the floor and disappeared. Alec and the others walked through the whole, and then it was gone.

There was a wave in the air like heat in the desert. Two men emerged from the wave as if they were a mirage on the porch of house in a jungle. As they walked through the doorway one of the men began to pace. The other took a seat in the shade.

"Sit down, Lord Montgomery and welcome to Calcutta. Some tea perhaps to calm your nerves?"

"No, milord, thank you."

"Why are you so worried? Stop your pacing. You're quite safe." Montgomery sat across from the man in the shadows. "My lord, while I know you would keep me safe, I heard, before we left, that my king has sent for me to return to the palace. He has even sent a centurion to retrieve me."

"Yes, I know. He has even put trackers on to you. Your quite the sought-after now, aren't you?"

"Yes, milord, but I am safe?"

"Trust me, I have great need of you for their trial. Continue to serve me, and I will keep you far more than safe. For now, relax. I have much still to do." The man in the shadows stood and walked for the door. "I must make preparations for Bael when he decides to leave the wizard's castle. I have something special in mind. If you need something, ring the bell. I'll return soon." In the wave of air, he was gone.

Thomas and Lisa looked around at their surroundings. At their feet was a stone path of orange-and gray stone; the fields were green at the base to a golden yellow at their tips. The ground in the distance had soft hills leading to a small mountain. Toward the top lay a small town of yellow stone. The trees and landscapes were beautiful as well. But it was the sky and the sound that brought all the beauty to a stop. There was something not right as they looked around. Everyone felt it. Thomas couldn't shake the chilling sensation on his neck. Lisa just felt sick over it. "Well, Toto, we're not in Kansas anymore." Thomas smiled and almost laughed. Alec turned around. "This is not a place or time for jokes, Miss Thory."

Jason stopped. "Alec that's enough! The children are here. They have been told what has happened in the past to some of those brought here. I think a sense of humor is perfectly acceptable." Jason took the children by the shoulders. "Don't let the robed wonder there get you worried. So far, so good. So let's be on our way." Bael bringing up the rear winks at Jason, who winked back. Lisa looked at the trees and was listening when she realized there were no birds or animals. Even the wind there seemed quiet.

"There's nothing here, is there?" Thomas stopped.

"She's right. I don't hear a single bird or rabbit rustling through the grass, not even our echo came back. There are also no clouds, but the sky is an unhealthy blue."

Lisa went to Jason. "Does anything survive here?" Jason looked down at Lisa's face. "Yes, but not as you know survival. Lisa, this place was brought here alone. For the existence of creatures here time does not move."

Lisa put her hands to her face. "That's horrible. Those poor animals." Lisa started to cry. Bael and Thomas went to her as the brothers looked on. Bael held Lisa till she stopped crying. Thomas took her hand.

"Come on, sis. Let's go. This place isn't for us." Thomas turned to the brothers. "You should have warned us. This place isn't dead, it's . . . it's just gray. Here but not there. Your lessons taught us. To a point, everything has a life. This stone of yours has a lot to answer for. Look around, this isn't right!"

Thomas had never handled seeing his sister hurt. "If we could, I'd say we leave right now. So let's get this over with." \

Alec and Jason said nothing; they knew he was right, they should have warned them of more than just the danger. The walk down the path took a silent turn. A mile or more went by when something caught Thomas's eye. Movement in the tree line. A shadow moved. "We're not alone here." Jason stopped and brushed his sleeves. "Stay close to the group and try not to notice them."

"Who are they?" Bael put his hand on Thomas's shoulder. "Their watchers, but I don't know what they're doing here." Jason hesitated. "They've always been here. When the town was brought here, they were as well. The watchers aren't affected by any magic that I know of. So when Anun was taken out of time, it had no effect on them. They still live here." Bael grabbed Alec's arm. "Watchers with nothing to watch for thousands of years, separated from the others. What has that done to them?"

"Most of the time they keep their distance, but they have on one occasion become aggressive."

"You two have to work on your conversational skills on *things you should know.*"

They continued down the path till they reach the foot of the mountain. The path turned to stairs and a winding path to the town. They started up, and along the way, they noticed the shadows or watchers were getting closer. It took over an hour to reach the town walls. Just outside them, the watchers were gone. The gates of the town were huge. Lisa laughed in her head when she saw them thinking back to the doors at Bael's house. As Bael pushed them open, the air moved as if it had been waiting for someone to stir it. A small wind seemed to move across the floor of the town. Lisa noticed that the dust it stirred wasn't dust. It came from small piles littered about the streets. Lisa swallowed tears in her throat that felt like a thick wave hard to get down. "They were people, the ones that lived and the ones that attacked. Piles of dust." She started to reach for a pile, but stopped short. Still holding back tears, she clinched her fist. "Is this all there is to remember them?"

Alec pulled her to him. "No, dear. We remember them. My brother and me. We knew them before this happened. We cried the day we left this place the first time. Walking through our friends remains. Now, we just remember them. Bael's grandfather told us many years ago where they truly ended up, and that was our relief. They are at peace."

Nicola paced the castle floor again and again. His daughters were nervously watching both their father and the circles on the wall, waiting for the whole to open again. Maliki waited in a corner, meditating. Remi and Harry were in the kitchen playing cards. Nicola leaned against the fireplace in the center of the room. Katja got up and hugged him. He put his arm around her. "I'm sorry, I know I should be comforting you right now, but the little ones still have far to go even if they make it through this. Sasha saw how worried her father was yet smiled. She too was worried. Worried about Lisa and Thomas, her friends, and as she looked up at her father, her family. She watched the circles. Lisa and Thomas were family. They all felt it. Even Remi who worried about nothing couldn't hide his anxiety. The whole castle was a match waiting to light. Beowulf sat in his chair; his eyes closed, remaining calm and making Sasha upset by staying calm. "Are you seriously not worried about them?"

"Yes."

"How are you so damned calm? I'm about to come out of my skin."

"Why don't you go for a run outside? It might take the edge off."

"Arrgh . . . there are times, little wulf, when I could just . . ." Beowulf sat in his chair, eyes closed, remaining calm, and smiled. While she was angry at him, she wasn't worrying about the others.

Alec led the group through the town; the stone of the buildings looked yellowed at a distance, but now looked a light gray with the shadows from the light it truly seemed dead. Now in the town, every step echoed. They moved through the town. Lisa saw how they lived. She even, from time to time, saw fires in hearths, frozen in time. Their life frozen. She was really beginning to hate the lessons they'd learned. Jason saw her face as they went, but didn't know what had her upset at first. It took awhile, and then he figured it out. "Dear Elisabeth, a flame's life isn't like that of us. Some grow, others go out that they exist is their point. Not when they go out, or when they start. It is the same for the water and the air."

She nodded and walked on through the town. Soon they'd reached a building at the top of the mountain.

"This is the temple of the stone." Alec wrapped his arms around the children and looked up to Bael.

"From here you must go alone. Inside the temple, you'll find the stone easy enough. The stone already knows why you are here, but you must ask for affirmation. Place your hands on the stone and ask then give yourself over so that all that you are is seen by the stone. What happens after, that I don't know. Be prepared for a slight pain if you're affirmed."

Bael started to walk toward the temple entrance when a hand stopped him. "No, Bael, I'm afraid this time you must follow." Alec looked to Lisa. "My dearest Lisa, you are the first to go through."

"Me, why me?"

"I'm sorry, but that is the order the stone has requested."

"Then it talks to you?" Jason took her hand. "It talks to us both, and you and your brother must go first." He smiled. "Now be strong and be brave. After all, it could have destroyed us all as we entered this plane." Lisa thought to herself, "Yeah, that makes me feel so much better." His hand held hers slightly tighter for a moment, then he released her. Lisa turned and walked through the archway following the hall to her right until she reached the archway to the temple's inner chamber. She looked up at the high archway and smiled when she realized "no doors." She thought back to the town. There were no doors. She walked into the chamber. The room was almost round; the walls were green with moss. Even the stone slab had some parsley over it. The room with the green in it had a warm feeling to it, but the air was musty. Then she heard something. A drip, then another. As she walked through the town, she heard nothing, but here it was different. *Time hasn't stopped here?* The moss had grown; the water dripped though from where she wasn't sure. Lisa was enraged to have stopped life in the town but have it here for itself.

"You need to know me. Well, fine, you get to know me! Know why you've pissed me off!" With that, she threw her hands on the stone. The stone seemed to shock her. Without electricity, it began to glow softly, and the stone became as sand and pulled her toward and into it, till her head, arms, and chest were enveloped. Only her back and legs were visible. But she did not struggle. Soon she felt the stone. In her mind and through her body. It felt her mind and her anger. It knew her thoughts. Little by little she felt a voice in her mind; though it said nothing, she heard it all the same. It apologized for her discomfort and understood the problem she had and her anger. The stone had never thought of so simple a problem. It had taken someone young to see what it had not. It saw the town needlessly frozen. Then she asked the stone from inside herself for the affirmation, but asked if it was truly needed. In her mind, she heard the word *yes* and was shown *why*. Those among her Vampiric family they needed to assure the royals that she was not only allowed but perhaps needed. She wanted to know for what, but no answer came. It was then that Lisa gave herself over to the stone. It moved through her feeling, syncing all that she was. Then she felt warmth around her chest and heart. It grew hotter till she felt it burn. The mark on her hand too began to burn. Soon she was thrust back to temple floor. Slowly she got to her feet. She looked beneath her shirt where she felt the burn. There she saw two symbols branded on her, but the redness went far past the symbols. Something in her mind made her smile as she walked out of the temple. The others were overjoyed when she walked through the archway again. Bael and her brother grabbed and hugged her.

"Are you all right?"

"I'm fine but"—she looked at her brother—"I won't be for long if you don't come back. Be careful, Thomas." He turned and walked in his sister's steps. Before going down the hall, he turned back to his sister. "Love ya, sis."

"Love ya back." And in he went.

Thomas walked in through the archway as his sister had. Unlike his sister, he had no anger; however, fear seemed to have found a home. He began to talk to the stone in front of him. "Okay, I'm here. I guess all I need to do is put my hands on you and that'll be it, right? Look, I don't care so much about myself here, but my sis needs me, ya know? Yeah, well, I guess here goes nothing." He placed his hands over the stone as they fell toward the stone; he wanted to pull them back. He stopped before they touch the stone. "In for a penny. In for a pound." Then landed on the stone. The shock went through him as he was pulled into the stone.

Thomas tried to fight, to resist being pulled in. He felt the stone moving through him. He didn't like the feeling. It took a few minutes, and then he started to relax. Instead of feeling like an invasion of him, it felt as if the stone was saying hello. The movement felt like a handshake. Soon Thomas could feel something like words form in his mind. Though it came through in blurred pictures. Soon they cleared, as he became more at ease. A question formed in his mind. "Why?" Thomas was confused. The stone knew why he was there. What did it want? Then he remembered what Alec had said. Thomas asked the stone for affirmation. Again, he felt "Why?" Thomas thought about what it was asking. Truthfully he didn't know. "I don't need affirmation. The royals need it from me. Without realizing it, Thomas had given himself over to it. "I guess I need it to survive being able to make my own choice. And to stay with my sister. Other than that, Thomas was happy with his life. Finally, he heard a question. "What if more was needed from you? Would you, could you be more?" Thomas had only known one thing for certain. Whatever his sister needed, he would be there for her. "What about others?" came the voice. Thomas thought back to Bael's house. "I don't know till I know them. Some are friends. Some aren't." The stone moved through him, feeling its way. "And what of the family you've not met?" Bael said that they would be safe when they reached the family's father. That he would protect them. "Of course he would help where he could," he thought to the stone. The stone seemed to build up in his mind, looking for an answer to something. Then all at once, his chest began to burn painfully as he was pushed to the floor. As he sat, he felt a pain in and on his chest. Keeping his hand on his chest, he got up off the ground. As he walked out of the temple, the others, glad to see him, rushed to him. Alec saw he was grasping his chest. "Are you all right?"

"Yes, I think so. It hurts though."

"May I see?" Thomas dropped his hand, and Alec pulled the corner of his shirt back to reveal two symbols branded to his chest. Thomas hadn't noticed his palm; the mark there had become more intense. Alec smiled as did Jason. *"They are affirmed!"*

Alec and Jason were happy and smiling; just then, they suddenly turned their heads as if they had seen something, or as it happened, heard something. The stone called out to them. Their smiles grew serious, almost sullen. Alec turned to Bael. "The stone is requesting you. I'm afraid it's time." Bael walked toward the arch. As he passed by Alec and Jason he patted them on the shoulder. "Well, I'll a . . . try not to be too long." Bael smiled back to the children to reassure them, but he himself couldn't shake the feeling going through him. For thousands of years he'd been in battles, fights and just recently met his grandfather, the God Baal. He'd been stunned a few times surprised even, but never worried. The stone's power. He'd been told and warned by his father. Was unknown even in the three pieces it had split itself into. It was a force to be reckoned with. As a whole, it had the power similar to a god. Bael turned back to the arch and walked through.

Just as the others before, he found the center of the temple easily and there sat the huge stone. He could sense its presence as he entered. He was there for a truth about himself. Was he right? Right in the way, he imprisoned those that broke the laws of their world instead of laying them to rest as his father had done? Was he truly the prince his father said? What did it mean to be the grandson of a god? And how much of that God was he? He had struggled with these questions throughout his life. Now he stood at the stone and worried about the answers. He looked at his hands for a moment. Then he placed them on the stone. Like a whirlwind, he was pulled into the stone. He had been pulled off his feet and brought to the heart of the stone. Bael felt his body burning as if it had caught fire. He could see nothing, but darkness in his mind he saw a redness from the pain. It felt as though he would be crushed from the pressure on his body and burned to ash. Then as he thought of his death, a coolness began in his mind. Little by little, the pain gave way to a cool sensation of almost floating in a spring. From a distance, he heard a voice. It came from no direction, but all directions at once. His sight went to a blue pale light. Then came the voice again, "*Welcome, Prince Bael.*"

"Hello?"

"You have come far for answers. Why? When the truth you already know."

"But I don't know?" A shock went through him. It moved through his limbs and heart. Through his body to his mind. There the shock took on a presence. *"Very well . . . you have found recently that there is more to you than you knew. You also are aware that there are still more abilities you may have?"*

"Yes . . . but what does it mean to . . ."

"Be a god?"

"Yes."

"Prince Bael, you are no *god, you are a prince. Immortal, but only a prince. As a prince, you have a duty to perform. Though you believe you should be lenient in that duty. That your father too harsh in his duty?"*

"He did his duty as he thought right."

"That is not the truth. He did his duty as told. As a hero and a king and as a son."

"But the killing. To kill so many?"

"To be king you must defend. To be a hero you must do what others cannot. To be a son, you must understand why a king, and hero do as he is told." Bael remembered the arguments with his father. "But I didn't. I fought his ways of doing things. To do the job a better way."

"That is not the truth. You fought to fight and to do things your way. Had you listened, you would know which to fight as your son has." Bael remembered how his son had to fight to get the others into Alec's castle. *"You fight, your father listened. You fought yourself. Your son listened to others.* Again, Bael thought of the past. The time wasted away from his family and friends while he mourned his loss. *"You do a job, your father does his duty. All of this you already know and have known."* Bael could feel his mind opening. The stone was bringing those past memories back for him to face. *The truth you came for was having no one to fight. To be made whole again to what you are and may yet be? You want that truth of a child to change from set ways? A rebirth of mind and spirit?"* Bael's thoughts were racing. "Yes, to change and yet be the man I could be, and once was." The stone went cold and silent. The silence seemed to last so very long. *"Because of whom you are, and what you may yet become, there is a price, a painful price. The*

111

stone tried to show him in his mind how much pain as a warning. Bael knew, if he were to become what he might, he would have to leave his stubborn past yet keep himself. To become the whole self he was. Not just for himself but for his son and Katja and for all of his family and his friends. The presence acknowledged his decision. Bael began to feel the burning sensation again, yet it was different. This was as if the electricity were burning him from the inside out. His body and mind were being pulled apart cell by cell. The pain crashed on him in waves, trying to yell and scream, but he had no voice. He could feel the pain as flesh ripped from his bones. His mind pulled apart into pieces of sand. This all seemed to last for hours. He could feel the presence of the stone pulling him back together. His seared flesh returning to their limbs. Then he heard something. It was a beating sound as if someone was beating on the stone. The sound got louder. Was it Lisa he thought beating on the stone to release him? He began to feel the beat like a wave over him. Still, the pain went on. It felt as though his bones were being fused. Muscles twisting like rags. Till finally it started to subside. And still, he heard the beating on the stone. No, it wasn't the stone; it was his heart. His body ached, and his head felt terrible but getting better. Then from nowhere, he felt himself moving through the stone till suddenly he was pushed from the stone. Bael's body hit the floor. He was naked wet and cold to the bone, shaking in a fetal position on the floor. As a demigod, he had never truly been affected or felt the cold. Soon, he felt a cloth on him and a hand trying to help him up. He was a bright red over his skin. "There there now. My boy, you're finished." Alec wrapped Bael in one of his robes. Alec called the others in. When all four were together, Bael looked at the children smiling and shaking.

"Piece of cake." Lisa got under his arm to help steady him. "Is he going to make it back? It's an awful long way in his condition." Alec shook his head that won't be a problem." They walked down the corridor to the entrance. But the archway had been walled up. "What's going on? Why can't we leave?" With that, the wall turned to sand and fell to the ground into nothing. As they stepped through, they were back at the castle's main living area. Katja saw them come through and leaped to Bael's side, still shaking.

THE CHOICE, THE FIRST OF THE THORY'S CHRONICLES

Alec gave her a wink. "He'll be fine, my dear. Still, you should take him to his room and put him to bed." She grabbed him in her arms and went toward the bedrooms. "Oh, and keep him warm till he is himself again." Sasha, holding Lisa and Thomas in each arm, turned to Alec. "Oh, I think he'll be warm enough." She laughs a little. One by one the others each came to congratulate them for coming back and getting affirmed. At the end of the line was Nicola, waiting till he could put his arms around them. With tears in his eyes, he squeezed them. "I'm so happy to see you. And was it a success? You are affirmed?"

Thomas pulled his shirt to one side, and there was the affirmation of his family line and through it the mark of the stone. Lisa bore her mark to Nicola as well, but there was something wrong. Nicola read it in her face. "What is it, little one? What is wrong?" She pulled her shirt open; her skin was red far past the mark. Her skin seemed to have a rash.

"Does it hurt?" Lisa shook her head "No, but it itches a little." Alec and Jason also saw the rash. Jason was waving his hand. "Don't worry, Lisa, you're fine. I know it itches, but it will fade." Alec agreed. They seemed to know what the rash was, or was from, and that made her feel better about it. Though it was still early in the day, everyone was exhausted. Sasha took Lisa to their room, and Maliki helped Thomas to his. Soon the entire castle was asleep and at peace.

8

A few miles away, Seidrich was still searching for Lord Montgomery. He stood silently in the snow waiting. In the distance, he saw the snow disturbed by a force across the ground. As it approached, the force dropped, and two women came from the wind itself. "Master Seidrich, so good to see you." The women bowed. "It isn't often you summon us. How may we assist you?" Seidrich bows back to the women. "I'm sure by now you have heard of the attack led against Lord Bael. I need you to track Lord Montgomery for me. When you find him, notify and leave him to me. He must answer to my king."

"A vampiric attack on Lord Bael is within our mandate, as for our payment? Ten will suffice to locate him."

"Seidrich reached into his pocket for a leather pouch and handed it to the woman. "Here are thirty, my dear, Tisiphone for you and your sister. I assume you know where it took place?"

"Oh yes, Seidrich. We will return when we know where he is."

"Thank you, my dear furies." He bowed and left. The sister's carefully count the silver coins in the pouch. "Always the gentleman that one."

"No, Alecto, not when he gets his hands on our quarry." The women laughed and disappeared into the whirling snow.

The next day the sun has risen as had Harry sitting in her chair reading the paper from her home outside Los Angeles. The clock began to chime as it was ten o'clock when she heard the others down the hall, the yawning, the talking, the water running, even a few roars seemed to come rolling down the hallway. One by one they came through the kitchen. She had made an assortment of food for breakfast. As each made a plate, and a cup of tea, or coffee, they would say how good everything smelled, and a few gave her a kiss on the cheek.

It felt nice to her to have a house full of people. Even the tigers didn't hunt that morning. Lisa had gotten a cup of coffee and a muffin. Nicola was sitting on the sofa when Lisa came in and snuggled next to him. He put his arm on her shoulder and smiled. Sasha walked by, kissed her father good morning, and sat down next to Lisa. Thomas and Remi walked in the kitchen starved. They made two huge plates of food—eggs, bacon, pancakes, and sausage, muffins, toast, with butter and syrup over all. Bael and Katja were amazed as the sipped their tea. Alec and Jason were in the living area cleaning the wall of the spells from the day before. As the dishes were being done, a bell rang out.

"That's the bell for the door!" Harry said. Startled. "Who the devil would ring our bell?" Alec started for the door. "I suppose we'll have to open the door and see?" Harry got to her feet, shaking her finger. "Not you, you old fool, you're not dressed for company. Now, go and change while I get the door!"

Lisa shouted. "What if they're the vampires?"

Harry shouted back. "I doubt that they'd just ring the bell, dear!" Lisa sat back down, feeling a little foolish.

Harry opened the door. There stood Seidrich. "My apologies Miss, Murray, for the early hour. Might I speak with Lord Bael?"

Harry called back to Lisa. "I was wrong, dear, it is the vampires." Harry turned back to the door. "I'm sorry, please come in." Seidrich followed Harry to the living area. "Bael, dear, you have company." Seidrich entered the room and bowed. "Good morning to you all. If I may, my lord?"

Bael stood and shook his hand. Seidrich came in, of course. "What brings you here?"

"I have come to bring Lord Montgomery back to the king for questioning. I have also been asked to apologize for the attack on your person on behalf of the crown."

"Seidrich, I already know who ordered the attack. Please tell his lordship that our friendship is as steadfast as always. No apologies are necessary, but thank him anyway."

"Thank you. Lord Bael. Sir, I don't wish to be impertinent, but you seem different somehow?" Bael turned to the children. "Lisa,

115

Thomas, I would like to introduce you to Seidrich Kael, an enforcer to the families. Seidrich, may I introduce the Thorys."

Seidrich bowed again. "Glad to meet you, Mr. and Miss Thory. It is a pleasure and an honor.

Lisa curtsied and Thomas bowed. Seidrich stood in awe.

"Are you all right, Seidrich?"

"Yes . . . I just. I can feel their power. Lisa smiled. "A benefit of the stone, I guess?" Seidrich's reaction to hearing the stone mentioned made him take a step back. He looked at Bael in a panic.

"Yes, they went before the stone."

"The Paragon stone?"

"Yes."

"But, Lord, why?"

"They were affirmed. Seidrich, I must ask you to say nothing till the court has met."

"But if they have been affirmed, the court would be unnecessary?"

"Seidrich, there is more going on than we know. The royals must decide on this."

Seidrich felt that it might be seen as a betrayal. "It worries me, Lord Bael. But it shall be as you ask. My king will understand."

"I think he will."

"Lord Bael, I must complete my mission in the meantime."

"Of course." Seidrich bows and is escorted to the door.

Harry came back to the room. "Well, I guess Montgomery won't be a problem anymore. Bael and Nicola shook their heads. "Nicola and I aren't sure he ever was. Someone's behind him, though we're not sure who. Though I believe I know at least one that may be involved. I just can't figure out why he's involved."

Harry, with her hands on her hips, was getting impatient. "Care to let us in on whom?"

Bael rubbed his head. "I'm a little reluctant to say the children's minds might be read by the royals, and I want the fact that I know to be a surprise."

Lisa grabbed her brother's hand. "Come on, Thomas. They need to talk and get a plan together. Bael we'll be outside practicing what we know about our magic. You guys talk." Thomas and Lisa left the room quickly. Bael and the others took their seats around the room. Bael spoke one name: Ea-Bani. They all looked shocked. Even Nicola looked puzzled.

"What makes you think he's even alive? As far as anyone knows, he was killed thousands of years ago."

"Yes, but he must be involved. With the queen and Lord Basarab supporting the kids' side of things, who else has the power with the royal's council? Who else could voice an opinion that would have effect on the vote?" Maliki sat back and thought about what Bael had said. Remi's anger had gotten the better of him. His hand on an end table had changed. The bear claw forming as he thought about this man, stopping the children after so many years. Sasha had only heard about Ea-Bani as a myth or legend. He had been the first vampire, given an immortal life by the god An himself. He feared what might happen to his people, so he went to the wilderness till he could control what he had become. It didn't make sense to her. He cared so much then, and that would make him one of the good guys. Now to stop the kids after all they'd been through. Her own anger was on the rise. Katja saw how they were taking the news and became a voice of reason. "Even if he is involved, you don't know if he's necessarily the problem." Bael nodded his head. "She's right. Someone else may be pulling all these strings, including ours. Again, but why?"

The night was dark little to no moonlight. A man in the shadows was tired and breathing heavy. Before him were two sets of eyes. Huge and bright, shining cold in the dark shadows of the surrounding trees. He put his hands out and pat them on their heads.

"There now, wait for him, my boys, wait for him. The beasts bowed their heads then lay in wait. The man raised his hands to the air. "I think you could use a little cover, if you're to be my surprise." He waved his hands and brought them down, and it began to snow. "Ah . . . much better. Now, you two behave and remember who you're after." He placed a piece of cloth under their noses and put it on the ground in front of them. The beasts bared their teeth. "That's my boys." As he turned, the air shimmered, and he's gone.

The bus was opened; they swept through it as a breeze. Two women search the ground then the air. Their hair blowing around in that same breeze. "He was not in the assault on Lord Bael." Her hair reacted to something in the air, and then her nose picked up a scent. "This way, I feel it . . . Yes . . . they move across the field of snow where the attack stopped, working their way back till they find it. The presence, the scent of Lord Montgomery. "Ah . . . ha . . ." They smiled. He was watching from here. Then he moved back toward the area at the bus. Again, they moved this time back toward the bus where their chase began. Far from the bus, but close enough to see it. The women stopped and searched the ground. "How unlike a vampire." Her hand picked up snow from the ground. "He must have been so worried, sister. Look here, he was sweating blood. They began to move over the ground till they reached a point they could see the forest and the wall that had the entrance to the sorcerer's plain and castle. Her hair bristled; her nose could no longer pick up the scent. However, they felt something in air. Something that should not be there. Both of the sisters picked out of the air. "Do you feel it?"

"Yes."

"Something or someone took him away here. She brushed her hands through the air. Till it had presented itself. A wrinkle in the air, a shimmer."

"Can you follow it?"

"Oh yes, I believe so. A wave of her hand and the shimmer reopened. They walked through slowly. It opened to a porch. The air told her he was close. Through a window, they saw him. She moved back from the window and down from the porch to the sand. Her hand moved openly across the front of them till a portal had opened. They stepped through and returned to the snow. The woman Tisiphone turned to her sister. "Inform Master Seidrich of Montgomery's location and inform him of what else was found. I will inform Lord Bael. He will want to know." Within a turn of the wind, they were gone.

The afternoon was filled with practice for Lisa and Thomas. Bael too had continued his lessons. Thomas had taken a break from the magic. Maliki had decided to work with him on something else. They went into the forest where Maliki found a tree that had fallen and had broken in three at the trunk. Thomas sat down on the broken stump. "Why did you wanna come out here for?"

"You and your sister have worked hard on your magic, but your bodies are capable of more as well."

"Yeah, Bael said something like that when we first met him, but . . ."

"No buts, that is why we are here. For you to learn your abilities better, and time is running fast, far too fast, so let's get started." He took Thomas to a branch of the fallen tree. "Can you lift this?"

"Sure."

"What about that?" he asked, pointing to one of the pieces of trunk. "A . . . no, I think you might, but as strong as I am, that's a bit much."

"Close your eyes and grab the tree. Don't hug the tree grab with your fingers. Now then, forget what you know. Remember all that was a lie. Think about who you are. You are more than you were." Thomas did as he's told. He closed his eyes. He tried to lift the fallen trunk. Nothing happened. He tried again and again. The tree wouldn't budge. "Thomas, what is the most you've lifted?"

"Oh . . . about two hundred and fifty or a little more."

"Then Thomas lift the tree."

"I can't."

"Thomas, the tree is hollow."

"Oh well, it felt solid."

"That's why I chose this part of the trunk, it's solid enough to stay together. Now pick it up." Thomas pushed it with his foot till it began to roll, then stopped. He grabbed the trunk, and his fingers strained, his legs strain as he pulled. It began to move. He rolled it toward him and pulled it up his arm till it's cradled. It still felt heavy to him, but he tried to stand. Maliki helped steady him. Slowly he stood. Maliki looked pleased. "Well, how does it feel?"

"Heavy."

"How heavy?"

"Well, I can hold it. Is this thing really hollow or is this a trick?"

"Well . . . a little of both. It is hollowed out. Bael did it for me, and then I filled it with some help over at the horse shed. I smelted the iron and steel there, then filled it, and Bael placed it back."

"Why did Bael put it back?"

"Just in case it cracked when I poured in the hot metal. He has a better grip."

"Ah, funny. So right now I'm picking up a bar of iron?"

"No, steel. About six hundred pounds of it."

"Right, it ain't that heavy."

"Good, I'll tell you what, just a . . . let it down any where you like." He took a step back. "Right on the other side of this log is close enough for me." Thomas heaved it off his shoulder, and as it hit the other log, it got hammered deeper into the ground, and his log cracked open. Thomas looked at the split tree, and there on the ground was the bar of iron and steel. He bent down to feel it. "I don't believe it. That could have killed me?" Maliki shook his head. "Neither Bael nor I would ever let you try if we didn't know you could lift it. The more you try the easier it will get." Thomas followed Maliki as he walked back to the house. Thomas was complaining all the way back.

Lisa and Harry walked across a field of barren ground. Harry looked over Lisa, trying to figure something out, but staying quiet. "Elisabeth, dear, you understand where your father's abilities came from I think, don't you?"

"Well, sort of. They came from nature, right?"

"Yes and no. You see, your father was a natural sorcerer, but what that means is that when he was born, he was already a part of the magic that exists everywhere. He was born with the knowledge to use it." Lisa stopped walking. "But Thomas and I don't have that. We're learning our magic. Through our lessons."

"Exactly. You are learning very fast. However, you're not like your father. This opens a few possibilities for you. You did very well with the elements the other day, or at least that's what Jason said." Lisa smiled. She was glad to hear Jason speaking so well about her. "I'm glad to hear that."

"Yes, dear, but I was wondering if you might consider a little help."

"What kind of help?" She had learned to ask before accepting. "In our world, things are different than they are back in LA.. Certain sorcerers can use or join with other things to increase their abilities."

"What do you mean join to? I don't like the sound of it."

"I understand that, I do. Just here me out. Here there are different kinds of demons. You know that there are good and bad of every species. Well, there are also different types as well. And if allowed, certain demons can join with a sorcerer, and as it grows inside, that sorcerer's power is increased many times over. You see you and your brother seem to have a good relationship with the elements. So perhaps joining with one could be beneficial for you both." Lisa stood quiet and still for a moment. "Are you asking me to be possessed by a *demon*? Are you kidding me? My name is Lisa, not Linda, and I hate pea soup." Lisa walked off, leaving Harry, rolling her eyes.

As Lisa returned to the house, she saw Alec and Bael on their way to his lessons. They had stopped on the path. When Lisa had gotten closer, she noticed they were talking to a woman. She looked to be in her twenties to thirties dressed in slacks and a burgundy leather jacket. She had flowing red hair and stood with an attitude. Either from LA, or New York, but she looked as though she could take on anybody who had the nerve to ask. Lisa was just glad to see another human. As Lisa walked over, she vanished like leaves in the wind. There than gone. "So much for human," she thought. Bael saw her on the path and waved to her to come over. She ran over to him wanting to know who she was. "So I see we had more company?" Bael and Alec didn't look happy from the visitor. "Lisa, I need you to go and find Jason and the others. Everyone needs to hear what just happened. We finally have some answers. Tell them to meet us back at the house in an hour. Alec needs to teach me something than we'll be in."

"Sure, but I'm not sure where everyone is?" Lisa turned and ran to the house. Bael, who was angry from the information, grabbed Alec's arm. "What lesson is so important? After all that she said, can't it wait?"

"After what she said. No, it can't wait at all. In fact, we should start now."

Alec cleared his robes, throwing them back. "You see those trees there?" Alec pointed to a grove of trees a mile or so in the distance.

"Yes."

"That is where we are trying for. An ability you've never used is the shifting or moving from place to place without really moving."

"You mean teleporting?"

"No, if you think about this as science, you can't do it. You must use your thoughts as motion to get there. Think of where you are, and then think of yourself there. Believe that all that is between the two doesn't exist. That you are the motion itself." Bael looked at the tree line and closed his eyes. Alec slapped his head. "Open your eyes! I don't want you to imagine it. *Believe* it. Oh, where is your grandfather when I need him?"

"As always, I'm here." From out of what seemed nowhere, Baal was standing beside them. "I take it your having a problem with the lesson?"

"There are some things, Lord Baal, that must be seen to be understood," Alec said as he bowed. "I can teach him only what he can learn from me." Baal stood with his hand to his chin. "You may be right. However, go on with the lesson."

"Lord Baal, I can't show him how to shift. I can't shift."

"You don't have to have an ability to teach it. You don't learn to sing, you learn to talk. The singing is an ability one has or not. Bael can shift, but you must teach him as if teaching a child to speak. Most of it will come from him."

"Yes, Lord Baal." Alec thought about what Baal had said. Alec looked at Baal, waiting. "Bael, you know through magic how to make a portal. Think of yourself as the portal, where you are, where you want to go. Instead of opening, your becoming, letting it move you as a wave would envelope you. Only you are the wave."

Bael listened to Alec and saw that what he said was right since his grandfather seemed to agree. Bael looked at the grove of trees and pictures himself there. "Ah. Ah. Ah" came from Lord Baal. "You're trying to imagine again. Once you believe that you can shift, you'll do it as a reflex, without even thinking about it." Alec took Bael's hand. "You don't try to visualize a portal. You simply make one."

"Yes, but I know how to do it. Dad taught me years ago." Baal nodded. "Very well." He placed his hand on his shoulder. "Shall we?" And they were at the grove of trees. Bael felt the movement, yet he didn't move.

"Now, you take us back." Bael thought about what had happened what he had felt. There had been no movement. Yet they got there. He took his father's arm. "Well, here goes nothing." As he turned to face Alec, he felt the movement. And they were with Alec.

"It wasn't pretty, but not bad. Keep practicing, and it will come." And with that he was gone . . . again. Alec nodded. "For now that will have to do. Now we should get back to the others."

"Alec, are you sure nothing else shifts?"

"Did the fury seem like she was unsure?" Alec and Bael rushed back to the house.

As they walked into the living area, Bael saw that some of their group was missing. Beowulf, Jason, and Lisa were missing. Nicola came to his side. "What is it? The little one came in and told everyone to meet here. That you had news for us."

"Where is she?"

"She went to find little wulf."

"Where's Jason?"

"He went to his study, and said he'd be back before we got started. Have patience, my friend. They will be here soon."

Lisa went through the upper rooms of the castle with no luck in finding Beowulf. On the fourth floor, at the end of the hall, was a staircase. She followed them up to a door at the top. She knew she was in a tower. At the top was a door leading to a terrace overlooking the entire castle. As she walked on to the terrace, the wind came up; as she turned her head, Beowulf caught her eye. "So this is where you've been? I've been looking all over for you," she said.

"Sorry, just wanted to get some air. I haven't been around so many people in years. I started to feel cramped."

Lisa didn't understand; they were his family. She had grown so close to them in such a short time. Wanting to be away from them seemed impossible. By the look on her face, Beowulf could see she didn't understand. "Lisa, I've seen more of my family than my father has, but I still spend a lot of time by myself. I know it seems great to live forever, but it has several drawbacks. True, the vampires have their houses, so it won't be a problem for you."

"Your grandfather Nicola seems close to his daughters, and he certainly loves you and Bael even though he hadn't seen either of you for a while. Why don't you stay in touch better?"

"It's hard to say. I just spend most of my time at home, or fighting someone else's battle somewhere."

"Well, you're here now, and your father needs you. He wants us all downstairs. He got news from some woman who showed up and then vanished."

Beowulf looked a little shocked. "I guess we better get down there then." Lisa turned around, but suddenly was picked up. "Come on it's faster this way." Without hesitating, he jumped from the terrace, over the lower rooftop. She clung to his shirt till they came to a stop with a small jerk as they hit the ground. Lisa looked up at him and saw him smiling down at her. He put her down. As her feet touched the ground, her face got upset. Are you trying to get me killed? I'm not a god, a demigod, nor am I a Weretiger. Hell, I'm not even a vampire. Are you crazy?"

Everyone heard the yelling and came out to see Lisa yelling at Beowulf with her arms still around him. "What were you thinking? Jumping off with me from that tower. Oh you, you . . . Oh."

Bael cleared his throat. "Is everything all right here?" Lisa looked at Bael. And realized she's still holding on to Beowulf and let go. "Ah . . . yes, fine, but that's the last time he better jump with me," she said as she stomped to the castle past the others. Beowulf was watching her stomp past and smiled.

Bael turned back to Beowulf. "Are you okay.?"

Beowulf shook his head. "Huh? Yeah, I'm fine. She just got a little surprised, that's all." Beowulf and the others went back into the castle. Katja pulled her father down and whispered in his ear. "Maybe I'm wrong, but it looks as though she wasn't the only one surprised."

Nicola started to laugh, but stopped. Something bothered him about what she said.

They all came in and found their seats. Harry, being slightly more impatient than the rest, asked first, "Bael, what's going on that's got you so upset?"

Bael, looking grimace, cleared his throat. "I just had a visit from one of the furies that Seidrich had looking for Montgomery. She found him, but more than that, he had been brought there by someone who has the ability to shift themselves and Montgomery to Calcutta, which is where Seidrich is off to by now. The problem is, the only ones that can shift are gods and demigods. Someone like myself or my father, and that must be who has been pulling all the strings of this puppet show."

Harry, again, was the first voice heard. "Any idea's on whom that might be?"

"No, not really, most of the demigods that caused problems in the past were killed by other demigods. Heracles, Perseus, Thor, Achilles, and Beowulf, the list of heroes were long but most chose to pass over to live with their human families. Father did his duty killing the worst of them long ago, or so I thought."

Thomas looked up at Bael. "Would your father know how many, and who might be left?"

Bael stopped before he could answer and thought to himself. "What about grandfather? He would surely know?" Alec could see the wheels turning in Bael's mind. "Remember the rules, Bael. Baal is forbidden to interfere between any of the demigods. That's why I had to teach most of your lessons."

"I know, damn it. I just need some answers."

Lisa stood, arms open. "But, Bael, you have answers now. You don't need a name. You know what you're dealing with, but whoever it is doesn't know that you know. That should level the field if we're smart." Bael hadn't thought of it. Lisa was right. "We know what, and he must know my limits. But he didn't know about the stone, or the other abilities I was perfecting. It did level the field."

"Alec, could you send Sebastian on a trip for me?"

"Of course. Where am I sending him?"

"To get word to my father that I need him." Nicola smiled, but didn't let anyone see it.

As they started to break up the meeting, Lisa, joking with Bael, said as she's leaving, "I'm still not getting possessed by demon. Demigod or not!" Bael put his hand out to stop her. "What do ya mean possessed by a demon. Who said that?"

"Oh, don't worry, Harry can't sell that as a good idea." Bael smiled and laughed it off till Lisa's gone from the room. "Harriet! What are you up to?"

"Now, Bael. It's not what you . . . Ah, hell, I just thought the kids could use an edge. It would triple their abilities. Maybe even quadruple them."

"NO, HARRIET, and I mean it."

"Fine."

"Just train them, Harry, that will be enough."

Days went by, and the children trained. As did Bael. Lisa had taken her physical training to a new level. Sasha and Katja were making her tough. Thomas too had gotten stronger than he thought himself capable of. Their magic was changing. Each were becoming powerful but in different ways. Thomas had spells and incantations from the books he read. While the magic seemed to flow more naturally through Lisa. She was in tune with the elements and them with her. Her magic was becoming as simple as thought. Thomas's spells were almost as fast, but some were far more powerful spells. As for Bael, his abilities were becoming as powerful as his father. It was just three days till they would be leaving for the royals. When the clock in the hall struck three, the bell at the door rang. Before Harry could answer it, there was a ripple in the air, and Bael's father Beowulf was there.

"Hello. Harriet, my beautiful dove, how are you? You look wonderful. If you don't mind me saying so." She gave him a blushing smile and a hug. "So . . . Where is my son?"

"He should be on his way back in for lunch."

"And where is the rest of his merry troop?"

"Oh, they're here and about throughout the house. Your grandson is out in the garden."

"Garden?"

"Yes. He's helping Miss Thory with her lessons."

"Hmmm, so how are the lessons going for our little marks?"

"Well. Now are you here with good news, or bad, or are you just here to fight with your son again?"

"I'm not sure, but my son sent a message that he needed me. So I put some things in order and rushed to get here."

"Good, it's about time, but I warn you right now. The first one who starts a fight, and I finish it. *Am I clear?*" Beowulf put his hands up and nodded. "Yes, ma'am." Just then from the top of the staircase, Jason exclaimed, "Ah, the king has arrived, I see." Jason gave a small bow. "I hope you've come to remove this group of rabble and pests from our happy home?"

"My dear Jason, if this is ever a happy home, you're out of it."

Jason laughed as he walked down the stairs. "So . . . how are you enjoying retirement?"

"I am far from retired. I like to think of it as on sabbatical, or hiatus. When the time is right, I will leave for the afterlife with a smile on my face." Again, he nodded with a small bow. "As will we all." Harry clapped her hands. "That will be quite enough of that. Now you come with me, both of you." Harry took both by the ear and led them to the living area. "Now sit, and if I hear one more dig from either of you. I'll put you over my knee. Understood?" Neither said a word as they both knew she would do what she said. Beowulf looked around the room. "I must admit it feels like home here." Jason turned to him. "It seems like that to me too. Oh wait, this is my home."

Beowulf rolled his eyes and waited for Bael to return. After a few awkward minutes, his grandson came in with Lisa carrying flowers for the table. "Little wulf! Ahhh, it's good to see you!" He walked over and hugged his grandson. And this must be Miss Thory." He bowed, and she curtsies.

"I am so very happy to have met you. You are quite beautiful."

"You sound surprised?"

"Not at all, and I am sorry for making it sound so. I had heard that you were through others. But they did not do you justice."

"Thank you, you must be Beo . . ., I mean BW's grandfather?"

"Yes, and Bael's father. Harriet went out to get him. He should be in soon and then I'd like to meet your brother Thomas." They sat down and exchanged pleasantries. Throughout the conversation, Beowulf the senior, was watching. Watching his grandson and Miss Thory. He saw that his grandson would barely take his gaze from her. Lisa, though she had been slightly embarrassed days before, but now seemed not to notice his attention. Bael and the others came in through the kitchen area and were in a hurry to see his father. As Bael came in his father noticed immediately he was different. Not just that Bael greeted him with a smile and hug, but that he was honestly happy to see him. There was no fight or anger in his eyes for him. Bael had changed.

"I've missed you so much, Father." Beowulf held out his son for a moment to look at him. Then pulled his son to him.

"And I you, son, so very much." As Beowulf and Bael patted each other's back; Beowulf shed a tear for his son's return.

Everyone came in and joined them in the living area. As all took their seats, Lisa stood. "Lord Beowulf, I'd like you to meet my brother Thomas Albert Thory." Beowulf stood up and bowed, then shook his hand. "Master Thomas, it's wonderful to have met you and your sister. I am honored."

Bael and the others exchanged their greetings. All but Alec who had not joined them in the room. As they all settled in their seats, Bael got serious and asked his father, "You know what's been going on, don't you, Father?"

Beowulf nodded his head and slowly looked up at Bael. "Yes, I know about the attacks, and I know what has happened with the families."

"Father, there is something else going on. Someone is trying to get to me through the Thorys. Pulling string after string."

"Yes, and I wish I could tell you who. You know that I'm forbidden to interfere. Or help you in your quest. I hope you understand how much I truly want to. I was warned by An and Ea before I left to get here about my limitations."

"Whoever it is has the abilities of a demigod." Beowulf leaned forward. "If you're sure of that, then you may be able to figure out who it is for yourself." Bael thought about what his father implied. He tried to read his father's face for some clue. He looked at his father. His father? Bael had done things different than his father. Any demigods that were dark in his time were killed by his father. So how many remained?

"I can only think of a few demigods, Father, that could even cause this much of a problem. Most were gone." Beowulf again nodded. "Yes, but not all. Bael, my son, remember this: you must defeat and destroy this enemy, or he will destroy you."

With that said, Katja took Bael's hand and arm. "Bael, you must be ready to kill. I won't lose you." Beowulf turned to his grandson. "Little wulf, you must teach your father quickly about the darkness. How to feel it out. He must also learn to kill."

BW wasn't happy about the idea of teaching his father. "Father, may I speak to you in the kitchen for a moment?" Bael and his son walked to the kitchen. BW placed a fast privacy spell up behind them. "Father, I've been thinking about this for a while now. Why don't you let me take the Thorys to the royals? I can keep them safe."

Bael shook his head. "I appreciate your concern, but I fought alongside my father for many years. I can kill, son, I just don't."

Bael could see that there was something BW was trying to say, but struggled with it. "Dad, you won't kill, and to keep them safe, it *will* have to be done." Bael understood what his son was trying to say. He had lost faith in his father's abilities to keep the Thorys safe. Bael dropped his head for a moment, then looked into his son's face. "Son, I know why you have doubts, but you're not strong enough to take on mine and my father's enemies. You must trust me. I will however need to practice. So will you practice with the old man?"

"Sure, Dad. I just thought . . ."

"I know. Come on, let's get back to the others."

"Sure, Dad." And they returned to the room. Katja met them. "Is everything all right?" Bael kissed her lips hard. Everything was fine.

Later that evening, most everyone had gone to bed. Thomas again couldn't sleep and went to Jason's study to read. In the short time they had been there, Thomas had read quite a lot of Jason's library. He was on the latter when he spotted a book on top of the shelf covered in dust so thick it was hard to pick up, his hand kept slipping. It was a small book compared to many of the others in the room. It was a brown leather book with simple English lettering. *Godspell* written by Jason Ashmoore. Thomas was intrigued to read Jason's book. After a few minutes, Thomas realized what Jason had written. A book that broke the rules and laws that Bael had shown him back at the cabin. Just as Thomas had finished the fourth chapter, he heard a voice from the doorway. "Good evening, Master Thomas. I see you couldn't sleep again. I think you spend as . . . much . . ." Jason stopped dead in his tracks. "What are you reading?"

He looked closer at the book, and his anger swept over him. "*What are you doing reading that?*" Jason flew across the room and grabbed up the book. "How dare you!" Without thinking, he swung his hand and struck Thomas, knocking him and the chair over. Back into the glass cabinet behind him, Jason took the book and returned it to the shelf. "I'm sorry, Thomas, for flying off that way. I just can't have this book read by anyone. I never should have written it." Jason turned on the latter to see Thomas lying on the floor, bleeding. A knife from the top of the cabinet had fallen, striking him in the chest. Jason called out for help as he came down the latter. Alec and Bael, Katja and BW arrived and saw Jason holding Thomas. "I lost my temper." Jason repeated over and over. Bael rushed over to Thomas, but couldn't find a pulse. He tried CPR, but the blood merely came rushing out. Thomas was dead.

Bael looked at Alec. "Is there anything you can do?"

"I'm afraid necromancy is out of my depth, Bael." Alec looked down at the boy's body. "Bael, your lessons! You might be able . . ." without Alec finishing his sentence, Bael placed his hands on Thomas's chest. Bael tried to focus on the wound to see in his mind the wound healing and to feel it in his hands. Bael could feel himself getting weaker. Finally, he removed his hand. The wound was healing, even the blood was fading back into his body, but no life.

Bael tried again and again with no success. Bael saw the affirmation mark on his chest. He placed his hand on the mark. His other hand on his mark. Bael tried again to focus. He felt a burning sensation in his hands. In his mind, all was quiet. Then he heard it, the beating. Bael's heart beating, stronger and stronger. Finally, he felt Thomas's heart beat with his, stronger and stronger. Thomas opened his eyes.

"What happened? What's going on?" Bael released from Thomas and passed out. Maliki entered and picked Thomas up. "I'll put him to bed, he'll sleep soon." Alec nodded. Bael was taken back to his room by Katja and Nicola. Jason sat on the floor, blood on his hands from Thomas.

"I just lost my temper" was all he could say. He had forgotten what happened when his magic reacted with his anger. Jason in tears was helped by his brother to a chair. "What happened, Jason?" The brothers went back and forth repeating the question, and Jason, the same sentence. Jason came out of his shock at last and explained about the book and what had happened. Alec understood the accident and put his brother to bed.

The morning came and went. Lisa had made breakfast, but no one had gotten up. Sasha and Remi came to the kitchen and had their breakfast. Still the others slept. Harry finally woke and came for her tea, which Lisa had made for her. She took the cup with a smile.

"Thank you, Elisabeth. I'm afraid I just don't handle excitement well anymore," she said as she looked at the clock. Lisa thought she meant the arrival of Bael's father.

The clock struck ten o'clock when Lisa heard the others coming from their rooms. Katja and Nicola, and then Maliki; a few minutes went by, Alec and Thomas followed. Alec turned to Thomas when he entered and asked, "How are you this morning?"

"Fine, I guess. I'm still not sure what happened." Thomas rubbed his chest as it was still sore. Alec put his hand up. "I'll explain later when I get my thoughts in order."

Alec explained what had happened during the night. As the events unfolded, Lisa got more and more upset. "How come nobody told me? Didn't even wake me when Thomas recovered? And where is your brother this morning?"

"Jason naturally feels very guilty about Thomas. I haven't heard a sound from his room this morning."

Jason sat in his bed. In his long life, he had never been so ashamed. He had lost his temper, and it cost someone their life. He looked at his hands. Alec had cleaned them before he left last night. Yet he still saw the stain there. He put his hands to his face and cried. "Thank god for Bael," he thought. He had saved Thomas when he himself could not. His shame closed in on him and made him fear to leave his bed, his room. He began to feel dizzy and passed out.

Alec understood her anger. Thomas went to her and hugged her. "Sis, I'm fine. It was an accident. I was the one in the wrong. I started reading his book, when I figured out what it was, I should have stopped. I didn't. I kept reading."

"Why? Why would you keep reading it if you know you shouldn't?"

"I'm sorry, sis, but you can't blame Jason. You've knocked me over plenty of times. I fell into the cabinet. It could have been you who knocked me over." Lisa nodded her acceptance. Katja put her arm around Lisa's shoulders. "Lisa, Bael and your brother will be fine. Bael is resting, and your brother is recovering fast as well." Lisa began to calm down. She walked out of the room toward outside to get some air. BW followed behind her. Lisa sat down on short wall around the garden and looked up at the sky the pink and orange hues were so different from her home yet so peaceful. BW came from behind her. "Are you okay?"

"Yeah sure, what's not to be fine about? I have vampires that want me dead, others that just want me, and that's a little creepy. Then there is a whole new world that I've been brought to where my brother dying is something I just need to get over because he's still alive. I have new friends that are like family, and I will most likely lose them when I make this choice that I may not survive to make. Clearly, it's raining sunshine. Have I missed anything?"

BW moved in front of her. "Well . . . let's see, as for those that are after you, they're not going to get you. We'll all see to that. As for those that just want you. That can't be anything new. Who wouldn't? Your brother is alive and kicking. An accident could have happened anywhere. I understand that's what started this in the first place. And as for losing any of us, I think you need to rethink that one. Cause my whole family loves you and your brother like family as well." He pulled her to her feet. "Lisa, your safe, and among people who care and love you. How many can say that?" He bent down and kissed her cheek. "Now . . . come on, and let's get back in."

Nicola watched his grandson as he and Lisa returned from outside. At first, he thought he saw something that wasn't there. Then he watched closer. The routine of the house had started late, but it had begun. By noon the children were practicing their lessons. Bael had rejoined the group, though still weak, he sat on the sofa with Katja. His father had not been seen all morning. At lunch, Nicola noticed Lisa and his grandson not watching each other, looking away from each another when the other was watching. This time to make sure what he saw was right, he watched Sasha as well. When Sasha saw what was happening, she would smile to herself. Nicola asked Lisa to walk with him after lunch. She loved spending time with Nicola. She clung to him on their walk. To her it was like getting to spend time with her father. They walked for some time till they came to a tree that had fallen, and they sat. Nicola put his arm around her shoulders with a hug. He had never said it, but he loved her too. He rocked her in his arm. "Elisavetta, how are you, little one? I worry about you having so much happening to you."

"I'm all right, but I sometimes feel a little overwhelmed. It takes me awhile to catch up to myself." She hugged him and held on to him. "It helps that I don't feel alone."

"You're not, dearest, you're not. May I ask you something?"

"Sure."

"I am not at ease to ask, but are you and Beowulf . . ." Lisa had her head at his chest. "No. I . . . I mean we. I mean there is no *we*. We're just friends." Nicola picked her up and looked in her eyes. "Elisavetta, I hope he doesn't ask you. You are far from convincing. Just so, I think he could not convince me either." Her face lit up a little. He sat her back down. He raised her chin to see her eyes. "I talk to you because there are things you must know. For as old as he is, he has spent far too much time alone, his heart is good, but his head is

133

awkward. Take time to understand if what he said comes out wrong. Sometimes you'll find you need a translator. Also, remember, if he steps out of line. I'll remind him of *who he is*." Lisa smiled. "Then you wouldn't mind?"

"Mind what? You? You are mine first. Okay?"

"Yes, most definitely okay." She hugged him again tightly and kissed his cheek. "Now other things to remember are that I don't think he is aware of his feelings. So don't bring his attention to them. Once he's aware, he will most probably fight them. Show patience. He's smart, not wise. Do you understand?" Lisa thought about what Nicola said. "Yes, I think so."

"Good, one last thing. I do not want you to fall deeply for him, or him you, so for now, focus on getting home." She could see the concern in his face. He was worried about more than just her and Beowulf. "I'll do what I can. You should know something though." Nicola stood. "What is it, little one?" I've already fallen in love with you and your family. Very deep."

"And we with you. Come, let's get back to the others before someone talks." Lisa laughed with Nicola, and they returned to the house.

Meanwhile, away in the hills of India, above Calcutta, two men meet. Lord Montgomery and Master Maris. The night had fallen, but the air was thick. Master Maris was summing up the man in front of him and was not impressed. "Why have you asked to meet with me here? This is neither of our territories. The Kali are not social to the other tribes, and their queen has the power to cause you a lot of pain before she has you killed."

"Right now, I have other things on my mind. I've asked you here to find out if I have your support at the meeting of the royals? What are you going to vote?"

"Ah . . . I see. Yes, you want to know how the court stands. And just how does it stand? I have heard rumors that you are not in good standing with the Magyar royal house. Your own people hunting you down. Tsk-tsk. What a shame?"

"I too am a royal, and my house will not stand for these marks."

"Montgomery, the queen is in favor of the Thorys as are the Vampyr, the Magyar, and the Vatala. Not to mention the house of Basarab. Other than you're Magyars, who stand with you?"

"The Abiku, the Azeman. And the wampyrs. The Nosferatu are also split as to whether these marks should be destroyed."

"Ah and what will happen when Lord Bael speaks for them? And the queen? How many will stand before the house of Basarab and deny him his human offspring?"

"Lord Bael has no voice in the royal counsel, and I'm not sure the Basarabs should even have a vote in this."

"You must really have something up your sleeve to try something like this. Very well, I will give our support. I'm anxious to see what you have to pull this off?" Montgomery bowed his head. As did Maris. As he left him on the hill, Maris smiled his repulsive smile.

9

The next morning, Bael and Alec discussed the fact that it's time to leave for them and how to get to the coast of eastern Canada. "Bael, you should be fine once you reach the boat at Churchill. That will take you to the docks at Newfoundland. There you can catch a ship to Europe. From there I can't see anyone stopping you."

"You make it sound real easy, Alec." Across the room, they heard the heavy footsteps of Bael's father. Beowulf, looking irritated, entered the kitchen. "Good morning, Father, what's wrong? You look upset."

"I am son, I am. You are leaving today, and there are forces at work against you. That you know, but I am forbidden to tell what or who or where you may meet these problems. I am your father. As such I should be allowed to keep you somewhat safe. I left to ask permission to warn you of a certain danger. I was refused. Perhaps a general warning might do. Something like look before you leap. Or perhaps don't pet strange dogs." With that the Lord Baal appeared. "That is quite enough, son. Bael, I too would like to impart a word to the wise. It is the only warning we are allowed to give you."

Bael listened closely to his grandfather. "There are times you must fight. There are times you must kill. Your duty is to protect your charges and yourself. A warrior places his trust lightly. And as you now know, more than faith can move a mountain. Your father taught you years ago. Remember those lessons." And they were gone. His father and grandfather left as fast as he came. Bael sat and thought about what was said. Their hints were vague, but perhaps not. "Look before I leap, and don't pet strange dogs?" Bael thought them over again. The first was easy enough. Look before they left the castle. Bael went to Jason's library to use his palentier, a kind of magic mirror that holds water. Bael placed it on the desk and poured a liquid into it. He reached into his pocket and pulled out his change till he found a small gold coin. Lisa entered the room, yawning "What's going on? I saw you two heading up the stairs in a hurry, so I got curious to see what's up."

Bael turned to Lisa. "We're just taking a look outside before we leave this afternoon." Bael tossed the coin into the water, the ripples formed the trees, the ground, the snow. Even the bus at the end of a path. Bael moved his hand over the mirror. The scene changed over the area. The heavy snow made it hard to see. "There," Alec said. They looked close and then Lisa saw what caught Alec's eye. Two small clouds rose from the snow. Just down the path on both sides, she saw them.

"What are they?" Lisa asked. Bael looked up. "You can't tell because of the snow. But my money says a strange dog I shouldn't pet."

Bael Alec and Lisa went back downstairs. On the couch Thomas and Maliki enjoyed some coffee. "Morning, sis, Bael, and Alec. I trust everyone slept well? What seems to be the problem *this* morning?" Bael looked at Thomas. "Thomas, what kind of dogs gave the gods problems?"

Thomas sipped his coffee. "Well, there was Garm, the two-headed dog that guarded the rainbow bridge, Cerberus who guarded the kingdom of hell." He drank another sip from the cup. "Oh . . . and the fenris—wolf who killed the gods at Ragnarok. But it was killed by Tir." Bael thought for a moment. "Would it be possible?"

"The fenris wolf came from . . . Loki, didn't it?"

"Yes, but I don't remember why?"

"That's all right, Thomas." Bael spent a few minutes remembering his childhood. His thoughts on his father no longer marred by his stubborn ways. He remembered playing with his father. His father and mother teaching him about family. His mother wrapping his arm from a bite he'd received. He had been bit by a pup of his cousin's. He tried to remember which cousin. The cousin was older and laughed with father that I had gotten bit as he had been. "Like father like son." His father hadn't laughed at him, but with him.

"There now" his father said, holding him in his arms. "The bite will fade. Like me though, you'll remember the lesson." Bael had forgotten the bite and the lesson. Till now he'd only remembered the laugh. Who had the cousin been? His father called him by name, but not Loki. The pup though. It had been a wolf pup that pierced his skin. What had his father said about the wolf? He couldn't remember. His father bent down to pick him up. He patted his sword and his chest, then took him to his mother. The words of his grandfather rang in his mind. "Remember those lessons," he'd said.

"It had something to do with father's sword?" Thomas turned to Bael. "What about your father's sword? I remember it hanging over the door at your cabin, and how Maris had not been willing to pass it. You said it would have killed him. How?"

"My father's sword is more than magic. It was made by the dwarves out of the living metal uru. It was made for a hero. The gods would not touch it. For the metal had the ability to cut or kill anyone against it. As all the uru weapons can. Thor's hammer, father's sword, and even the sword Excalibur was made by the dwarves for the beautiful lady of the Lake Ea. As a gift." Thomas loved the story, but still had questions. "What do you mean the weapon had the ability? You meant the hero, right?"

"Well no. Just as Thor's hammer could only be wield by him or a hero who possessed his traits, or as Excalibur broke at an unjust strike. The weapons have an ability that the user can call on to do the right thing. Only the dwarves can find and work the metal into its many forms." Lisa was fingering the chain Nicola gave her. "Have they made things other than weapons?"

"Yes, Lisa. They've made jewelry but not much was made of the magic metal though." Each had its own magic cast upon it. Thomas had one question left that bothered him.

"Bael . . . have the dwarves ever made weapons to do the wrong thing?"

Bael's face lowered. "Yes, Thomas, there have been a few. During a time long ago. There was a war. The dwarves were fighting in battle after battle against men who had found out about their treasure. They had made a deal with a group of warriors to fight the men for them. Weapons were made and spells of darkness were cast to turn the tide. The men were defeated, but the warriors were later found to be demigods in disguise, and the weapons were to be used against the gods. They were stopped and in the end destroyed by other sons of the gods. Most of the weapons were hidden away. Only a few warriors themselves had escaped the destruction. The other races, seeing the aftermath of the demigods, knew that something had to be changed. That's why there has been peace amongst the races. The laws and rules were set down by all the races to follow and keep that peace."

"But there was still darkness, and that's what your father fought?"

"Yes, one was given the responsibility to keep back the darkness and maintain the laws when the races could not." Bael's son came into the room. He had been listening from the hall. "Of course Grandfather killed those from the darkness. As well as he could. He did his duty," he said proudly. Alec knew the old family's argument. But before he could say something, Bael put his arm around his son. "I can only hope to do as well," he said to Beowulf. Bael understood his father now better than before. His son hugged his father.

Lisa though moved by the sight was focused on the problem at hand. "Does anyone have an idea about what to do with the dogs outside?" Bael turned to Lisa. "I'll deal with them while the rest move to the bus." The next hour was spent packing up and getting ready. It was about time to leave when Jason came from his library; he walked in silence, and no one even noticed him till he reached Thomas. He placed his hand on Thomas's arm, and he turned to Jason. "I'm glad you came down before we left. It wouldn't have felt right not saying good-bye."

"Thomas . . . I'm so sorry for pushing you back and for . . . I'm just so sorry." Lisa went to him. "Jason, he is fine now. And it was partially his fault. Please stop feeling so guilty. It's done and over with." Lisa and Thomas smiled, then gave him a hug. Jason turned his head for a moment in shame, then reached into his pocket. In his hand was a small book. "Here, this is something for you. It should be of some use when you've mastered your magic."

Thomas took the book, but when he opened it, it was empty. "When you've mastered your magic, you'll be able to read it." Jason turned to Lisa. "I have something for you as well, but I need you to wait to open it. For now put it away, and I'll trust you not to open it till I send word." Jason handed her a small box. He looked at Harry and Bael nervously as though he'd done something he shouldn't have. Lisa put it in her pocket. "Thank you, Jason." And she kissed his cheek. Then she kissed Alec's cheek. They all said their good-byes. Then they headed for the door. As they started through, Jason stopped Sasha and whispered in her ear, "You take care of yourself my, little kitten, and look after the children as well."

She turned and gave him a kiss on the lips. "You old softy." As the door shut behind them, they heard the movement in the snow. Bael raised his hands and formed the barrier on the path as before Lisa and Thomas were whisked away on Maliki and Nicola's back, and off they ran. Suddenly they saw it. The wolf. It was an easy full story tall. Its hair bristled, and teeth were bore. It ran at them, and when it got to Bael's barrier, it came through as though it was nothing but air. Had Nicola not been so agile a tiger, it would have had them. Bael saw that the barrier had no effect on them. The other wolf sprang from the woods and focused on Bael. The wolf moved through the woods as if had known every inch of it. The other wolf began to follow the other toward Bael. Bael tried to focus his power as he had with the vampires. The wolves kept moving. Bael's eyes had again turned black, yet his eyes glowed on. As the wolf reached him, Bael jumped high into the air. He looked down, expecting to see the wolves left behind him. But the wolves had jumped as well. As Bael began to return to earth. The first wolf steadied itself with its tail, reached out with its teeth, and struck Bael's arm. With its claws, it raked Bael's back. Bael punched at it till its teeth released him. Bael, using his strength, pushed the wolf far away. As it fell into the trees below, he heard it howl and land. As Bael hit the ground, he felt another swift jolt of pain. The other wolf bit deep into his leg. The pain had his heart racing. He reached out, struck the animal again and again. He could here the other moving in, circling behind him. He kicked at the wolf on his leg, but before it could release, the other bit into his shoulder. Again, with all the force he could muster, he struck the wolf at his shoulder. Bael was bleeding badly as the wolf released him and began to circle again. The other too had begun to circle. As the wolf charged again, Bael moved into position and kicked the wolf in its chest and leg till it went flying backward. But the other took advantage of the move, knocked him down while he was off balance, then bit into the wound at his shoulder. He began to feel weaker as he punched wildly at the animal. Then the beast let him go. Bael opened his eyes to see his son had ahold around its head. Beowulf pulled at the beast's head and fought on. Bael reached out for the beast's throat, and with the last blow, he had struck the wolf, giving Beowulf the chance he needed with the turn of its head, the beast's neck had broken. Beowulf lay the head down. It was dead. He went to his father who was bleeding from every wound. He picked him up and ran quickly to the bus.

Remi started the bus and began moving before Bael was laid out on the floor in the back of the bus. Lisa and Katja began wrapping and bandaging the wounds, cleaning each of them as they went. Blood still flowed at his shoulder. Lisa looked through the first-aid kit till she found the suture kit. She tried to sew a stitch, but the needle wouldn't penetrate his skin. Lisa looked at Thomas. "Tom, I don't know what to do. He needs stitches." Thomas's mind was racing for an idea, but none came. The blood kept coming. Then Lisa had an idea. She took the suture needle and soaked it in Bael's blood and held it out in her hand. She got Nicola to strike a match. The flame moved from the match to her hand; her thoughts went to the flame, and it began to burn brighter—the needle within began to glow, and the blood in her hand boiled, yet like before, she felt no heat herself. "Now stop!" she said to the flame. The blood cooled the needle; she wiped it as clean as she could and put the thread through the needle. Then she began to sew the wound. The needle pierced through without a problem. Katja held the pressure till Lisa had finished. The blood stopped and wound was sown. Katja washed the wound lightly till it was clean. Lisa took a deep breath and smiled. Smiles seemed to fill the bus. Bael was still unconscious, and Lisa came down from her adrenaline rush to sleep soundly next to Bael. Katja and Sasha looked after them through the evening and into the night.

Lisa woke first at a little after one in the morning. Thomas had taken over the driving from Remi who had taken a nap. Sasha was looking after both Bael and Lisa for a while. While Katja had a nap as well, Nicola sat and watched over the bus. While Beowulf kept his senses alert for any other trouble, Lisa went to Nicola when she got up and sat close to him. "I guess I kinda took a little nap, huh?"

"I think you earned it, my dearest." Nicola nodded toward Bael. "He's been sleeping soundly, and the bandages are almost dry. He is healing, thanks to you. Though I'm not sure how it was done." Lisa snuggled next to Nicola. "I used a flame to fuse Bael's blood to the needle, then it went in. It was all I could think of. Believe it or not, I got the idea off a comic book Aunt Lucile would read to us when we were little. Who would have thought?"

Nicola gave a light laugh. "You did well, Elisavetta, very well." But Lisa had fallen back to sleep. "You know, she loves you? Don't you, Father?" Sasha said, watching from her seat. Sasha wiped her eyes as they teared up again. "Sasha, stop now. Why do you cry now?"

"I'm sorry, Papa, but no matter how this ends, she will be gone. You know the tribes. Their friends, but we never see them anymore. I know it's selfish, but I want to keep her with me. She's like a sister. Maybe more so than Katja."

"How can you say that about your sister?"

"Papa, don't misunderstand me. I love Katja with all my heart. But she and Tara were so close it didn't give us much of a chance to bond. Not to mention, we aren't quite the same, are we? But I do love my sister."

Nicola nodded. "I understand, and I would miss her too. But she will be safe with them. Remember that."

"Yes, Father." Sasha put her head down on the back of her seat and fell asleep.

The sun hadn't risen. No bird sang but the morning had arrived, and so they had reached the docks at Hudson Bay in Churchill. The boat was waiting that would take them to Newfoundland; it was a nice ship, if not the largest. The captain came down to greet them.

"A nice man," Lisa thought. A portly gentleman with rosy cheeks and blue eyes; his hair was gray what there was of it. He held a pipe in his mouth, blowing rings as he walked. The man behind him was about the same age, a little boney and thin. He had more hair, and it was a little darker. His smile lacked a few teeth, but he was friendly and proper to the captain's orders. After talking with Nicola, the little man went back to the ship for a stretcher for Bael. It took the rest of the morning to get everyone bedded away in their cabins. Katja stayed with Bael while the rest went to the café for breakfast. Beowulf had been on guard since the attack though he could sense no one around. Lisa noticed a look in his eye. He wanted vengeance for his father. He hadn't even glanced at Lisa since then. The meal was huge. Remi and Maliki had enough fish and biscuits to close the café. The rest made due with the specials. They returned to the ship, got settled in, and waited for permission to leave the dockside. By eight o' clock, they were under way. Beowulf stayed on deck. Lisa and Sasha talked on the aft deck away from the others while Nicola and Maliki played cards with Remi. By supper everyone had finally relaxed. Even Beowulf came down to eat and seemed to take notice of Lisa again.

Master Seidrich exited the plane in Calcutta with four members of the royal guard. His anger at having to chase a lord of a house to a remote location in another house's territory made his teeth gnash. If Montgomery had any honor, he would have come at the king's request. That Montgomery was a lord was bad enough over the centuries. Now to have to chase this spineless creature was disgusting. The information the furies brought him made him sick. Montgomery had been used by someone with abilities of a higher nature. What or whoever it was—it was no vampire. "The sniveling puppet," he said under his breath.

Through the valley and the city, they drove. Up the mountain road, they went till they found the mountainside house he chose to hide in. They stopped short of the mountain drive and walked to the house. They came through the door, and Montgomery turned to run. Seidrich called out, "Lord Montgomery, by order of the king, you are to come with me."

Montgomery stopped dead and turned to leave with his escort. "Ah yes, gentlemen, it's so good of the king to send someone for me before the trial. He shouldn't have gone through all the trouble. Though I do appreciate the effort. However, did he know where I was vacationing?"

"Lord Montgomery, may I be so bold as to ask you a question about your vacation?"

"Of course, Seidrich. Feel free."

"Where on your trip have you misplaced your luggage?"

"Excuse me?"

"Your luggage? You've been here for several weeks. Yet you have no luggage?"

"Ah yes, well you see . . ."

"Lord Montgomery . . . get in the car," he said nothing more. He just got into the car with a man on either side of him. Seidrich sat in the in the passenger's seat with a small smile he couldn't get rid of.

In the shadows of the house, a figure watched in amusement as Lord Montgomery was taken away. He too wore a smile. He still had plans for him, but they could wait. The man in the shadow's smile deepened till Seidrich rolled down the window in the passenger's seat and flipped off the darkened doorway of the house as they left. He had felt the shadowed man's presence and wanted him to know it.

At Bael's cabin, Lisa cleaned and wrapped Bael's wounds again. Katja went for her dinner. Lisa had relieved her to dress Bael's wounds and to check on him. Beowulf watched as Lisa took such care of his father. Thomas knocked on the door and entered. Bael was still unconscious. "Is he any better?"

"No."

"I don't think he's healing the way he should." Thomas sat down and watched his sister. Thomas kept thinking that there was something he might do for him. He sat and thought for hours. Katja returned, and since Lisa was taking care of Bael, she finally slept. Beowulf left to be on watch. Lisa too had begun to get tired. Thomas had remembered a spell from the book that Jason had gotten upset about. He knew he could cast it, but he didn't understand it well enough to use it. Later, Lisa had fallen asleep in the chair, leaning against the wall. Thomas covered her shoulders with a blanket.

It was late in the evening and Thomas faded. Just before he started to nod off, he heard footsteps in the hall, and the door opened slowly. Thomas kept his head down but eyes open enough to see. Bael's father entered the room. Silently he looked around the room and then knelt at Bael's bedside. "You are so weak from the fight." He took Bael's hand. My son, my poor son. I'm so sorry I could not help you anymore." Thomas watched till he spoke from guilt. "Sir, I don't mean to interrupt, but I believe I am more to blame than the wolf." He turned questioningly to Thomas. "I would by dead if Bael hadn't brought me back." Thomas explained the events of his death and resurrection to his father. Thomas believed that he was the reason why Bael was so weak. Bael's father looked to his son, then placed his hand on his chest. Thomas watched as around his hand Bael's skin began to turn red as if it was burning. For several minutes, Beowulf Sr. said nothing, just sat with his son. Finally, he removed his hand and got up from the bed. "He shouldn't play with death. It could have cost him far more than I would have him pay." He turned to leave the room. "Are you all right?"

"Fine, tell my son when he wakens that I stopped by, will you? Tell him I'm proud of him, but give him my warning." Before the door was open, He had disappeared.

By morning Bael had begun to heal. By ten he had awakened. Thomas told Bael of his father's visit and warning. Katja was so happy to see him awake. Bael thought he might break from her hug. Everyone laughed at the joke. As Bael got better over the next few days, Everyone started to lighten up again. Laughter was heard more often around the ship. Still, Beowulf stood, watching on deck as if waiting for the next attack. Bael and Nicola told him several times to relax and that they were safe on the ship. Bael explained to Lisa and Thomas that most vampires had a great fear of the water as their bodies would no longer float. Though they could not die, they can and do for some reason freeze below the cold water after a while. Some that have been brought back were said to have gone mad. Beowulf would smile at this and say what about the other. The one pulling

145

strings. Then he would go back to his watch. Thomas used the time to practice his magic. He had learned to focus it to work his natural magic and casting spell magic and then have the spells work together to accomplish a task. He wanted Jason and Maliki to be proud of him. Lisa and Sasha spent their time in more athletic pursuits, learning tactics in fighting that honed Lisa's instincts. Sasha found that Lisa was getting to anticipate her opponents faster and faster. Even Sasha was feeling worn out. Remi though would come to keep Lisa on her toes. Yet at the end of every match, Nicola would watch and say, "Very good, Elisavetta, but you *will* do better." Lisa loved being urged on by him.

The first voyage lasted less than a week. When they reached Newfoundland, the next ship was waiting. A huge ship compared to their first one. It was a converted utility ship and looked beautiful to Lisa. Nicola pointed the ship out to her and Thomas. As they were leaving the boat, Lisa and Thomas saw the captain and crew in an argument of some kind. When it was over, the captain shook the crew's hands. On the dock Lisa and Thomas waved to the crew and thanked them. All but the captain and his first mate. They were nowhere to be found. Bael was able to walk off the ship. When they reached the end of the dock where the other ship sat, Bael stood silent for a moment. "She really turned out well, didn't she? I had Ramon get her ready and bring her up from Boston."

The boat was white with a red striping. There were three decks above and three below. Down the gangway came a man in a black suit. He had a look to be in his forties, clean shaven with dark hair and light brown eyes. He bowed to Bael when he reached the dock. He greeted all of them. Something about the man seemed familiar to Lisa. As she walked up to him, he bowed and proceeded to give her a hug. "I am so happy to see you again, Miss Lisa. You have grown even more beautiful than your aunt had said." Lisa returned the hug, but was still unsure of how she knew him.

"Please forgive me, but though you seem familiar, I don't remember you."

"Of course, I'm sorry it has been almost twenty years. I used to help take care of you and your brother. When your mother left, I helped your aunt till you were seven and then I went back to work for Lord Bael. Still, I was the one who had taught you to speak your first words and take your first steps." He thought for a moment. "Do you still have the little bear I gave you?" Lisa knew the bear and, slowly, remembered the man. "RJ! I remember. You helped me make breakfast for Mother. You got me out of the fishpond when I fell in. In the backyard." She gave him another hug. Ramon smiled. "I'm glad that you remembered me, miss."

"Lisa, please." As they were talking, a large black crow flew down to Ramon's shoulder. "Oh yes. Lord Bael Sorrow arrived days ago. He seems to be upset."

Bael held out his arm and the bird flew to him. It began cawing and screeching to Bael. When he finished, Bael told all to get aboard.

After they had boarded and were shown to their cabin, Bael called for a meeting in the galley. They all arrived as quickly as they could. Something in Bael's humor had dried up. He had become irritable and grumpy as far as Katja could see. It had something to do with his crow Sorrow. When everyone arrived, Bael sat at the head of the table, hands crossed with a scowl and deep in thought. Suddenly, the door behind him opened. It was the captain from the other boat. He bent down and said something to Bael. Bael nodded back and the captain left. Bael looked up and noticed that all were present and waiting for him.

Bael stood up. "Sorrow went back to my house after I sent him to find out what he could about what might be behind Montgomery's outrageous attacks on both the children and our troupe. It seems someone else is pulling his strings. After the wolves that attacked at the brother's castle, I would have thought I knew who was behind them, but I was wrong. Sorrow got a glimpse of someone at my house. Someone he or his community has never seen. Someone whose abilities match, or better my own. He is a demigod. With the arrival of the wolves, I thought it might be my uncle Loki. Sorrow knows Loki and can see through his disguises. This was not Loki that Sorrow saw." Thomas had pencil and pad he'd borrowed at Alec's. He had been writing in it since Bael's father dropped his hints. Something added up for him, but what, he wasn't sure. Thomas looked at his notes carefully. What he *had* figured out was missing too many pieces. His information on the demigods was incomplete. "What exactly did Sorrow see?"

"A man standing outside the house, staying in the shadows. Well dressed in an overcoat. Sorrow cawed in the corner of the room. He said that he had something metal attached to his side. Possibly a weapon, but not a sword. He was clean shaven, accept for a moustache. When he spotted Sorrow, he disappeared. Thomas scribbled more on his pad. Well, Thomas, what do you think?"

"How many dark demigods are left? Who planned the uprising? And last, how many demigods are left?" Bael tried to remember what his father had taught him. Beowulf also began counting in his head. Finally, they had their answers. Thomas wasn't surprised when they had two different answers. Bael came up with three dark and fourteen demigods left. Beowulf's answer was higher, five dark and twenty-three demigods, but both said that Loki was supposed to be the mastermind. Thomas shook his head. It only added up one way. "Bael, someone has been trying again and again to get into a position of power. But he was before Loki's time, or Eris, and Hades. Someone behind the scenes every time manipulating others to get rid of whoever defends the triad of gods. They seem to fail in the end because of the unknown factor. Those heroes that change the odds. Do the unexpected, what shouldn't be possible. Ragnarok had survivors. The Greek gods were not overthrown due to Hercules. Your father should have been killed by the dragon. Fighting so soon after defeating the Grendel, he even broke his sword, but replaced it with the magic sword that hangs at your house. I believe someone has been making others do his dirty work for quite some time. I think the only reason he's doing things himself this time is he believes he can take you, Bael. He's been watching you. You've refused to kill and opted for your ice prison. He believes you're unable to kill if you must and therefore weak. I think he's used this opportunity with us to force you to fight. If he kills you, his way is clear to the gods. It's the only thing that adds up. However, he has no idea what you've done since this started. The wolves were meant to test you. In the end, Beowulf killed one, while the other you sent to your ice prison. So as far as he's concerned you're still no threat."

"But who is he?"

"Bael, right now it doesn't matter. That's just a name. What matters is, we know how he operates, and that's through others. That leads me to think in the physical confrontation he may not be that strong. My only question is, is he right? To stop him you'll have to kill as your father did. Can you kill, Bael?"

Bael remembered the stone and the lesson it taught him. His father was right, and he knew it. His time to do his duty was clear. "Yes, Thomas. I can. Whoever he is, this must end." Nicola and Maliki sat back in their chairs and nodded to each other as if they knew some secret. Remi stood up. "As for the young ones, that will still depend on the royals? Their foolish trial and rules of the tribes?" Nicola raised his hand in objection. "The vampires tribal rules are no more foolish than ours. They serve a purpose you and I know very well."

"Aye, Mon'ami. Not that I care for our rules either. Look at your own situation. You can no longer step in. Aye." Nicola waved off any further conversation. Bael nodded his head as he looked over the room. "Well, my friends, if Thomas is right. And I think he is. We may have the upper hand here. Whoever he is has no idea of the changes back at castle or the stone." Thomas couldn't help but wonder about Maris. "What might he say, or give away if he wanted. Yet if he were going to cause trouble, why would he help us in the first place?" Thomas could think of no easy answer.

Lisa went to Remi. "What about these rules? I know we're not supposed to exist, but we do. Are there any other rules that we may have broken or maybe bent?" Remi picked her up as a parent picked up a child. "Mon' cher, don't worry. There are enough people on your side at the royal houses. You will be fine. I swear."

"How do you know their rules so well?" Remi smiled at her. "A very beautiful woman made me study and memorize them bottom to top. She made quite a pleasure of it."

"Why? I mean, why go through the trouble?"

"As I said, she was very beautiful." He put her down and gave her a hug. "Remember, we are here for you as well." The meeting was apparently over and was breaking up.

The hall echoed with heavy footsteps of the guards and their escort. Lord Montgomery was being brought to the royal presence. The king in his throne room was expecting to hear him pleading with the guards, but Lord Montgomery walked with the guards as though they were his to command. The calm demeanor he showed was that of righteousness. He truly believed he was in the right with his actions, defending the laws of the tribes by destroying the Marks.

The queen sat in her throne holding the hand of the king trying to keep him calm. "My dear, remember, as king, you must remain impartial. Hear him out. Let him defend the charges against him before a judgment is passed. Then you have him dispatched." The king smiled at her attempt to calm him with humor, though it was not far from the truth.

Lord Montgomery was led to the podium facing the king. He bowed to the king and queen. A slight nod was returned. Montgomery cleared his throat. "My Lord and Lady Draugur, if I may ask? Why have I been summoned to the palace in this manner? Treated as a criminal under guard?"

The king leaned forward. "You would stand there and act as though you had no part in the attack on Lord Bael. That you would use our subjects without our command, permission, or knowledge?"

"My lord, I too am a father of the Magyars. I have the responsibility to uphold the laws of the tribes. The Marks were being protected by Lord Bael. Therein are my rights to have the guilty destroyed. He as well was judged in error. Therefore, he was in violation of the laws as well."

"Lord Bael is bringing them to a court of the royals. It is the high queen's wish to hear and review the children of the house of Lord Basarab. As they are his tribe, he will sit in judgment as will we all. As is procedure and Prodi call. You are in violation of those rules and laws. How do you plead?"

Montgomery walked around the podium. Looking around the room, he turned to the king. "My lord, I do not see Lord Bael present, nor do I see the others that led the attack to serve as witness. As for not notifying Your Highness, I thought only of expedience as Lord Bael is capable of escaping with the Marks."

"Ahh. I see you had no time to request. What if any action should be taken so you took the responsibility upon yourself, correct?"

"Yes, sir." The queen reached to a servant with a tray. She smiled at Montgomery and lay her finger on the tray, which was followed by electronic buzzes and sounds. Then from Montgomery's pocket came a few musical notes, then they rang out again.

The king gripped the throne and smiled, baring his teeth and fangs in anger. "It would seem that it takes very little time to reach you. It also seems that you could have reached our countenance as well."

"Well, you see . . ."

"THAT WILL BE ENOUGH! One more word from you and I shall let the queen have you." Montgomery returned behind the podium. The king settled back into his throne. "So you want to face Lord Bael. Very well. Understand that you *have* been found guilty today, but I have decided to let you stand against the children when they arrive. And face Lord Bael as well. I'll even go so far as to release you if they are found guilty by the royals. However, as you took the responsibility, let it be known, after their judgment, you will no longer be the father the Magyars in title or name. You shall stand as one. *Alone.*" The king waited to hear him beg, but none came. "TAKE HIM AWAY TILL THE MEETING!"

Montgomery was led out of the chambers. The queen was so proud of her husband's restraint. "You handled that well, my love."

The king took her hand and kissed it. "Thank you, my dear. I could not have remained calm without you." He sat back and thought to himself. "Now all that is left is to wait for Lord Bael."

10

All were hurrying around the castle of Lord Basarab. Queen Lilith herself had arrived to oversee the preparations for the meeting. The Ravenna family was busily at work to help the queen. Lady Valarie, Ravenna sister to Peter and David, had voiced her opinion that perhaps the Marks, meaning the children, should be destroyed for safety's sake if nothing else. Her voice had in fact carried some weight with the tribes. However, her brothers had been the children's advocates since their return from America. Soon all the tribes would arrive. The entire town would be playing host to them, some in the castle itself. The kitchen and banquet hall were being prepared to the queen's requests. As was the main chamber set for the meeting. Lord Basarab made plans to welcome his family regardless of the royals.

On the ship, the seas were calm. The winds were cool. Beowulf sat on a stool, still watching for trouble. Lisa brought him some coffee to keep him warm and kept him company. Below deck Bael and Katja stayed in his cabin. She looked after him till he had his strength back. Nicola and Maliki along with Remi were in the estate cabin, talking about the situation with the children while Sasha and Thomas play cards. Maliki sat with his head in his hands. "I know how much she would like you there, Nicola, but you know that it's impossible. True, you wouldn't be in their territory, but it's just too close."

Remi stood and paced the floor. "Mon'ami, there is no reason to go. You will not be allowed in the chamber anyway. You know she would prefer you safe." Nicola placed his hands on the arms of the large chair, as they started to change to paws. "But the only one with them will be Bael and, possibly, Beowulf. They are not going to be very comforting to the children."

"Don't worry, Mon'ami, they will be looked after, I promise."

There was a loud crash on the rear deck, and Beowulf and most of the others rushed to see what had happened. There on the deck caught up in some of the deck lines was Miss Murry. Thomas went to help her get untangled. "Thank you, Thomas my boy, I didn't see them lines before I walked through. The deck was too dark."

Thomas helped her to her feet. "What are you doing here?"

"Oh, I started thinking. As your aunt can't be there as a witness, I'm the only one with the information they might want. So here I am. Besides, you need to keep up with your magic, right?"

Thomas nods and smiled, and they all went back inside.

At the top of a full-size bed, Bael sat up. His shoulder still bandaged but now healing fast. Katja was lying next to him, asleep at last, after looking after him for the last few days. Only sleeping when Lisa would relieve her. Bael watches her sleep, thinking to himself, "The irony is, I have her father, a world-class surgeon with us, and Lisa figures out how to stitch me up and Katja and her are the ones nursing me back to health." He smiles, realizing how much the people on board care so much about him. And how much he loves them.

"It's nice to see you up and looking so much better. So much better than the last I saw you." From out of nowhere, his father was sitting in a chair across from him. "And keeping good company as well."

"Good am glad." Bael looked down at Katja then back at his father. "Don't worry she won't awaken, I promise. She hasn't the last few times I stepped in. So how are you feeling?" Bael rotated his shoulder. "I've been better."

"Have you?"

"Well, the bites not . . . you're not asking about the bite, are you?"

Beowulf smiled back at his son. "No, not really." He stood and walked to him. You'll heal from the bite, and I think your family problems are working themselves out quite well. I'm worried about you. You understand that you can be hurt, and even die. For years you haven't had to face any enemies more formidable than you. Now, you have been injured. So I ask again, how are you feeling?"

Bael looked up at his father. "Weaker. I feel weaker. Almost afraid of what's coming."

His father took his son's other shoulder. "Perhaps you do, but you're not. You haven't turned around. You're getting yourself prepared to battle, not run. That bite hasn't made you weak. It's showing you your strength. What does a knight do, son?"

"He *stands*. He holds the ground beneath his feet. Till it's the last ground to hold."

"And why does he do that?"

"To protect the land and the people." He took his father's hand at his shoulder. *"As my father did."*

"You, my son, are stronger than the beast you face. Hold that ground and protect who you must."

Bael closed his eyes and remembered his father's lessons and stories of knights and quests. He remembered them all. As he opened his eyes, his father was gone, but he had no bitterness in his absence. He could remember things now without his stubbornness getting in the way. The stone had given him truly a new start without changing who he was. Bael put his arms around Katja, and from the sound of their hearts beating together, he fell asleep.

The ship was swiftly moving through the waters. The thrum of the engines could be heard throughout the ship. Beowulf, finally taking some time to relax, sat with Lisa and Sasha on the foredeck. Sasha was taking in the air and keeping an eye on her nephew. She was all for Lisa and little wolf's relationship, but her father said it would have to wait. "You must chaperone," he told her. Just what she wanted to do. "Play the fifth wheel." Lisa understood, but that didn't mean she liked it. Beowulf didn't mind because it took off the pressure. "So, nephew, are you going to get any sleep tonight, or are you staying on guard?"

Beowulf threw up his hands. "I've already been told by dad and Nicola to be in bed before midnight and to stay there till I had eight hours of sleep. I know when I'm beat, so yeah." Both Lisa and Sasha said at the same time. "It's about time!" The ladies laughed as did Beowulf. "Well, you better get going. You're running out of time."

"Yeah yeah, I know." A few minutes later, Ramon walked up to the group. "I am sorry, sir, but I was instructed by Mr. Lazar to inform you of the time and, if necessary, to remove you to your quarters." Beowulf shook his head. "Have I really been that bad?" Ramon took his arm. "This way, sir. I believe the question was rhetorical?"

"I guess this is good night, ladies."

"Sir, please don't break into song." The gentlemen left the deck and Lisa and Sasha looked over the bow at the waves. "How much longer will we be at sea?" Lisa asked Sasha. "About three days. Then one day by train. Bordeaux to Milano where my father will leave us, then to Romania where you're grandfather waits for us."

Lisa rolled her shoulders. "I'm not sure about meeting him. It makes me nervous. I mean, he's a king, right?"

"Yes, but he's also your family." Lisa cocked her head. "So does that make me a princess?"

"Ah, no, it makes you family."

"Oh, so what are the royals like anyway?"

"Just be yourself and keep an open mind."

"Thanks, the last time someone said that, I got put on this rollercoaster ride." Sasha laughed. "I guess you have had some ups and downs."

"Yeah, but I got you guys in the mix so . . . I don't mind so much." It's all Sasha could do to hold back her tears. "You know, it's getting pretty late. I think we should get to bed, yah think?"

"Sure, I'll see yah in the morning."

Queen Lilith had the royal arrangements nearly complete. She took her seat and looked over the room. It was quite to her satisfaction. A man walked in with a tray and a letter on it. "This has just arrived, Your Highness, by special courier." The queen thanked him and opened the letter. As she read the message, the air in the chamber grew cold; her teeth gnashed and fangs glistened. Her anger was almost in a fury when she called out. A servant rushed in as she told him to retrieve his master as fast as possible. "The man must be insane?" She crumpled the paper in her hand. Lord Basarab enters the chamber. "You requested me, Your Highness?" She turned to him.

"Ah, than I am the queen then? I almost wasn't sure. For him to send this to me is an . . . an . . ."

"Who has sent what, milady?" She gave him the letter, and he quickly read it, "He's gone mad." The note drops to the floor.

To Queen Lilith, Queen of the Vampiric tribes.

This is to inform you that I, Lord James Edward Montgomery, is suing for Royal abstention in the judgment of the Thorys as well as that of Lord Basarab due to his bias in the matter as well as your own. As you have shown a preference in bringing them before the royals in refusing to destroy such abominations as the laws state. I therefore insist you abstain from the proceedings.

Sincerely,
Lord Montgomery of the Magyars

The queen calls for her page. She tells him to inform the families to come to the palace a day early due to an unforeseen circumstance that bore their immediate attention. And gave her thanks. The palace pages leave the castle to the village as fast as their legs can carry them. The affirmative answers came in short order.

The king of the Magyars was sent the message as well as being informed by Lord Basarab as to the contents of the letter. They in turn sent Lord Montgomery ahead to the castle under guard. The King and Queen Draugur will follow as told by Lord Basarab. Seidrich makes the arrangements with pleasure.

Dawn broke over the sea. As one by one the travelers awaken, the aroma from the dining hall brought a healthy appetite from crew and passenger alike. Lisa smelled her coffee in the air, seeming to call her. The crew ate at dawn; the passengers, at eight.

Bael calls Ramon to his cabin where they whisper in private. At the end of the conversation, Ramon nods. "I believe that can be arranged, sir, as well as the other matter. I believe there is one aboard, sir, I shall endeavor to find it as fast as possible, sir."

The dining hall was a hurricane of hungry people, and after the meal, Ramon entered the hall with something in his hand. He passed it off to Bael who looked at it and thanked him. "It looks perfect." By ten thirty, everyone was into different projects. Bael saw Katja, returning from the chart room. She walked to him and kisses his cheek.

"Well, we should be there tomorrow evening. We've made good time." Bael kissed her back and saw that the room was empty except for a pair of eyes at the porthole. Bael pulled her close. "You know, I was thinking last night after you fell asleep and came up with a great idea for today and tonight."

"Oh, and what was that?" Bael dropped to one knee. How would you like to be married by the captain? He then pulled out a case. Inside, as he opened it, was a beautiful ring. She took his hand.

"Are you sure about this?"

He gave her a look. "I know you may think it's too fast since we just got together only a short time ago, but I've loved you for a very long time. I've known it since the beginning. Your sister knew. Hell, everyone did. All these years I've mourned, yet I still loved you. I have always been sure. I just don't want to wait any longer."

"Then yes, I would love to." She pulled him up, and he placed the ring on her finger. "Now I'll wait here, while you tell your father." They laugh and kiss.

"Oh no, you don't. We'll both tell him and then everyone else." It was as he embraced her that she noticed. "Hey, you're using your shoulder?"

"The bites are fine. I feel great."

Ten minutes later, a roar of laughter was heard through the ship; everybody came running to see what's happening. When Lisa, Sasha, and Beowulf arrived, they found Nicola with Bael and Katja up in the air being hugged and a smile on Nicola's face. Whatever it was, it was good news. Thomas, Maliki, and Remi came running in, followed by Harry who was bringing up the rear. Beowulf went in, holding up his hands. "OK . . . OK . . . can you guys settle down long enough to tell us what's going on?"

Sasha spotted something, and Lisa's attention followed hers to the ring on Katja's hand. The ladies screamed and rushed in past Beowulf to join in the group hug. Ramon stood off to one side, waiting with a grin, letting anyone who noticed that he knew what was happening but probably knew first.

Remi tapped Ramon. "Pardon, Mon'ami, would you care to relate to the rest of us what's happening?"

"I'm sorry, sir, but it's just not my place to tell, sir." Finally things started to settle down, and Katja came to middle of the room. "As some of you may have guessed, we have some news for you all. Bael and I are getting married tonight." She held her ring out for her friends to see. "I hope you all will be there." Everyone came up one by one to congratulate the couple. Beowulf at last walked up and took his aunt's hand and looked at the ring.

"So you finally caught him?" He pulled her hand and hugged her as she fell into him. "Well, it took you long enough!" He smiled to his father and shook his hand, not letting go of his aunt. "I wish nothing but the best for you both." The men left. The girls grabbed Katja and pulled her off to get her ready for the wedding. Bael was left standing in the room with Nicola. "Now then, Nicola said, sit down. I think there are a few things before this wedding that we must talk about. First is, I'm very proud of you. You have found your heart again. Second, *I am wanting more grandchildren!* Third, continue to grow in your happiness. And last, where is Ramon?"

"Here, sir. I thought I should take the liberty." Ramon brought in a bottle and glasses.

"Ah, you are a man who understand traditions." Ramon poured three drinks and passed them to the others, then to himself. "Sir, if I may?"

Nicola raised his glass. "Of course you may join in. You're family. But I make the toast."

"Of course, sir." Nicola raised his glass high. "To my son-in-law, may he and his bride live happy and healthy lives and may their love be eternal." They tapped their glasses and drank and drank. Ramon left to prepare the room for the wedding.

The chamber was round with ornate chairs encircling half the chamber, each with a small desk paper pen and gavel. At the far side sat the ceremonial thrones for the queen. Behind each house's seat stood their page. Fourteen tribal leaders in all and a place for their spouses. The royals began to gather and take their places. Lord Montgomery was escorted to his seat. The guard remained. The clock struck the hour of eight and the deep chimes rang out. The queen entered and took her place as well. Most of the royals were present, but the king and queen of the Magyars had not arrived. Lilith used her gavel and struck three times. "My lords and ladies, we are here tonight because an issue has been brought by Lord Montgomery that I and Lord Basarab should abstain from the trial of the Thorys. That myself and Lord Basarab are perhaps bias and would not be fair in our judgments of the Thorys. While I can assure this council of my own mind and opinion, Lord Montgomery has his right to plead his case for our abstention."

Montgomery stood and proceeded to the floor. "My lords and ladies, while I am sure our queen knows her mind, well . . . I believe there is bias here. As by now you are aware, the Thorys are Marks in the views of our law's abominations, a crossing of the worlds of magic and our own abilities. It has long been one of our most held traditions that each of our people in dealing with humans be limited. Compel the minds and actions of humans to a point but are forbidden to interfere with the innocence. And have done so in the noblest of efforts. The sorcerer's magic has no known effect on our people, and we cannot compel them. Once the choice is made, our ability to procreate is gone. We therefore must rely on our bloodlines. The Thorys are from one of the strongest of the bloodlines. Yet they are tainted, *marked*. By our laws, this is forbidden and with good cause. It keeps the piece between our peoples. Even as the Thorys travel, there are no Vampiric elements on their journey. They are brought by Lord Bael and members of the werepeople. Noble persons all, but none of her own people? Because we are not her people, and Lord Bael knows this. They have in them the possibility of the destruction of our race. Or worse yet, the end of the races themselves." He turned to the queen. "Yet instead of having them dispatched, they are brought to the royal houses. I am sorry for Lord Basarab as they are his line. But if they were my line, I would uphold the laws and have them destroyed."

There was a knock from a gavel. Lord Ravenna stood. "So far I have heard you prosecute the Thorys and remark that it is your opinion that they should be destroyed. We have understood that. So you may stop saying it again and again. As for the bias of either of house named, I have heard nothing to suggest that their judgment has been bias at all. In fact, the only bias I have heard is yours for their destruction."

Suddenly there was a loud ring as metal to stone. Montgomery turned to face King Draugur and the queen. "And that is all you will hear from this pathetic fool." He escorted his queen to her seat and returned to the floor. He bowed to Queen Lilith and the other royal houses.

"Today, my friends, what you have heard are the ramblings of a once great house. Now he has brought that house down. The man before you is no longer a lord of his people. He has tried to negate not only the will of our queen but taken it upon himself to attack Lord Bael. Against, and without royal approval of any kind. Putting in danger the very peace he claims to protect. Lord Bael has kept order amongst all the races. Without breaking the individual tribal laws. When the Thorys were only but humans, he was told to bring them to the royal presence for the choice to be made and to keep them safe. When he found out that they were indeed marks, he proceeded to let the royals have judgment over their offspring. He is, I understand still, bringing them here. His duty fulfilled. Lord Basarab will bring them here as we have always brought them. There is no bias. There is our tradition. This must be upheld. As he has disgraced himself going against our queen as well as his own. Our judgment was that he is now one and stood alone. He is no father of this tribe. Merely one he tries to kill those to save his own life."

The royals stood. With the information from the Magyar king, they placed the pens down at the top of each desk and left. Montgomery was sent down. There was no judgment to make. Lord Draugur grabbed Montgomery. "When you lose your case against the Thorys, I can't but wonder who will get to you first?" He dropped him to the floor. "Take him to a cell."

The guards came and escorted Montgomery away.

The Queen Lilith sat in her throne as Lord Draugur and his wife came forward and bowed. "Your timing was perfect as always, my lord."

"Thank you, my queen. Are we prepared for the Thorys yet?"

"We are . . . I only hope that Lord Bael is."

Beowulf stood on the top deck of the ship while below everyone scrambled with things to do. He waited, praying his great-grand-father will hear him. There was a breeze on the deck. In a whirl of wind, he appeared. "Oh, thank you for coming. I need your help. I need something from my house, and I can't leave."

"What is it you need, Beo?"

"I need a box from on top of my dresser."

"Is that all?" He opened his hands, and there was the very box needed.

"Thanks, Grandfather Baal. This day would not be the same without this. Baal smiled and vanished in the breeze. Beowulf ran to his aunt Sasha who's got Katja and Lisa in a frenzy. He broke in on her ordering around. "Sasha, can I borrow you for a while?" Katja took his arm. "Borrow, steal, or just tie her up. Take her."

"Well, I like that, here I am just . . ." With that he took her arm and pulled her from the room. They ran to his room and closed the door. "What's with all the mystery, sweetie?"

"I have something for you." He opened the box on his bed and handed her folded parchment. "I was told to give this to you today. Before the wedding."

She saw the writing. "This is from my sister?"

"Mom left some things for all of us and put me in charge of handing them out."

Her hand shook as she opened it. She started to read the letter. "Do you know what's in this?"

"I was there when she wrote it."

Sasha read the note.

My dearest Sasha, I have known of my condition for a while now. I am sorry to have kept it from you and the family. Bael found out days ago, but I have kept him with me. So not to worry you all. However, I need you to do me a favor. My son and husband are taking this far too hard. He is feeding his own darkness. His father will do what he can, but one day, his true heart will return. If he weds, give them our hearts and give her this ring. I love you, Sasha. Beowulf is now the keeper of my estates. He has all of my instructions and faith. I know Katja will love him as I have. You are our family's strength: keep father safe from himself.

You're loving sister, Tara.

Tied to the letter was the ring, Tara's ring. She untied it and put it in her pocket. Her tears flowing down her cheek. Beowulf held her for a moment, then told her, "Keep the ring till the ceremony, not before. And don't tell either of them about the letter. Just tell them it's a gift from Tara."

"Why not tell them about the letter?"

"Because . . . that's what Mom said to tell you."

"Well . . . okay then." She saw the box behind him. It is filled with letters. "I guess Tara isn't done yet?" Beowulf closed the box.

The rest of the day was spent on preparing for the wedding and reception. When Ramon was finished, the room was beautiful tables in linen and where he got flowers was a mystery that even had Bael stumped. Ramon had evening ware brought on board for everyone when he was told to get the ship ready. He like Thomas did not like surprises, so he tried to prepare for all eventualities. And as far as anyone could see. He did his job better than they could ever guess. He had the kitchen working in overdrive and, somehow, managed a cake for the wedding. Thomas, after seeing the main room, went to Bael and told him, "That Ramon, give that guy a raise. You would not believe the room upstairs." Bael smiled. "Ramon is the best." Ramon had even managed to find material for a veil and train.

Everyone took their places. Beowulf was the best man while Thomas and Maliki and Remi were the groomsmen. Lisa and Sasha were bridesmaids. While Harry and Ramon watched, the rosy cheeked captain stood with his book in hand and a pipe in his lips. Nicola led his daughter to her love. He was so proud walking her down the aisle; Lisa thought his chest would burst. Before Katja had reached Bael, a slight breeze entered the room, bringing Lord Beowulf with it. Behind him, in the doorway, stood a gray cat, which jumped into a chair and sat.

"Continue, please. I did not mean to interrupt. I just wanted to be here." Lord Beowulf bowed, and Katja continued to Bael's side. The captain cleared his throat. "Who gives this woman to this man?" Nicola stood tall and put his hand to his chest. "I do, Nicola Lazar, her father."

The captain turned to Bael. "And do you receive this woman?"

"Aye, Captain, I do." Bael took her hand from Nicola.

The captain took their hands. "We are here today to witness the joining of two souls. Two souls, who willingly bind themselves to each other. As one. Love has brought them here. Love is that which binds them and makes them whole. Is there any present who would dispute that love? Let them speak now before these witnesses. The room is quiet as the captain proceeded. "Do you, Katja Mia Lazar, take this man, Bael, to be your husband, to love, honor, and obey. To keep him as half of one?"

"I do take this man." He turned to Bael. "And do you Bael take this woman, Katja Mia Lazar, to be your wife, to love, honor, and cherish. To keep her as half of one?"

"I do take this woman."

"From this day forth, their two souls are as one. Place the ring upon her finger." Bael reached for the ring, but Sasha put her hand on theirs. "Wait! I have something for you both." She opened her hand to reveal her sister Tara's ring. She turned their hands over and placed it in his hand.

"A gift from Tara to you. Wishing you both to be as happy as she was." Bael slipped the ring on her finger. The captain again cleared his throat. "It is my honor, as captain, to pronounce you husband and wife. You may kiss the bride." Bael and Katja kissed and embraced each other, holding each tightly. When they released they looked down at the ring, knowing that Tara was with them. Confetti and rice were thrown. Everyone congratulated them. There were hugs and kisses, handshakes and pats on the back. Champagne was popped and glasses were filled. The party went on into the night. The bride and groom left while the others continued the evening's fun.

Hand in hand they walked through the ship to his room. As they approached his door, he quickly whisked her up into his arms. She held him around his neck.

"I love you," she said and kissed him. Her heart was racing as they reached his door. He opened the door and swept her through the threshold. As he put her down, she slid across and down his body. Her feet were slowly reaching the floor, but she still felt as though she were floating. His hand moved down her back, while the other reached to unzip her. As their hands met, her exposed back got a chill. He moved his warm hands to her skin. She trembled in her nervousness. Her head rested on his chest as her arms fell to grab his suit at the collar. Her hands moved down his shoulders and arms. The jacket fell to the floor. He brought his hand back pulling her dress forward. The loose dress fell next to the jacket on the floor. She unbuttoned and removed his shirt. Their breath quickened in anticipation. They stepped out of their shoes and moved toward the bed. He lifted her again gently and placed her on the bed. She watched almost breathless as he unfastened his pants. She tugged playfully at his leg till his pants fell to the floor. She reached for his hand, and as they clasped, she pulled him down. They rolled across the bed till she was lying on top of him. She held his head in her hands, and he held her by her side and thigh. They kissed again, long and passionate. Their tongues were tasting their lips; they began to lightly bite and gnaw at their chin and necks as their passion released. Their hands moved over their bodies. They rolled again and again. Their bodies writhing as one as they'd moved across the bed. Each panting and gasping. As he filled her again and again with his love, her eyes began to blaze. She held on to whatever she could to maintain control of her passion. He could feel her body as it tried to change to its tiger form. But she brought herself back and kissed him. Their passion went on and on through the night. She continued to hold on to her human side till at last together. They had an explosive release that left them both exhausted and exhilarated. Breathing heavy and pulse pounding, they looked into each other's eyes. They laughed light and short and then kissed. They smiled and kissed again and again. It didn't take long until their passion again took over.

At the party, some were talking about the events of the last few weeks; others, of what's to come. Nicola was still somewhat upset about leaving them in Spain. Maliki and Sasha finally quieted his resolve. Ramon was brought up-to-date on most of what had happened over the past month. He was amazed at how much Thomas had grown and how far his abilities had come along. Harry sat back in a comfy chair, smiling at the party, looking quite satisfied at how things were playing out. Lisa and Remi were talking about where they would go after they'd dock in Spain. As they talked, she noticed Beowulf leaving to the foredeck. Remi saw her attention change as Beowulf left. "Be careful, Mon' Cher. He is a good man, but watch your emotions, little one. Your people respect Lord Bael, but Beowulf is his mother's child. The royals are friends, but they frown on . . . Well, just be careful." He kissed her cheek and waved her off. Lisa kissed him back and followed Beowulf.

Montgomery sat in his cell, calmly waiting. In the back of the cell, he heard a voice. "Well . . . not quite what I had in mind, but you will be at their trial." Montgomery bowed. "Yes my lord. It seems the royals are set against doing what is right."

"Don't be so sure of their victory just yet. You reached a few ears, and there is still the trial itself. You alone may have an opportunity to set things right. I still have a few cards to play as well."

"Either way, my lord. Those abominations will die at trial's end." The man in the shadows smiled with a smirk. "You will be rewarded, Montgomery. I'll see to that." With that the man disappeared as dust in a breeze.

In the queen's chambers, Lilith waited till she heard a knock on her door. "Yes?"

"Your Highness, the Ravennas are here as you requested."

"Send them in and leave us."

"As you wish, milady." The Ravennas were shown in and the door closed behind them. Peter, David, and Valarie Ravenna approached and bowed to Lilith. The queen returned the bow.

"I called for you because you know the Thorys. The trial will begin at the end of the week. I have looked over our bylaws, and Lord Montgomery has a few points that might hurt their case."

Lady Valarie came forward. "His case stood on the fact that the Thorys are a danger to the houses. That what they are may change the rest of our kind. He can in fact state that they are not truly Lord Basarab's blood at all and therefore. Need not be judged, but destroyed. In truth, there is no proof. Not to mention are their powers effective on us. If so, that will play a part in proving his case."

Lilith looked at Lady Ravenna. "What do you think of the Thorys' chances?"

"My queen, I'm not even sure if they can stand for judgment. As it is, they have no one to stand for them at the meeting. As you well know, a royal cannot stand for them. And as their fate will be sealed as well. I don't see a tribal member taking the risk."

"And I can't ask one too."

Beowulf stood at the railing, looking over the dark water. He closed his eyes as the wind and light spray hit his face. From behind him, he heard footsteps. He recognized them without opening his eyes and smiled. "So is the party finished or could you just not go without my company?"

"Neither. I just thought you could use some company, but if you'd prefer to be alone, I'll leave you to yourself. Have a nice evening." She turned and started to walk back in when Beowulf turned and put his hand on her shoulder. "Please wait. I'm sorry. Of course, I would love your company. Thank you." Lisa came back with her hands on her hips and a little pouty. "Why do you do that?"

"What?"

"Act as though you're one of those elitist jerks one minute. And then you act all nice and apologetic." He turned back to the rail. "I get nervous sometimes . . . then I overcompensate. Then I feel guilty . . . You get the picture, don't you?"

"Sort of, but you and I have been around each other for a month now. I would think you'd stop being nervous by now." He turned his head with a jerk. "I am most of the time. I just don't spend much time with people, even in the *were* community. I'm a little out of place."

Lisa walked up to him. "You get along fine with your family, and I remember you said that you had been in the military. So you've gotten along with people before?"

Beowulf rolled his eyes and looked back to the ocean. "Yeah . . . but you really don't remind me of them. You know?"

Lisa had a little smile on her face, starting, "Oh . . . so it's just me? I guess I just make you nervous?"

"Okay, fine, yes." He turned to her. And she was quite close behind, now in front of him. "Just you." She stepped even closer. "How do I make *you* so nervous?"

He took a few steps back from her. "I think you know how."

She looked at him and smiled. "Mmm, maybe. I guess I should go back in then?"

He breathed a sigh of relief. "That might be best?"

She jumped and put her arms around his neck, then kissed him strong. After a few seconds, she let him go and walked to the door. "Well . . . you have a nice night. And I'll see you later."

Lisa went in. Sasha saw her come in and looked out the doors window. Her nephew saw her and turned back to the ocean. Sasha grabbed a napkin off the table as she headed for the door. Sasha stood next to him. Both looking around. "Yah know something, little wolf? You a . . . might think about doin' something about that?"

"Huh . . . what?"

"Uh-huh." She threw him the napkin. "You wipe that lipstick off, and it still won't sound believable."

He wiped his mouth. "Oh that. Well—"

Sasha cut him off. "Honey, don't even try. I'm not saying it's the best idea in the world, but when this is over, I'd suggest you recognize a good thing when you see it. But I would be nice about it, or Dad will have your hide." Sasha went back in. Beowulf wiped the sweat off his head and sighed. He leaned on the rail. "Whoa . . . Am I in trouble here?"

The next morning, the captain could see the coastline. Lisa and Nicola were on the deck, taking in the morning air. Remi arrived next with his hangover, taking aspirin and a Bloody Mary. He saw the coast.

"Ah, the next land you see will be France, then Bordeaux, and finally Spain."

Lisa asked Nicola, "Will we be safe in Spain?" But Remi answered, "Aye, cher, we all will. The territory is run by the Ravennas, and they are powerful allies. Till we reach your grandfather's territory."

The morning seemed very slow. If it had not been for the breakfast bell, Lisa thought they wouldn't have seen Bael and Katja. They awoke with a ravenous appetite and rushed to get dressed for breakfast. Everyone was happy for them. A few jokes were made. But they were taken in stride. The rest of their time was spent packing up. Ramon organized everyone. He had called ahead for transportation. Thomas watched as he instructed everyone. What they should take, what they could take. Thomas was getting dizzy watching him go from one person to the next for inspection. Nicola rested in a lounge chair, eyeing his daughters. Ramon bent down to him and whispered to him, "Sir, I was able to reach your brother Alexi, and he will meet you in Barcelona tomorrow at the hotel you requested. He said to tell you that you were right after all."

"Thank you, Ramon."

It was after one o'clock by the time they'd reached Spain. By four they had docked at the port of La Caruna. They said good-bye to Ramon. Thomas shook his hand. "Well . . . I hope to see you again, sir, it's been a pleasure."

"Indeed, sir. I hope things go well for you and your sister."

A bus was waiting to take them to the train station.

At the station, Bael got their tickets. Nicola and Remi went off on their own to talk. Lisa was watching and tried to listen in. But couldn't hear over the trains. Remi put his hand on Nicola's shoulder. "Don't worry, old friend. I promise I'll look after them."

"I know you will. I do. I just want to be there. Bael is ready to do his duty now. I think? Good-bye, my friend."

"Good-bye, Mon'ami."

As everyone boarded their train, Nicola wished them well. He held up Thomas. "You remember what Maliki taught you? You're stronger than you think, and powerful, but use it wisely. Foolish and stupid is what they fear."

Nicola hugged him and put him on the train. Nicola looked around till he spotted Lisa.

Lisa stood back away from the platform. She was hiding her face. He could see she was crying. He bent down to say something, but before he could say a word, she grabbed him around the neck and hugged him tight. He held her as she sobbed into his chest. Her muffled voice. Begging to let her stay. He found a bench and sat down with her. It was quite a sight, but she didn't care. He pulled her chin up lightly to see her. As she looked into his face, she saw that he too had tears in his eyes. "I want you to stay I do, but you can't run from yourself. You are far too brave for that. When you get to their meeting, you will have enemies in the room. Show them who you are. Show them no fear, but let them know your heart. Then their fear will lessen. They are a good people, little one, or how could you come from them." Lisa smiled and hugged him again. Her voice choked as she pulled herself together. "I can't say good-bye to you. You understand, don't you?" He set her on her feet and wiped his eyes. "Go to your train. I'll be with you." He brushed his hand against her necklace. She turned and walked to the train holding her necklace to her heart. As the whistle blew, she jumped and ran to the train steps. She turned and saw him standing tall and proud of her. The train began to move, and she stepped inside to find her seat.

11

The countryside was beautiful as she looked out the window. The towns all had an elegance to them that Lisa found warm. She wished she could stop and look through the shops. As they went through the larger cities, she understood why writers had painted such macabre about them. The cities had the sensation of keeping old secrets. She saw horse-drawn carts in the country. And the gray stones of city buildings. Yet each seemed to have beauty in mind when they were built. The rolling hills and the sun going down made her sleepy. Thomas and Harry were going over spells he had learned at Alec's. Sasha and Katja were talking and occasionally laughing. Lisa thought it was probably about her wedding night. All the while Bael, Maliki, and Remi went over their plans for the meeting. By the time the sun was down, so was Lisa.

They arrived in Romania by eleven forty the next day after changing trains twice. They had gotten sleeper cars for the long ride. Katja woke Lisa and Thomas before the station to refresh themselves with the train's facilities. At one point all Lisa could think about was the warm bath she had at Alec's. Now she had her head under a sink, washing her hair and face. The train had provided nice hair products. Obviously she wasn't the first to do it. Thomas too was having troubles. After washing he had tried putting the beds up and got knocked in the head for his efforts. Only afterward did Bael come in and say that the stewards would put the beds up.

"Thanks" was Thomas's only reply. They joined the others in the club car. Lisa was scrambling for the coffee and Thomas was still rubbing his head. By the time Lisa finished her cup, the train was slowing. They arrived at a small station at the edge of town. What town? Lisa didn't know. Bael grabbed the large backpack again.

"From here it's not far, but there aren't many cars this far in the country and the roads through the mountains weren't made for them. So . . . they all chimed in, "We walk!"

They only got a few feet when they heard the clopping of hooves and saw two horse-drawn carriages coming toward them. In the back of the first carriage was a man with a narrow nose and thin moustache. He had a smile they could see down the street. As it pulled alongside, he almost jumped out of the carriage to see Lisa and Thomas. "I'm so sorry, I wanted to be here when you got off the train, but you arrived early, and I was all thumbs today getting ready." He took a deep breath and calmed himself.

Bael dropped the bag and went to the Thorys' side. "Lisa, Thomas, may I introduce you to your grandfather, Lord Basarab."

The Thorys' bow, and he returned their bow, then he grabbed them up in a group hug. "Oh, how I've waited to see you. Look at you. You"—pointing at Lisa—"are so much like your mother. Even lovelier perhaps. And this is your brother. Though I never met your father, he must have been magnificent to have had a son like you."

Lisa had seen many things since their adventure started, but at their grandfather's words, Thomas began to cry. He had always wanted to know if his father would be proud of him. His grandfather's words were like a song he'd waited too long to hear. His grandfather took him in his arms. "We have always been emotional at family gatherings, my boy, always." He held him and rubbed his back. "Welcome home, Thomas." When he released him at last, Lisa saw her grandfather wipe tears from his eyes as well. She didn't know what was coming at this meeting, but she knew her grandfather would be there for them. Lord Basarab got into the carriage, never letting go of either of them. Bael was told to get in with them, and Katja took the seat next to him. The others got into the other carriage. As Beowulf, Maliki, and Remi got into the carriage, the horse could sense the animals within them. It took a moment or two before it had settled enough to follow.

Thomas and Lisa were happy to find that their family was glad to see them. Bael though had other matters on his mind. "Have you heard from Lord Montgomery? I don't know what he's up too, but he's not working alone."

"It's funny you should mention him. Your trip has lost you some information. Right now Montgomery is sitting in his cell, waiting for the meeting. And on his way here, he has misplaced his title. Though the king and queen of the Magyars aren't hopeful, it shall ever be found. However, after the meeting, I have been told that a title will be filled. So Montgomery will be the one advocating their demise at the meeting."

Bael sat back and thought about what he's just heard. "But without his title, how can he be heard by the royals?"

"Oh, he was given special dispensation to go against you. Knowing of course what that would mean for him in the end. So yes, he must think he has an awfully big ace up that sleeve of his."

As they reached the castle, both of the Thorys were amazed. It was beautiful. Outside the stone walls were gardens of flowers and small buildings surrounded by trestles with flowers running down them. Next to the wall was a stone building with an iron gate for its door. Through an archway to a main yard they went. People were busy all around them. They stopped at an enclosed archway the doors were opened to a hall of beige gold and white with a burgundy rug on the floor with patterns of flowers woven throughout. There grandfather was telling them about the castle as they walked through. At the end of the hall were huge doors. Which were opened by servants of some kind. Inside was a grand ballroom with red and gold patterns on a few walls. The ceiling was white with intercut shapes in them. Everything was beautiful and busy. It was then that Lord Basarab informed them that he was having a ball in their honor tonight. They were introduced to their handmaid and valet. "They will see you to your rooms and that you are properly attired for the party.

When Lisa got to her room, she felt like Cinderella. The wardrobe, the canopy bed, the huge mirror. She was excited about the whole idea of a ball. Then she stopped as she saw herself in the mirror; she had been fingering her necklace faster and faster. As wonderful as it all was, she wanted her tiger, she thought. She sat on the bed missing Nicola. In the new world, she had become a part of his as he was hers. He made her feel secure.

The handmaid made sure of her size and brought her an assortment of dresses and apparel. When she announced that her bath was ready, Lisa turned to her. "Show me the way, please!" She bathed in the hot water far longer than she should have. When she got out, the maid had everything ready. Lisa was dressed so quickly and then her hair was fixed. Her maid was amazing. Lisa looked at herself again. She couldn't believe it was her reflection. She saw the maid in the mirror behind her. "Are you a . . . human or vampire? "

"Human, madam."

"You don't mind working for vampires?"

"Ma'am?" She smiled at Lisa. "We here at the castle have worked under Lord Basarab for many generations. He has seen that we are clothed, educated, and has been kinder at times than many of our own family. While I should be more formal. I will say I would rather be here than anywhere, ma'am." Minutes later there was a knock on the door. Thomas and her grandfather were waiting in the hall with a corsage to escort her to the ball.

The music playing below was more old-fashioned than she would have preferred, but the room was filled with people much older than they looked. She reminded herself. Her grandfather laughed as they walked. She looked up at his face. "You're reading my mind?"

"I do apologize. I wanted to know what you thought of our home." She and Thomas both laughed. "I guess if I could, I would to." Lisa and her family were at the top of the stairs when a man at the bottom announced them. "Lord Basarab, Lady Elisabeth, and Master Thomas Thory!"

All eyes turned to them as they walked down the staircase. Halfway down, the people began to clap. Thomas in his tux and Lisa in her light blue gown, the white lace accents, framing her as they walked down. At the bottom of the stairs, she saw a familiar face or faces, Peter and David Ravenna.

"Miss Thory, you are truly a vision." David bowed and stepped back as his brother continued his banter with Lisa. "If I may, after the procession, I would love to introduce you to some of the other

guests. In the meantime, I would like you to meet our sister Valarie."
Peter brought his sister forward. Lisa bowed to her, and she bowed
in response. Lady Ravenna did take her in though. David came from
behind her. "I told you you'd like her. When have you met another
with her presence?"

"She does seem to have a spark, doesn't she?"

Lisa and Thomas walked down the presentation row with their
grandfather. One after another, they met the tribal royals. Finally,
they were taken before three individuals sitting down in lavish chairs.
Their grandfather snapped his heels and bowed. "Queen Lilith, I
would like you to meet my grandchildren, the Thorys: Lady Elisavetta
and Master Thomas Thory."

"I have heard so much about you two over the last month or
so. The Ravennas were especially taken with you, my dear, and I see
why." The queen waved her hand for the others to stand. "This is the
king of the Magyars, King Draugur, and his wife, the queen. They
have been most interested in seeing you as well." They stood and
bowed. The men returned the bow. Lisa returned hers in a curtsy and
bowed. Queen Lilith looked and studied the children. She looked
deep within Lisa and smiled. She did the same to Thomas. "The
Ravennas were right," she thought to herself. She looked at Lord
Basarab and he nodded.

They took their place at the long table in front of the dance
floor. Again and again, they met the families. Lisa fingering her necklace when she felt someone had sat beside her. Bael and the others
had shown up and sat beside them. With her friends around her. She
began to relax more.

Sitting in a hotel room in Barcelona, Nicola waits as he started
to get up to pace again. There's a knock at the door. As he opened
it, his brother pushes in and hugs him. Nicola greeted his brother in
an embrace. "I'm glad to see you, Alexi. Right now I'm a bundle of
nerves."

"Why, what is wrong? I had heard that you were helping Lord
Bael with the transportation of vampires, and he met with some
problems, but you're here, and they're there all should be well."

"Alexi, my brother, you don't understand. The little ones we brought are still in danger. They'll go before the royals soon." Alexi looked at his brother with a question in his face. "What are these vampires to you?"

"They are not vampires yet. They have been brought there for the choice and for judgment. They are marks! And I fear for them."

"If they're marks, then there is nothing to fear. For they won't be allowed to exist. You know how the vampires are about that?"

Nicola turned to Alexi with tears in his eyes. "That is the problem, Alexi. I love them too much to let them go, especially my Elisavetta. She is as family to my heart." Alexi noticed his brother's hands as his emotions heightened and his claws extended. As Nicola paced, he began to change, not to the tiger but to the form in between.

His brother went to his side and held him. "Nicola, calm yourself. You must calm down. The vam . . . the marks or children will be fine, I'm sure. They *are* under Lord Bael's protection."

Nicola slowly reverted to himself again. "That dammed Montgomery. I would have his head if I were there."

Alexi began to laugh. "You definitely should relax. You haven't heard? Lord Montgomery is no more. He has been stripped by the king of the Magyars of his title and denounced to stand alone. Everyone is talking about how the queen herself wants his head." He laughs a little more.

Nicola knew that someone else is was behind Montgomery and wondered what might happen now. "So who will be advocating the charges against the children?"

"Oh, that's the best part. Montgomery was granted dispensation to charge your marks, but without his title, no one will hear the charges!" Alexi held his laughter back. "At the end of their trial, chances are, Montgomery is dead."

Nicola sat back in his chair, stunned by his brother's news. "Whoever was behind him could not have thought of that? What will happen now?" he thought.

At the ball, the celebration of the children's arrival was going as Lord Basarab had hoped. More and more of the families were talking to the children, getting to know them. The Queen and Lord Basarab were syncing out the room. Worries were settling. The ball was a success.

Lisa felt a tap on her shoulder, but there was no one there. She felt it again. As she looked behind her, she noticed a woman slightly hidden behind drapes. She felt a pulling sensation. Lisa excused herself for a moment to her grandfather and went to see the woman. Queen Lilith watched as she left.

Outside the party stood the woman. Lisa remembered the dress; it was Lady Ravenna. Lisa walked to her. "I was wondering if would be able to reach you or not," said Lady Ravenna.

"I wasn't sure what I felt was real?"

"That's the point, Elisabeth, my dear. You can be reached. Sorcerers can't be reached at all, but you can. That will serve you well at your hearing or trial. I must admit my brothers were right. You do have something as does your brother. I think most of the families here have been won over by you two."

"And what about you?"

The lady turned away. "Half a month ago, I wanted you dead. You're a mark, and that was that. But my brothers couldn't stop saying how you had my spark." She turned quickly. "My flame. Oh, they never told me, but I hear far more than I let on. And I got more and more curious about you both. Then the queen I found was defending you in conversations. I was shocked. Then I met you at the stairs. I couldn't believe it. My brothers were right. I liked you immediately. I went through you to see if I could. And I do apologize for that. You will have to be taught how to resist being gone through, but it was difficult, most wouldn't have been able to. I promise I won't do it again, at least not without your permission."

While Lisa didn't like being *gone through*, she had to admit to herself that she too liked this woman. She did seem like a friend. Then she thought about her, knowing her plans. Before Lisa could say anything, Valarie saw her face. "Don't worry, Elisabeth. I understand, and I know how to keep a secret."

"Thank you, and please call me Lisa."

"I am Valarie. I cannot do it now, but I'll teach you how to guard against us going through you. Right now, it is best that they can a little. It will be another thing in your favor during your trial. Trust me. Right now, in many ways, the trial has already started. Your grandfather wanted to show you off for many reasons. One of which is to win over the families. They've all been watching you both since you arrived. And I don't know if you noticed, but he is more than a little proud of you both."

"Yeah, that much I figured out, without being able to read people."

"I just wanted you to know, they were watching, so you'd be careful. I . . . uh, oh, someone is looking for you. You better get back."

Lisa headed back to the table. When she heard in her head, "Good luck."

She returned to the table and started to sit down. When she's taken by the hand, startled, she found Beowulf standing there. "I thought you might care to dance?"

She smiled and nodded.

On the dance floor, he took her by the waist and hand. He led her in the waltz. They glided around the floor, circling each other, barely aware of the other guests. The band played another song, and they continued to dance.

Bael and Lord Basarab were looking on. For Bael, a lightbulb had lit in his head. For Lord Basarab, a certain concern. He looked to the queen. She smiled and gave her nod of approval. Bael however was slightly less enthused. But as he watched them, he saw they were happy. He started to rise, until a hand held him down, Katja shook her finger at him. "Leave them be." He settled back in his chair.

Beowulf felt a tap to his shoulder. Paul Ravenna stood and gave a slight bow. "May I cut in?"

Beowulf turned to Lisa; she nodded, and he bowed. Paul took her hand and continued the dance. Shortly followed by David Ravenna and then by others. For an hour or more, she danced, and Thomas as well had found quite a few dance partners. The evening wore on, and all were having a fine time. A chime sounded, and they all went to the dinner table. Each place was assigned. The food was brought from the kitchen in terrines on carts. The food was amazing. Each item better than the one before. As one cart was returning to the kitchen, it had snagged on the carpet and fell over. The heat canister from below rolled to a wall where it lit one of the drapes. The servants rushed to put it out. But the flame reduced in size before they could reach it. It was then that everyone noticed the flame was moving, slowly across the floor. Thomas stood by the side of the table. The flame was responding to his control.

Thomas went and picked up the small flame from the floor. As he turned, smiling, he saw the guests with worried looks on their faces. Thomas extinguished the flame and returned to the table. His grandfather patted him on the back. "Thank you, Thomas. Someone could have gotten hurt by the fire. Well done." Thomas felt as though he had done the wrong thing, but he felt he had to put out the flames.

After a while the guests could see that he had merely tried to do what he could to protect the guests. Some had indeed thought that his powers might be considered an asset, but many had concerns.

When the party was over, Lisa informed Thomas of the problems they were facing. His grandfather was still proud and defended Thomas. "He did what anyone would. He saved the guests." He looked at Thomas. "You did fine, my boy. Don't let anyone tell you different. You saved lives." He hugged them both. "I'll see you both in the morning. For now, sleep well."

Lisa and Thomas went to their rooms. As their doors closed, Lord Basarab's face changed to concern. He walked down the hall, shaking his head. He knew that some of his plans had been undone.

Down in the crypt, Lord Basarab again made a plea to their mother. "Elisa, your children are here, and they are wonderful, but there are those trying to destroy what is ours. What is yours! Please. I know you hear me. Your senses *must* hear their hearts beat. Your mind hear their very thoughts. Please awaken from this darkness. They need you."

Below the soil their mother's body lay still. Her body, white and hard. No blood flows, no air had it breathed; she had gone down. Lord Basarab now waited and listened. He could he hear the insects that moved about the soil? He could hear the guard's footsteps around the chamber in the castle, but from their mother, he could hear nothing.

The next morning, Thomas woke and went to his sister's room. She was still sleeping from last night's party. He noticed her hand was holding and fingering her necklace like a nervous habit. He realized why; Bael had power and strength, but Nicola was who made her feel safe. He left the room and went to find Sasha.

Down the stairs, he heard voices coming from the hallway. He followed them until he was at the doors to the ballroom. He looked inside and saw Bael and his grandfather talking with the queen and others from the party. From what he could hear, they were trying to figure out how to undo the damage of him using his magic the night before.

One of the servants came and whispered to his grandfather. He excused himself and left with the servant. Thomas raced around to another hall where his grandfather walked with the servant. He followed as far back as he could. The servant pointed down a stairwell and left him. His grandfather went down the stairs and disappeared down another hall. Thomas went after him and, after a few minutes, found him. He was talking far too quietly for him to hear. As he got closer, he saw Master Maris. He saw them shaking hands. Then he was gone. Thomas crept away till he found the stairs up; he ran till he found Bael and told him what he saw. "It'll be all right, Thomas. I'm sure whatever Maris said to him was taken with a grain of salt."

"A note came from the queen. It told him the meeting would begin in a few hours. Prepare the children to the procedures of the meeting."

Bael got the children together and brought them down to the chamber. "When the meeting starts, you will stand here behind the podium. The royals will be seated in the chairs there around the top. The queen will sit in the thrones here in front. Your grandfather will be seated first seat to her right. Montgomery will be seated in the boxed area next to the podium." The children nodded and continued to listen.

"First, the meeting will be called to order. Then Montgomery will make his charges. Say nothing to the charges. Because once he's made his charges, he can't add to them. If you say something and he's reminded of another charge, it will have to be addressed."

"So you're saying we should keep our mouths shut?" Bael put his finger to his nose.

"Montgomery will try to goad you into speaking out of turn, forfeiting your right to defend yourselves. If you think you're getting mad, look at the royals. As Montgomery has lost his title, you'll notice that they will be trying not to hear him. However, they must hear you. So don't get upset by what he says. After the charges are done, he will make his case to the queen. When he's finished, the queen will ask you what you have as defense of the charges. You tell her you have an advocate and witnesses as well as your testimony. From there, you can say what you like, but not till she asks you. Understood?"

The children nodded and stay quiet.

12

The royals entered the chamber and took their seats. The queen and Lord Basarab entered and bowed to the royals. Lord Basarab remained standing while the queen sat.

"I thank the families for this meeting to verify and, hopefully, welcome my human descendants to our tribes. Before they may join our families, I have heard that there are charges to be addressed. So let us hear these charges now and, if possible, lay them to rest. Again, I thank you."

The Thorys were brought in, and they stood at the podium. Montgomery entered and took his seat in the box. In the wings behind the children wait the witnesses.

The queen looks to Montgomery. "You may proceed."

Montgomery sat back in his chair. "Before I begin my charges, who will stand for the defendants?"

The queen had hoped he would forget or forgo that step. She waited for an answer. Montgomery smiles. "Are there no vampires willing to stand for these . . . a . . . defendants? Then I'm afraid this meeting must be dropped and the charges be instated." Before the queen could say anything, a voice from behind the children was heard.

"I stand for them." Into the chamber walks Remi and stands by the podium. Montgomery bangs his gavel. "My queen, this is an outrage! This meeting is of the tribes and families, this werebeast cannot stand for them."

Remi stood tall and opened his shirt to reveal the bite marks from a vampire. "I am Remi Pasquenelle married to Michelle Rosette Juene' of the house of Lorient and tribe Vampyr. As her husband, I invoke my rights."

The queen looks to the Lorient family. "Is this true?"

"Michelle Juene' was of our house, and the marriage was performed by Father Sebastian. He was bitten and has the right." Remi bowed to his family.

The queen smiles wide at Montgomery. "Master Remi Pasquenelle stands for the Thorys. Your motion is denied. The meeting will continue. Proceed with your charges." Montgomery sneered at Remi. "Yes, my queen. The charges are that the defendants are not just human but have the mark of sorcery upon them. As vampires cannot affect sorcery, they cannot be made vampires. Just as sorcerers cannot be affected by vampires will. This makes them a danger to our race. One cannot be both. It is against the laws of the tribe. As well as all the other races of the realms. As their blood holds the abilities to be of our race. This too put us in danger. Furthermore, there is no proof that they are truly of Basarab decent? We have seen no line here. What we have here are abominations. It was set into law long ago for good reason. The races have no effect on each other to prevent chaos and war between the races. As such, they must be destroyed. They are marks, and as hard as it is for Lord Basarab, there is no other choice." Montgomery looked around the room, so few of the tribes were listening at all.

Suddenly, a throat cleared. Master Maris tapped his Gavel. The queen is shocked. "You have a question, Master Maris?"

"I do, Your Highness. I know he should not be heard in this chamber, but I make it a point to hear as much as I can from all sources. It's my failing. So I have a question."

Montgomery smiles; his agreement with Maris had paid off. The others must listen while he'd ask and the answer given.

The queen had no choice. "Very well. Ask your question."

Maris looked down at Montgomery's face happy at winning his right to be heard. "Montgomery, what if it were possible, even legitimately confirmed, that they were the first and only marks that were legal. That they could be both. And yet have no effect on the other races. That would be a third choice. Would it not?"

"But that's not possible. That is why the law was put in place."

"I see, of course. In that case, the Thorys must be destroyed. You are certainly in the right."

With that the royal families had heard Montgomery they would have to make a judgment. The queen looked at him as he smiled. "Have you any further charges?"

"No, Your Highness."

"Does the advocate have a statement?" Remi stepped forward. "Not at this time."

"Do you have any defense of these charges, Mr. and Miss Thory?"

"Yes, Your Highness. We have our own testimony as well as witnesses, and I'm sure by then our advocate will have a statement as well. There is also physical evidence as well."

"Very well. Make your case and call your witnesses."

Remi stood behind the Thorys, his hands on their shoulders. "As our first witness, I would call Lord Bael to the chamber."

From the hallway, Bael walked. Lisa hadn't noticed before, but in his walk, he seemed to walk as a prince. He had nobility in his step. He took his place between the Thorys and the queen. Remi began his questioning. "Lord Bael, how long have you known the Thory family and their lineage?"

"Well, over a thousand years now. It was before Lord Basarab became a vampire. He had settled the region through many battles. His wife and children were brought here when peace had been achieved. His child was Lydia and his daughter's line married into the Tepes family line. Decades before an emissary from the south had visited, and she had brought the Basarab name to the tribes, he brought his son-in-law Lord Tepes, but his daughter remained human. Their children were taken in secret out of the territory to keep safe due to a new war. Lord Tepes was betrayed, and his wife lied to. At which time she died. At the death of his son-in-law, Lord Basarab had his line kept secret till, as the law states, they reach their twenty-third year and are given the choice."

Montgomery, sounding superior, cut in, "If the children of his line were taken in secret, how can you be sure these children are even related?"

"*Because* I was the one who took them away. I in turn gave them to a blackthorn for safekeeping. She is still alive if you would care to ask her?"

"Enough of the Basarab history. I will concede their lineage. But they are still illegal abominations."

Remi thanks Lord Bael and dismissed him.

Two men entered the palace. They walked in from the storm that had arisen suddenly. At the gate, the guards were made to stop and kneel as the two continue inside. Their faces hidden by the rain.

Remi called his next witness. "I call Henrietta Murry to the chamber."

She strolled into the chamber as if ready for a fight. Remi addressed the queen, "Your Highness, I have been informed that this witness has information for the court to address the issue of their legitimacy. What the information is I have not been told."

Shocked again, the queen waves her hand. "Very well. Miss Murry is known to this body. Please proceed with your testimony."

"Thank you . . . Before their mother made her choice, she had met and fallen in love with her husband. Two secrets were kept. One was hers. That she may one day have to choose the vampire race. The other was his, that he was in fact the sorcerer, Thomas Oaken. At the time of their second child being born. The time of making the choice had already passed by a few years, that was when she told her husband her secret. He too gave her the truth about himself. The children were too young to have their marks visible. What happened to their father is on record to all. And their mother's fate is known to all here as well.

"The blackthorn that watched over the babies kept their marks secret from all but me. She had me find out how it could be that they were not Vampiric or sorcerer but seemed to have both abilities. After several dead ends, I went to the watchers. After some coaxing, they told me why it was and what it was. No one knew Thomas Oaken's lineage, not even he knew the truth. In his veins ran a unique blood. He was a descendent of Albrecht, 'the Dwarf.' His only heir."

The royals were at the edge of their seats, listening to her tale.

"You see, it's his ancient bloodline that let both exist in harmony. It will never happen again. For they are the last."

The queen and royals were stunned. What to do next? they had no idea. The queen looked at, Bael but could see that he didn't know either. The royals began to talk among themselves till the queen brought the chamber to order. "This case will have to be rethought before we can go on."

Finally, the Thorys spoke up. Thomas cleared his throat. "Your Highness, if I may, I think our testimony may solve your problem. If we may present it?"

The queen looked to the royals as they gave Thomas and Lisa their full attention.

"If you can clear this mess, by all means, please continue."

Thomas let his sister take over. "Your Highness and royal families, our journey here has been long, and we have learned much along the way. Most of which has been in the last few minutes. However, it was suggested that we take certain steps to make easier our acceptance here with you. We were allowed to go before the Paragon stone to affirm what we were to ourselves and to you." The information hit the royals and the queen like an ice-cold wind.

Montgomery was hit the hardest of all. He took to his feet. "Your Majesty, the Paragon stone is nothing but a myth. It doesn't exist. And without taking us to it, there's no proof."

The queen knew the truth, but there was no one to second her knowledge. She had to rule despite what she knew. Before she made her ruling, a voice from behind her spoke.

"The Paragon stone is as real as all vampires are." The voice was deep and had a power to it. A tall man came from the shadows and sat in the throne next to the queen, throwing one leg over its arm. The royals were outraged that he had taken a throne. The queen stood and raised her hands for silence.

"My lords and ladies, though he has never taken his place before, I assure you, the throne is his. This, lords and ladies, is his lordship, King Ea Bani, my king."

Bael could see an outline of a man behind Ea Bani's throne. He was here. The one pulling the strings. The man saw him as well and smiled. Montgomery was pleased at his master's arrival. In his mind, he now had the children. He would kill them himself. Within his robes, he felt for his knife. Yes, he would kill these abominations for his master.

As his dark thoughts whirled through his mind, at another part of the castle, deep and dark itself, a heart beat. One beat, then a moment later, another. As his thoughts turned to rage over what had happened to himself over these insignificant children, his own breathing deepened. He nodded to his master and moved from the box.

At the other end of the castle, the heart beat, and black blood coursed through veins. Suddenly, eyes opened white. As Montgomery moved closer to Lisa, his knife in his hand beneath his robe, in a single motion, he moved in front of her and pulled his blade.

Through the halls there was a movement yet nothing was seen. No breath taken, no eye could have seen, not even the eye of a god. As Montgomery's blade swung, he was pulled back, hit by a force that pulled him apart, leaving only his blood in the air. Standing in his place, soaked in his blood was their mother, the Lady Elisa.

Lisa and Thomas were shocked and slightly splattered. The woman in front of them was facing away from them, her hands red with blood. At her feet were what remained of Montgomery in pools and slivers. The Lady Elisa stared past the thrones. Her voice dry, she whispered, "So much for the believer."

Bael, Katja, Sasha, Beowulf, and Harry came running in when they heard the royals all gasp and go silent. Bael hadn't seen the Lady Elisa for years and certainly not in her current state. He didn't recognize her. As he grabbed her arm, even with his strength, she was able to remove his hand as she stepped toward the thrones.

She at last took a breath, her first in two decades. She bowed to the king and queen as drops of blood fell from her hair.

"I believe, Your Highness . . . you were going . . . to make a . . . judgment?"

King Ea Bani took no heed from her tone or her actions. "No, my lady, I merely commented on the validity of a certain stone.

However, if a judgment on the Thorys' legality is what you're asking for, I'm not sure you'd care for my opinion."

The man behind the throne stayed in the shadows, smiling. Montgomery was a useful tool, but his end wouldn't change the outcome here. He had stacked this deck with more than a joker. He had the king and an ace. He had brought the winning hand. The man from the shadows could hardly hold back his laughter in his triumph.

Bael faced the king. "Lord Ea Bani, we have never met I am . . ."

"I know who you are, Lord Bael, but this is not a matter for you. Though your help in bringing them here is appreciated, I'm afraid you have no voice past that of a witness." He turned to Queen Lilith. "Am I correct, my queen? I have been away for some time." She closed her eyes and nodded. "I thought as much. Please, Lord Bael, take your place, but be silent during the proceeding."

Paul Ravenna hit his gavel to be recognized. "Sir, I'm afraid you as well should have no voice here. While we are glad to have you back among us, our laws say you must be present for other meetings during the year to preside here today. You have not."

Ea Bani bowed and smiled. "I know the law you speak of. However, again, due to the circumstances of special dispensation by the queen, the rule doesn't apply any more. Despite the fact that person is no longer here. I too know our laws as I wrote most of them."

Bael could see his plan had not worked as he had planned. Ea Bani turned to the Thorys. "I'm sorry, my dear, I believe you were saying something about the Paragon stone before you were interrupted."

Lisa could see by Bael's and the queen's expression that all had gone wrong. Lisa now splattered with Montgomery's blood was nervous and swallowed to get her voice back. "Yes . . . Your Highness. My brother and I went there to be affirmed by the stone."

"I see. And what happened?"

"We were affirmed, sir."

"Do you have any proof of this affirmation by the stone?" Lisa and Thomas pulled open their shirts to reveal the marks made by the stone. Ea Bani leaned forward to see the marks as did every vampire in the room. The queen herself had not been made aware of the marks.

The king looked around the room to the royals, each family knowing that the marks of the stone were real. King Ea Bani stared down at the marks. "Truly amazing, Miss Thory, and I must admit that usually those marks would have turned this body's judgment around. But you see, I'm afraid that is not the case. You see, I must also admit that I came here with my judgment already committed. Though I did want to hear your side of things to perhaps change my mind." He shook his head. "Nothing at these proceedings have altered that judgment. You see, even though I've been away from our people, I've stayed very well informed." The man in the shadows fell back deeper into the dark. He smiled, waiting for the king to deliver the bad news.

The king continued, "You see, I've known of your family line in the tribes as well as the others. I don't believe in surprises. I was the victim of one once. It's never happened again."

The king rose from his throne and asked for the queen's hand to join him. They stepped toward the Thorys. The king looked at the Lady Elisa, and she stood straight and bowed. "So you, see I've known you were both legal and legitimate, far before I was approached by Lord Ninurta here." He pointed to the shadows where a man stood. A very shocked and angry man, whose identity, was at last known.

Bael understood at last who and perhaps why this had taken place. Ninurta, the Samarian god of war, who had caused the death of so many demigods over the millennia. But he had failed to defeat his father in battle long ago. He was the one who had manipulated Loki and Aries as well as so many others. And why? To get put in a position to use his weapon against the gods themselves. Bael reached back toward the hall. From the bag that Ramon had packed came movement within. Then it came to him, the sword of his father's. Naegling, the sword his father said, would always protect him. Bael's father had taught him well how to use it. How to win the battle when it came. The stone had brought all those memories back with clarity he had not had since he was a child.

The king raised his hands. "There will be no battle here amongst anyone but the tribes, gentlemen. Take your fight elsewhere."

The king walked back to the shadows. "In the future, if you have one. Never forget this moment. Vampires aren't puppets. We do not manipulate well. You had lost before we met. My mother was in so many ways the goddess Ea. We have been ready for you. You should have stuck with your own kind."

Ninurta grasped his weapon at his side. "You'll pay for this, Bani. I'll see to it." The king laughed. "You're not even sure about the next few minutes. Learn to focus. It could cost you your life."

Bael stepped forward. "Where would you like to finish this, Ninurta?"

Ninurta came from the shadows, and as a portal appeared, he pointed down it. "After you."

Bael walked into the portal, followed by Ninurta. Lisa started to follow but was stopped by the king. "It's not your fight, child. It's Bael's. Have faith that he'll win." The portal closed. Lisa looked back at Harry. Harry nodded to her. Lisa looked up at the king. "The hell it ain't." She ducked under his arm and raised her hand as the portal reappeared. Lisa, Katja, and Beowulf ran through as it closed.

On the other side, the battle had already started. Each hitting harder than the last. Bael with his sword and Ninurta with a kind of bladed mace. Back and forth, the blows went, then Beowulf noticed something moving behind the fight. From out of the trees came the surviving Fenris wolf and behind him was another. They charged before anyone could move. Bael swung and missed one and nicked the other, but was cut by the blade of the mace.

Beowulf grabbed Katja and turned to Lisa. "We'll hold the wolves. See if you can help Dad! With that they changed to the halflings, giving them the most strength and speed. They attacked the wolves head-on. Lisa watched as Bael fought on, holding his left arm back as it was bleeding.

Bael swung fast and battled well. He had struck home with his sword, but the wound was superficial. In a bold maneuver, Ninurta rammed forward and struck Bael's sword at the same time, knocking Bael down to the ground and the sword from his hand. As Ninurta came for the final blow, Lisa grabbed the handle of the sword, but found it wouldn't move. Ninurta laughed. "You thought that sword would work for you? Stupid child, you're not a demigod." As he swung his mace, it's met by the blade. "No, I'm family!" She held the blade, shaking in her hand.

Bael was lying on the ground heard his father's voice in his head. "What do knights do?" He rolled over and took the sword from Lisa. "Haven't you learnt anything? Stick to your own kind before she kicks your ass."

Meanwhile, Beowulf and Katja were fighting the wolves. Katja was circling the wolf when it jumped past her to get at Bael. She turned and jumped herself. As she hit the wolf, her teeth and claws plunged deep into its neck and throat, twisting its body; she pulled it down, though still alive. Beowulf saw the animal down and moved in to take it from her. He stepped back and grabbed with both hands at its head, as the other came in for another attack.

As Katja released her grip. The wolf's neck broke under Beowulf's hands. Katja ran at the other wolf. Beowulf tried to stop her, but she was at full stride. The wolf was at the perfect angle for a kill. When Bael rolled away from Ninurta to throw his sword at the wolf, striking its chest and pinning it to the ground, he held out his hand as the blade returned.

Ninurta saw the wolves were dead. Though Bael was injured, he wondered if he had enough advantage. Bael returned to the fight while the others watched on. Ninurta reached for his dagger and threw it at Lisa so hard to distract Bael.

But Bael caught the knife. And before Ninurta could open a portal, he grabbed his arm. As Ninurta turned, Bael swung the blade, piercing his head and continued down. He was dead. Bael pulled the blade from the body. He felt no joy at the victory. He did what had to be done to protect those he loved. Nothing more.

Lisa came up, hugging and kissing him. Then Katja joined in. Bael was hurt, but would mend fast enough.

As his son walked up, a breeze came up and brought his father and grandfather along with it. Both Beowulfs congratulated him. His father patted his back. "I knew you could do it, son, and I'm proud of the way you handled it as well. We do this because it's our duty, not for pleasure." His grandfather Baal as well was proud of him.

Bael finally looked back at the body on the ground. "I just want to go home with my family." Bael opened the portal and walked back with them, leaving his father and grandfather behind.

Baal turned the body to dust. "He did well, didn't he?"

He walked to his son. "Yes, I truly have never been so proud."

"He's a good and strong man and demigod."

"He'll have to be more than that to face what's coming." Baal put his hand on Beowulf's shoulder. "I hope he never finds out that you set this all up for him."

"He can't. He just killed the only one who could have given him any clue." And then they disappeared in the wind.

13

They returned to Basarab's castle, Thomas, Harry, and Sasha. All waiting for news. Lord Basarab had nearly worn out the rug pacing. When they came back and told what had happened, everyone was elated that it was over. Lisa and Thomas were happy to take some time to get to know their grandfather better and to just relax for a while.

It was hours later when their grandfather asked them to come to the library. The valet brought them down and showed them to the right room. He bowed and then curiously he left. Thomas pushed open the door, then knocked slightly on the door.

"Hello, Grandfather?" They entered the room. Their grandfather sat in a large chair. Looking out the window was a woman. Lisa took a moment till she realized it was the woman from the chamber, the one who stopped Montgomery. She had cleaned up and was wearing a beautiful dress.

It wasn't until she turned around that Lisa recognized her. Thomas had never seen her before, but knew there was something familiar about her. Lisa was both happy and angry, relieved but sad. Her emotions were so mixed that she couldn't raise a tear.

Their grandfather stood up and told them to come in. All of sudden, the Thorys were nervous. As they got closer, Lisa started getting dizzy. Then Lord Basarab began to introduce the woman. "Elisavetta, Thomas, I don't know if you remember her, but this is Elisa Oaken, your mother."

It was just too much for Lisa. She was tired, and it had been the longest morning on record for them. Lisa was overwhelmed and passed out again. Thomas managed to catch her and get her to the couch.

Thomas turned to his mother. "Not to be rude, but it might help if you had an iris and pupil." His mother gasped; she hadn't realized what the time below had done to her. She was as white as paper. Lord Basarab called for his servant. "Klaus blut!"

The servant ran from the room and returned with several packs of blood. Which the Lady Elisa consumed in seconds. As she drank, her eyes began to show color, and her skin to soften. By the fifth pack, her eyes were a violet blue. Her face was easily recognized by Thomas. She continued to drink till the tray was empty. Klaus removed the tray and waited. Then Lord Basarab waved him away. When her mother looked more herself, he began to wake Lisa.

Sasha was on the phone listening to it ring on the other side. Finally, Nicola picked up the receiver. "Father, it's Sasha. It's over, and they're fine. We'll be spending a few days here, then we'll come back to get you." Nicola was relieved to hear the good news. "What about Montgomery?"

"There is no Montgomery. Lisa has a little over a week till she chooses. We'll be here till then." Nicola had nothing more to say. "That's fine, Sasha. I'll be waiting for you. Thank you for calling and letting me know." Then he hung up. Sasha knew what was bothering him; it bothered her too.

Bael, Beowulf, and Remi were sitting with Katja, Maliki, and Harry in Bael's room, talking over the events of the morning. Ninurta's death and the battle of the wolves versus the tigers. Remi was impressed that Katja could take down a Fenris wolf by herself. Beowulf too seemed surprised when she pulled it down the way she did. Katja just sat there. "I don't know what to tell you. I just had a surge of strength. My adrenaline, I guess."

Bael sat, deep in thought for a moment. Then a look took over his face. Everyone was a bit puzzled. Bael took Katja by the hand. "I know why you were able to take it down. I'm a fool for not noticing till now."

Katja waited. "Well, don't keep us in suspense. Tell us!" He kissed her cheek and looked into her eyes. "My love, you're pregnant." Katja sat back, stunned.

Remi and Maliki nodded. "Of course, we should have guessed. Congratulations, you two." They started their congratulations when Sasha came back to the room. She was shocked as well. No one had noticed that Katja was looking pale. Sasha shook it off and went to Katja. "You all right, sis?"

Katja nodded. "Yeah, I just a . . . need a minute to process this." She thought about it again and again, Bael was right. She was pregnant. Somehow, she knew it.

Lisa was coming to as she saw her brother Thomas standing over her. "What happened?"

"You did it again. You saw Mom. It was a little more than you could take. And plop, down you went."

"Oh yeah, right. Mom?" With a little help, she sat up and cleared her head, keeping her eyes closed. She took a few deep breaths and opened her eyes. It was her mother. She stood in front of her on the verge of tears.

Lisa didn't know how to feel about seeing her. She didn't know what to say. Lisa turned to Thomas. "I need a drink."

"Sure." He started pouring some water into a glass. "Thomas, I think you can do a wee bit better than that, huh?"

"Oh, you need a drink, duh?" He changed glasses and set it in front of her. She drank faster than her mother did.

"Okay. I'm sorry, Mother, but I'm just not that glad to see you. You left so long ago. I don't remember you that well and Thomas not at all. So I don't know what I'm supposed to do here?" Lisa could see she'd hurt her. "Mother, I understand being sad about losing Father. I do. But you made us lose both our parents. And we faced it, lived through it. We had Aunt Lucile, but you should have been there. We thought you were dead and mourned you. Now all that was a lie. You were still alive and not wondering about us. You were still mourning Father alone. Thank you for stopping Montgomery, but I'm confused at how I'm supposed to feel."

Thomas had stayed quiet for his sister. He had a different opinion. "Mom, I know Lisa's right in a lot of ways, but even though I never met you, I've missed my mother." He came around Lisa and hugged his mother. She kissed and held him. Her true voice was returning as she whispered to him how much she loved and missed him. When they were finished, his mother went to Lisa and took her hand.

They sat down together. "Elisavetta, you don't have all the story."

Lisa looked at her mother, hoping she could explain. Her mother smiled as though she knew what she had thought. As she had. "When your father passed away, I had already passed my time to choose to try and raise you and your brother was on the way. You were three when I first noticed the light mark on your hand. I had been looking for it, hoping it wouldn't be there, but it had. I called Lucile and explained what I had to do. I came to your grandfather and made the choice. With my husband gone, I was depressed. But that was not why I went down. The tribes could read my thoughts, and if they had known about you then, you could not defend yourself, nor could I. When I went down, my thoughts could not be read, but after a while, I could hear the thoughts of all who entered the castle."

Lisa was trying to put her puzzle together in her own head. She remembered Lucile, but her memories of her mother were tainted by anger. They just seemed muddled. Of course, she was only three at the time.

Her mother continued to explain, "Lisa, Lucile told Bael I had left because of my depression. But I was trying to give you both time. Time to live, grow, and develop your mind, your bodies, and your gifts." Lisa realized what she was saying made sense. That was why Bael didn't know about the marks until after we arrived. Why Lucile never told anyone but Harry; she couldn't be read or gone through.

"I had to stay down until it didn't matter."

Lisa at last understood. Her feelings welled up as she grabbed up her mom. Holding her and crying, Lisa had her mother back. After a few minutes passed, Lisa stopped and had a panicked look on her face. Her mother took her hand and patted it. "It's all right, Lisa, *I know*. It will be fine, I promise.

Lord Basarab was glad to see his family together, but there was a look on Lisa's face. "What is it, what's wrong?"

Lisa looked back and forth between her family. Finally, her mother nodded. "You might as well tell him."

Lisa swallowed down her fears. "Grandfather, I've waited till the trial was over. I was going to wait till we had gotten to know each other better before I told you." Her grandfather sat down with a thud in his chair. "What is it that has you so afraid?"

Lisa leaned forward. "It's the choice. I've made it. I think? I made it a while ago . . . I don't want to be a vampire."

Her words hit him like stone. "I see, so you wish to live in the mortal world? That's fine. You aren't the first to choose that . . ." Lisa cut him off. "No, that's not it either. I want to be with Nicola and his family, a weretiger."

Lord Basarab got a puzzled look on his face. He stood up and paced the room. Thomas could not pretend to be shocked. Lisa started to say something, but her mother waved her quiet. He stopped and gazed at her. "Does Nicola know of this plan of yours?"

"No." In a loud and deep voice that rang through the castle, he called Katja and Sasha to the room.

Minutes later, they all showed up at the door. Lord Basarab asked the ladies to come in. He told Maliki to wait in the hall and politely dismissed the others. They took the hint and went downstairs to wait.

It was a fact that everyone in the room was nervous. The ladies sat down on a small love seat, remaining quiet. Lord Basarab walked to the middle of the group. "My granddaughter has a plan. A plan which involves your family. So I thought you may have some thoughts on her idea as well?"

The sisters were more than a little curious. "We don't know what the plan is. But we'll help her in any way we can."

"Yes, I thought you might. You see, she has made her choice as to her future in the tribes. She doesn't want them in her life as much as I would like. But she does want her family." He took a knee and looked into their faces. "Her family being your father and you."

Sasha's face lit like child at Christmas. Katja began crying, and then her sister followed suit. "We'd love to have her" came flying out of Sasha. Katja wiped her eyes and looked back at the Thorys's grandfather. "I know how much you wanted them with you, but I also know how my father felt about her. He loves her as much as we do."

The great lord rose from the floor. "I thought as much." He called for Maliki to come in. As he entered, he saw the ladies' faces and tears. Sasha was still lit up. He made a guess as to why he was brought in. "Good news, I take it?"

"As I'm sure you can guess. My question? I want to know. Would it work? Could it work?"

I believe so, but Nicola is one of the few who knows the ceremony."

"Very well. Sasha, call him and explain."

Several minutes later, Sasha came running down the hall. "He says he can. He says he can!" She repeated down the hall. The others were informed of Lisa's plan. Everyone seemed happy about it except for two. Thomas and her grandfather wanted her to stay, but they wanted her happy as well. Thomas knew they shared a connection from the first. Lord Basarab told Thomas. "Well, at least the family line will continue" trying desperately to find a silver lining.

Days later, as they were leaving, Thomas said good-bye to his sister. The others had taken time to get used to the idea. So the tears were few as everyone knew they would see each other again. They were out in the courtyard loading the carriages when a car drove into the courtyard. It was the king and queen. They returned to give their farewells. The king got out of the car. "So, Mister Thory, I see you'll be staying with us for a while?"

The queen called to Lisa. She got into the car. "I have something for you, Elisavetta. A gift." She handed Lisa a small box. "Give this to Nicola when you see him. He'll know what it's for, and this is for you." It was brooch, beautiful but simple. On the back were the names of vampire families. "The families here are the ones you can trust, my dear. No matter what. You are family, remember that."

Lisa hugged her unexpectedly, but the queen ate it up.

The king told Lord Basarab and Thomas to see him when they could. That he was staying with his queen for a while. In vampire terms. That would be quite some time.

Lisa hugged her grandfather and reminded Thomas that they would meet back at their house in three months. For the men, the trip back was hard. The talking, laughing, and giggling to all hours was bad enough. Before they reached France, Katja was having emotional problems due to the pregnancy. Bael had lived through it once before, but Remi said something about the commotion one night and nearly didn't escape.

Lisa was fingering her necklace as the train pulled into the station. From the stairwell, she looked for Nicola. She had been nervous seeing him again after she had made her choice. Though Sasha and Katja had been wonderful about her being family, her role, she wasn't clear yet. If he could turn her, would that make her his daughter or wife? She only knew. With him was where she was supposed to be.

She finally saw him standing by a pillar; he was searching for her as well. She jumped off before it stopped and ran to him. He was happy to have her back safe. When the train came at last to a stop, the others departed.

Ramon was waiting with transportation to a hotel and, in a few days, the boat. As usual he had everything ready. At the hotel, everyone had their own room. Lisa was relieved when she saw the tub. She unpacked her backpack and remembered the queen's box.

She walked it down to Nicola. Lisa knocked on the door. When Nicola answered it, an aroma flowed into the hall; he had been cooking. There were pots and herbs from one end of the room to the other. It smelled great, but what a mess, she thought. "Nicola, Queen Lilith gave this to me for you. She said you'd know what it was for. What are you making in here?"

"You and I are having a meal together tonight."

"What about Sasha and everyone else?"

"Tonight it is for us. Alone. I have missed you so much. At dinner you will catch me up." He opened the box, and his eyes widened. "The queen gave this to you?"

"Yes, what is it?"

"It's a seasoning for our meal tonight."

At eight thirty, there came a knock on Lisa's door. Nicola was dressed well in a new suit. Lisa too had gotten dressed for an occasion. He escorted her to his room where he had everything cleaned and prepared for dinner. "So how was your grandfather?"

"He was great, and I got to spend time with Mom as well. She's coming home to California in a few months. She wants to make up for lost time. Thomas is coming home with her."

Nicola sat her at the table and went to the kitchen area. He came back with two plates filled with a kind of thick stew. He placed both of them in front of her. "It looks and smells wonderful, but there's a little too much food for just me."

He turned and sat at the other side of the table. "This meal is very special, Elisavetta. This meal is a part of me. It will make you what I am. Before you on those plates are two choices. A white like me or an orange like my Sasha. But this is something you must understand. This is who you will be. Are you sure this is what you want?" Lisa looked at the plates. "Which is which?"

"The plate with color is the orange."

Lisa finished her plate and smiled. "I've known for a while what I've wanted. I feel different around you. Like I fit in. I feel home."

He smiled. "That is how I have felt with you as well. That you were family." Lisa started to get up, but she began to get dizzy. The room wouldn't stay focused; Nicola took her in his arms and laid her to rest on the sofa.

As she fell asleep she was taken to dream of a place where there were trees and rocks. There she began to run at first on two legs, then on four paws. She ran through a forest, jumping and moving at tremendous speed and agility. She saw rabbits and a fox; she heard some kind of deer making its way through the trees. She noticed behind her was a tiger. It had joined her in her hunt. She waited, crouched, her legs ready to spring her claws to pounce. She sprang from spot and killed the fox. She slacked her thirst with its blood and picked at its flesh. Then the rabbit was found again and chased down and eaten. Yet another tiger came to her, but this tiger challenged her for territory. She fought and fought till it ran off.

In the morning, she woke up with a headache. The room had been torn apart; the sofa was in shreds. Nicola was nowhere to be found. Her dress was in taters on the floor. She felt sick and stumbled to the bathroom. Blood and something yellow came out of her throat. Her head was swimming when she stood up leaning on the sink. In the mirror she saw herself. How she had changed. Her skin was almost glowing. At first, she thought something was wrong with the mirror. She was taller by a few inches, and her hair had turned from its light auburn to a white blond. She could see beneath it to the stripes below. It had worked; she was a weretiger. She smiled at the mirror, and there she found fangs; her canines were long and white. As she looked at them, they pulled back to a slightly normal size, but they were still prominent.

She heard a door open. Then she heard Nicola, and she could smell his scent as well. He began placing plates from a cart to the table. He took a box off the bottom and placed it on the floor next to the bathroom. Inside she found new clothes, and she dressed. She came out, and Nicola was stunned. She truly took his breath away.

She came back to the table and had a huge breakfast. Her head cleared. She went back to the mirror as Nicola watched her pose. "Well, little one, what do you think?"

She didn't have to think anymore; she knew. She was who she was meant to be and with her family. She was home.

There was a knock at the door. When she opened it, Beowulf nearly fell over. The others were down the hall. Sasha was the first to catch her scent. As Sasha looked down the hall, she saw she had changed, even her scent was stronger. Sasha rushed down the hall followed by the others. They all told her how beautiful she had become. Beowulf just didn't have the words. Remi looked at her. "We are cousins now, cher." He gave her a hug and kissed her cheeks. Harry stepped back. "I'll bet you a dollar right now, that old grouch Jason has his nose to the palentier watching you, dear." And then she started laughing.

After a while, everyone began to leave. They wanted her to get used to herself. She returned to her room and went over herself in the full mirror in her room. She was quite pleased with the results. While posing in the mirror, she heard Bael and Katja talking with Sasha in the next room. Sasha was overjoyed at Lisa staying with her. Bael was hoping that Katja was feeling all right and what she might need or want. Katja just sang a song.

Lisa was so happy for everyone. She knocked on the door to come in. There was no answer. She could hear them in there, so she knocked again. Nothing? She opened the door to ask why no one would answer. The room was empty. She went out into the hall. It was the wrong room?

It was then she realized she didn't hear them from the room; she had heard them in her head. She could read them and go through them. She heard others as well. She wanted it to stop. Then there was nothing. She heard nothing. She stood in the hall, listening. She heard the elevator ring. Her hearing was fine.

She went back to her room. She paced for a minute and tried it again. The voices were clear as crystal. Then she made them stop. She looked in the mirror. "How is this possible?" She tried to make sense out of it. "How could . . . *the queen's box!*"

CPSIA information can be obtained at www.ICGtesting.com
Printed in the USA
LVOW11s0839270416

485546LV00001B/17/P